BLOOD HIGHWAY

Also by Gina Wohlsdorf

Security

BLOOD HIGHWAY

A NOVEL

Gina Wohlsdorf

ALGONQUIN BOOKS
OF CHAPEL HILL
2018

Published by
Algonquin Books of Chapel Hill
Post Office Box 2225
Chapel Hill, North Carolina 27515-2225

a division of
Workman Publishing
225 Varick Street
New York, New York 10014

Printed in the United States of America.
Published simultaneously in Canada by Thomas Allen & Son Limited.
Design by Steve Godwin.

LIBRARY OF CONGRESS CATALOGING-IN-PUBLICATION DATA
Names: Wohlsdorf, Gina, author.
Blood highway / a novel by Gina Wohlsdorf.
Description: First edition. | Chapel Hill, North Carolina :
Algonquin Books of Chapel Hill, 2018.
Identifiers: LCCN 2017061146 | ISBN 9781616205638 (hardcover : alk. paper)
Subjects: LCSH: Teenagers — Family relationships — Fiction. | Children of criminals — Fiction. | LCGFT: Thrillers (Fiction) | Bildungsromans.
Classification: LCC PS3623.O46 B56 2018 |
DDC 813/.6 — dc23
LC record available at https://lccn.loc.gov/2017061146

10 9 8 7 6 5 4 3 2 1
First Edition

For S. N. S.

To the bitter end.

To be ignorant of what occurred before
you were born is to remain always a child.

—Cicero

BLOOD HIGHWAY

Somebody'd punched the mirror. The web of cracks reached high and wide, spiraling to a center indented from the impact and brown-maroon with old blood. The splinters created a hundred fractals. Funky parallelogram shapes gave back the room each in its own dimensional miniature. It would have been beautiful, except all they had to reflect was five toilet stalls, three outdated hand dryers, dingy green tile, and me.

I dumped the Rite Aid bag on the counter. The girl on the box was blond. She was on a swing for no reason, her teeth these little white pearls, like she was trying to sell toothpaste instead of hair color. I tore her in half, poured the small glass bottle into the big plastic bottle, shook it up. The gloves were huge plastic hand muumuus. The directions said to test it first, but I didn't waste the time. I squirted rows down my roots and smeared it in, noticing belatedly there was no clock in here.

I pictured it. I couldn't not. The woman who threw the punch must have broken her hand. A hophead or a schizophrenic or a chick with a temper. She brought her fist way back, used her hips and legs like you're supposed to, and blam-o! The shiver it must have sent up her arm. How her screaming must have reverberated in here, drowning out the tinny Muzak I was humming along to. "Manic Monday," the Bangles.

But the Bangles were old enough that they'd begun the transition from ironic to nostalgic likability—an odd process, as I'd never stopped liking them. "Eternal Flame," c'mon. That dumb Bubble Yum was the perfect accompaniment to raining acid on my head, monkeying with what the hair gods gave me.

I chunked my empties and boosted onto the counter, turning my back. Another mirror was on the opposite wall. I duplicated, shrinking with iterations, into homunculi. It was the primping mirror. No sinks. There was a shelf underneath to hold makeup. Did the men's room get one of these, or was this was our trade-off for urinals?

Why did traveling for three days exhaust me so much? It was like I'd run the miles instead of sitting in a seat, watching the country pass. Plains turning into mountains, turning into desert, into other mountains. Turning into Sacramento, whatever it looked like. It looked like a Rite Aid, looked like a bathroom. My route got me here at four fifteen in the morning. It was a refueling stop and a change of drivers, so I had an hour 'til the last leg. I hadn't wanted to fall asleep in the lobby, since bus people creep me out, and I'd asked myself: What would a teenage runaway do with this hour?

Answer: Dye her hair.

When the time came to do it for real, I'd go red or jet-black. I'd be unrecognizable on my fire escape at sunset, strumming a guitar I bought at a pawnshop. If Audrey Hepburn could cold-learn those few simple chords, so could I. And people would be walking down the boulevard, rushing, late for a meeting—and they'd hear a whispery rendition of a ballad that hadn't been cool in decades. Only they'd be alone, in their head, and that's the last private place, the last place you don't have to be cool, the place you can be you in all your nightmare glory. The place you can hear a happy song and think for just a second—

"Five thirty to Los Angeles will board in ten minutes. Ten minutes 'til boarding, five thirty to Los Angeles. Thank you."

I startled awake and fell off the counter. The wall where I'd been leaning: its stained green had gone markedly paler in patches and streaks. The burning in my scalp was as hot as napalm. I dove for the taps, cranked them full blast, got my head under, and constructed incredible cussword hyphenates, bodacious compound swears. 'S fine, 's nothing, this is how bleach works. Rinse it out, erase.

The bathroom door blammed open, a stall slammed shut, a woman peed like a frightened racehorse. She flushed, and heavy clogs appeared by my sneaks. "It's leaving soon," she said.

"Okay."

"I told the pecker taking tickets to wait for me, and he was his pecker self about it."

"Okay, thanks."

"I'm trying to help you, dear."

"I said thanks."

My friend Ally wanted to be a hairstylist. She'd cautioned us about bleach. She said if you botched it, all your hair could fall out in clumps, and though that didn't seem to be happening, the texture was definitely different. I poured on the conditioner, and it helped. The strands went from straw to straw soaked in conditioner.

"Five thirty to Los Angeles now boarding. Now boarding, five thirty to Los Angeles. Thank you."

I shut off the water and wrung out handfuls. The rim of the sink was cool on my forehead. It was the fumes making my eyes water, the bright tang of fried hair. The bright white on my head in the mirror was incandescent. I thought of the magnesium we'd lit on fire two weeks ago in AP Chem.

"Five thirty to Los Angeles, final call. Final call, five thirty to Los Angeles. Thank you."

The lobby was empty. A diminutive man at the ticket pulpit was putting stubs to right angles with fussy hands. He didn't look up until I gave him my license. The contrast between my photo and my brand-new do meant he had to double-check. That was the last thing you wanted when using a fake ID.

He pushed his round glasses higher on his nose, ripped my ticket, and added the stub to his pile. “Have a pleasant journey, Holly.”

The Greyhound idled under harsh lights. It gave off heat, a relief when the cold morning was biting my wet scalp. I climbed steep steps. Most of the seats were vacant, but I sat right behind the driver. It was people’s least favorite spot, which made it my favorite spot. Out the window, bugs were frantic under streetlamps. Then we moved and there was nothing else to watch but black night cut by cruel electric, a median dry-dyed yellow, and across it the occasional northbound car driven by someone with a reason to be on the highway before dawn.

“LA, huh?” the driver said. His jowls rippled in the dark of the windshield. He tipped his Broncos cap at me. “Actress or model?”

“Yeah, you got my number.”

“I see a lot of you girls on this route. Makes me worry.”

“Sorry.”

“Lots of sharks, and I don’t mean in the water. They take advantage. You think you’re different, but there’s too many of you girls and too few gigs. It’s lonely.”

I didn’t mean to smile.

“Sure, old fart like me, what’s he know? You take care, sweetheart. Take care and know when to call it a wash. Will you do that for me?”

Other girls probably giggled, asked his name. I considered playing the part to find out how much of his concern was concern and how much was that brand of perviness unique to horrid old men. So self-awarely unfuckable that they crank their charm dials to eleven to see if this naïf will chortle and coo.

"You smoke?" he said.

"No."

"Thought I saw you smoking. Back at the station. Those things're poison, sweetheart."

I picked at my cuticle and found a stray flap of skin. I tore it. A gutter of blood ran down my nail.

"Okay," he said. "I got it. I'll leave you alone. Pardon me for caring."

The sky faded through successive washes of blue. The ocean crept up, foaming over black boulders whose sharp points caught more and more sun. People boarded, disembarked. Civilization never seemed to end here—it thinned and thickened, but there were always buildings and bridges and streets. Nobody wanted to waste an inch, even as the colors changed, becoming jaundiced, and the plants turned anhydrous, except for the palm trees flashing coconuts when wind caught their wide fronds. I got off the bus as little as possible, afraid the driver would speed off without me if he got the chance. Meaning the Marlboro Reds in my back pocket staled, and I ripped every miniscule excess of flesh that could be termed a hangnail, and my own blood made up my whole diet for the day, so that by ten to six that evening, when we pulled into LA's downtown station and the bus doors sneezed open, it surprised even me how spry I was jumping out of my seat and flying to the sidewalk.

"Hey! Don't forget your luggage!"

The sun angled low, elongating every shadow. I put mine behind me, running west. Ahead was Any Street. It blatted with traffic. A trio of girls wearing tight neon nothing Rollerbladed through the blocked crosswalk, catching their hands on hoods. A bistro was crowded with outdoor diners—expensive shades, capped teeth, the newest flip phones, the best blouses they could afford. I hit the button for a walk sign. Under Yugos and Rollses and Beamers and Bugs honking for the right-of-way, I heard an effortful picking apart of "Hotel California."

At the bus station's squat entrance sat the Caucasian version of Jesus. His guitar case lay in front of him, its blue lining pimpled in spare change.

He grinned at me. "You the next big thing?" he said.

I walked, though the sign still said don't. I caught another bus; this one was local.

I could tell I was getting closer by what the shops sold—Korean food and dry cleaning to bikinis and surf accessories. Traffic got worse, amazingly. People became populace. I heard it and smelled it before I saw it. I hopped to the street, and the shriek and reek of humanity faded. I remembered being thirteen, turning this corner for the first time. The way everything changed. It was, no metaphor, where the sidewalk ended. Stepping from cement to tan sugar, how crazed I was to get my shoes off. I did it leisurely now, and I walked into the soft scratch, the funny ground-shift. It had made me laugh back then. I'd been laughing and laughing, and nobody cared or even looked for long, and I knew this was the place.

Today was Any Day, and I could be Anybody. The Pacific Ocean at sunset was a sight I could come marvel at anytime I wanted.

A few volleyball courts had games going. Numerous couples walked hand in hand, far enough inland to stay dry. A girl, who couldn't have been two yet, didn't want to leave her sandcastle; she batted her mother's hand with a plastic shovel. I perpendiculared all of this, went right up to where the tide licked, and sat down. I balled up my coat and put it behind my back, with my shoes, and set my toes in the salty fizz, my chin to the divot of my knees. The sun was still above the water. Sparse clouds chose a palette of magenta and slopped it everywhere. Waves overshot my feet. My butt got soaking wet. A parasailer way out there cut a wedge from the juicy orange sinking to the horizon line.

The thing that still haunts me, and probably always will, is this: I could have stayed. It was my fourth dress rehearsal, and I'd aced it. Except for the hair, and from a certain perspective, that was a win. MISSING posters with my school photo would feature me dirty blond.

The sun skinnied down to a red rind as it slipped behind the edge of the world. The sea turned to blood. The stratosphere bulged with veins, draining its contents into the sea. I listened for silence, yet the sandcastle kid was still crying, a woman was telling her walking partner that she felt like he was using her for sex, a frenzied male was shouting, "Over! Over!"

I took out my cigarettes, found a dry one, and corked it in my mouth. The seagulls wailed while I lit up. It was over.

FOUR DAYS LATER, I got in a cab. It was four thirty in the afternoon. The streetlamps were on. A cold spring shower washed dirty slush into drains and brought night early, turning the last of rush hour into a bunch of gray dead ends. I'd considered taking the crosstown, but I was sick of buses. Plus, the Saint Paul station wasn't in the best neighborhood.

I regretted it when my driver tried a sucker route. I was just as sick of being a bitch to strangers. "Thirty-Five E, please," I said.

"Dis vay ees—"

"Thirty-Five to Five to Sixty-Two or let me out."

Most of the snow had melted. Parking lots had white borders, the last of the mountains that plows scooped to a side after blizzards. I thought it was nice our spring break actually looked like a spring break, albeit the Midwest's version. I was ready to go back, to hear about road trips to relatives in tired Wisconsin towns. I'd put together my own account of a week in Grand Forks, North Dakota, visiting my awesome

Aunt Vi, who taught English lit at UND and lived for live concerts. We went and saw James Taylor. I'd say I was the youngest person there by about thirty years. If there'd been a fire, I'd have so survived, because everybody else would've been using walkers and canes to get to the emergency exits.

I smelled great. My freshly albino'd head was even sexier after ninety-six hours without a wash. I was curious where I ranked on the driver's scale of foul passengers he'd ferried through the Twin Cities, but he didn't seem curious at all. He was turning up Bob Marley's "Three Little Birds" and whistling.

Had he been curious, he might have asked what was making me so uneasy. After exiting at Cedar, the streets ran a standard grid. They were stocked with houses that could have been drawn as a dictionary diagram definition of "normal." The Krenelka boys were hotdogging at their b-ball hoop, exploiting the last, most fleeting gasp of daylight. Ms. Suther juggled groceries out of her trunk while Max screamed in his car seat, scared his mother wouldn't come back for him. Good cars were socked away in garages for the night. Hail-pocked beaters sulked on the curb. Soggy leaves turned the yards into mulch piles, and lights in windows glowed warm caution, intimating meals inside: lavish, home-cooked, served with a side of convivial chatter.

My house was no different, except the blinds were closed. She did that so neighbors couldn't see in. During the day, the blinds were wide-open so she could see out. Preferably into neighbors' windows.

"This one."

He pulled in. I tried to see what he was seeing. Snow on the mountain under the front bays, lovingly tended. Potted purple mums hanging from either side of the door, garish old-lady earrings. Paint and siding in good condition. Clean gutters.

I gave him all the cash I had left—"Keep it"—and got out before his gasps could form cohesive thanks. The rain felt incredible. Clean, light, new. Our front door was purple, to match the mums. She loved color. She used to color-code my outfits: Stirrup pants and matching sweaters. Socks and underwear coordinated, too.

"Perfection is a secret," she'd said.

The heavy knocker thwacked, announcing me. The evening news was cranked in front of an empty purple couch. Blue TV light darkened it navy. End tables held vases full of artificial irises. The gray carpet was thick and plush, lined from recent vacuuming. Easter decorations were gone, replaced with more general spring flourishes—pink and lavender ribbons on the lampshades, green plastic grass in a basket on the mantel. Around the living room's corner, sink spray shushed from the kitchen, and angular light, and the smell of baked ham. In between, the dining room strobed its darkness, the mirror on the antique hutch reflecting a news segment about flooding in Duluth.

I took off my shoes as the sink shut off. A cupboard opened, a drawer. Her bowl met her spoon. She opened the freezer. It required that extra step, an audible fit-and-twist.

It was the kind of noise you'd dismiss, if you even heard it, and you'd never put it together, with how she didn't allow you past the front door.

The kitchen went dark. Her heels clopped a few steps. She appeared wearing her blue housedress, the nude pumps. She was eating as she walked. She got to the couch and turned on the lamp, sitting in its disc of light. She watched the news, and I watched her like a TV. She was brown-bobbed, rail-thin from mall walking, her nose a tad beaky. Its severity leaked to the rest of her face, sharpening it. She had perfect posture, but her bites of ice cream were greedy. White dribble progressed down the sides of her mouth. She didn't wipe it away.

Why would she? She was alone.

The anchors said good night, and their jingle played. Mom cut it off by aiming the remote. I heard the *Friends* theme's twangy opening. I got up, went toward her, sat beside her—all she did was set her bowl on a coaster, finally wiping her chin.

I recognized this one. It was where Ross and Rachel first kissed. I didn't get the appeal of these two; I saw no cliff-hang about them. Mom laughed at a weak punch line from Monica. Monica was her favorite. She'd told me a long time ago, and she'd asked who my favorite was. I'd said, "But they're not real, Mommy."

I thought: One more time.

I'd thought "One more time" so many times.

"Mom?"

Her eyes were silver, stuck to the screen.

"Mom, look at me. 'Kay?"

The knocker thwacked. It made me jump. Mom stood and smoothed her skirt, shoes leaving crags behind her as she went to the door. Her face changed. Vibrancy infested it. She was so happy to see whoever it was.

"Hi there!" she said. Her thick Minnesota patois took every vowel and turned it babyish. "You come on in out of the rain now. My goodness. What the heck're you doing with shorts on, you silly goose?"

"Thanks, Mrs. Cain. It was warm when the sun was out." Kyle Krenelka had his official *Star Tribune* billing pad. He tore off a slip and handed it to her. "Same as last week."

"Well, okeydokey then. I've got some oatmeal-raisin for you, how's that? How's that for a tip from the crazy lady down the street?"

Mom didn't give him a chance to answer. She flipped on the hall light and opened the closet, getting her purse. Her heels clunked into the kitchen—writing the check, getting the cookies. It took that extra few seconds again, but Kyle was busy noticing me.

"Hey, Rainy."

"Hey," I said.

"Is your hair different?"

"Yeah. Needed a change."

"Is it, like . . ." Kyle was trying to think of a euphemism. He gave up pretty fast. "White?"

"Needed a big change."

"Wow." It was not a positive "wow." But old crushes die hard. "I like it. It's awesome."

"Here we go now," Mom said. "There's three cookies in there, so you give your brothers one each."

"Okay. Thanks." Kyle's spitty smile said those fuckers were as good as digested. "Bye."

The "bye" was to me. I waved.

"You put on some long pants next time," Mom said, following him as far as the threshold. "And a coat and a hat, mister." Her wagging finger and maternal sternness held until she stepped back inside and shut the door. Her lips drooped. Her brows wrote a pitiless V on her forehead. She turned the lock and looked through the peephole, transitioned to the living room windows and cracked a blind.

Her nose twitched. She smelled something.

"Mom," I said. I went to her. While she watched to make sure Kyle left her property, I touched her blush-pink cheek.

She spun, grabbed her bowl. I ducked as she threw it, and a line of milk-melt cooled my hot throat. The dish's crash into the wall was enormous, completely obscuring the sound of the studio audience as Rachel got the door unlocked and Ross mashed his lips into hers. Mom flinched in every direction. Pale, stooped. Battle-ready and breathing hard. I stayed on the floor, not moving.

She looked around the room. Up, like her tormenter might be floating above her head. Down, where I was, then behind her. Nothing. "You wait," she said. "You just wait.

You'll find out soon. It'll happen soon, and then you'll be sorry."

She went and collected her broken bowl, smaller pieces clicking into a large crescent that remained intact. She left and came back with a rag and rug shampoo.

The theme song played again. They danced around the fountain, struck poses on the couch.

The clock on the mantel said 7:30. She came for the remote. I drew my knees way up so she wouldn't trip. Her skirt skimmed the air in front of me, the lavender craze of her dryer sheets almost making me sneeze. She shut off the TV and the lamp, but when she got to the hall she turned the light on, and she'd leave it on, for no better reason—I'm guessing—than fear of the dark.

I moved a few slats of vertical blinds and set my temple to the chilled glass. The rain was picking up. Its sounds mixed well with her bathwater running. The rush and gush and swish became a tide. I sang, very quietly, about rainbow's ends and huckleberry friends—fuckever those are—and thought how the joke was on her. Everything had already happened. I'd found out more than I'd ever need to know.

But Mom was right. I'd learn what it really meant to be sorry seven months and change later, on December 6, 2001. Any Thursday.

I

RAINY

ONE

I'm not a morning person, especially in winter, when dawn isn't dawn but is instead an extension of night. I watched my clock radio and waited for it to blast an oldie at 6:30 sharp. I had eight minutes. The red numbers made my room seem bank-vault black and a tiny bit evil. I wrapped tight in my blankets. I read somewhere that adolescents' brains need more sleep than adults', because ours are in the final, crucial stages of development. Yet homeroom started at seven forty-five. So figure that one out.

My alarm clicked. I slapped it before it played three notes. I still recognized the song—"Turn! Turn! Turn!" by the Byrds. It was my test for whether the day would be a good or bad one. Do I slap the button fast, and do I know the tune anyway? Yes to both meant I'd score breakfast without a problem, ace every assignment at school, and find an effective method to stay out of my house tonight until after she was already in bed.

Meaning I was oddly ebullient putting on whatever clothes I grabbed, leaving my room, locking up, heading downstairs. I only paused a second when I saw her at the dinette, wearing a short robe that showed too much leg. Her hair still undone, no makeup, skin blank and stale. Mesmerized by the *Early Today* show's carnival of colors splashing our dark walls. It was the single second I always spared, to confirm her mere presence, her adherence to routine. Is she ballerina-upright at the dining room table, pecking at buttered toast, a cup of black coffee turning with the fidgets of her knobby knuckles? Is she watching the morning news at too high a volume?

Is she pretending you don't exist? Yes? Okay, proceed.

The sidewalks were iceless. The sky was going from ink to navy-blue ink. My optimism was holding, was growing, because I could feel a warm day waiting to happen. The cold had a humid quality, teasing my arm hairs, promising forgiveness for my lack of a coat. Winter coats suck in high school. It takes up half your locker space or you walk around like Mr. Stay Puft or you forget it somewhere. I had an alternative heating system, and I employed it now. It's the best inhale, always, that first drag of the day. It tastes like a long, empty road.

I noticed the cop car as I exhaled. My reaction was instant instinct: I put my arm down straight, cig clamped ash-out against my thigh. I played my throat cloud like cold-air steam, which it partially was. A citation for underage smoking would take a nice juicy diarrhea all over my morning. I'd never been caught, but I'd also never seen a cop car plunked in a direct eyeline to my house. I flicked cinders, nervous. Somebody sat in the driver's seat. Streetlight hit his badge. His sleeve rose, and a McDonald's cup disappeared into his dense shadow. I figured he was getting his a.m. caffeine, bound to set a speed trap nearby. He didn't get out of the car.

I turned the corner. Smoked cocky.

Starbucks at six forty-five on a weekday. Suits of varying quality, lurkers on laptops at little tables, housewives in the good chairs sipping their extra foam. There were two other Sbuxes on my way to school, as well as a Caribou and a Dunn Brothers, plus two noncorporate locally owned coffeehouses—I never went to those; their profit margin was narrow enough that it couldn't handle too many of me—and I used a rough schedule, rotating them.

I popped to the bathroom, peed, brushed my teeth. Then I went to the pickup area and watched. Five minutes was my limit. Longer than that, and I became conspicuous. I was probably wrong—the baristas attacked their espresso makers and steam wands with the kind of focus that can only come from a brutal gig that pays shit hourly but nets you health insurance in a bad-joke job market. Still, five minutes. I was beginning to despair at four and a half, when a guy with three chins said into his phone, "Hang on a second. I *said*, 'Hang on a second,'" and interrupted the cashier's

"Good m—" with "Grande nonfat latte and a cinnamon scone." He threw a five at her and scuttled to the far wall with a finger in his free ear.

So walking to school, I dipped the scone in the latte, letting chunks fall off and wallow to the bottom, where my last few sips would have a sort of puddingy texture. I surrendered the sidewalk to kids in bright winter wear. My coffee was mostly cold by the time I reached Dewey Street, with Dewey High its dumpy crown jewel. I went a block up, to a single-story house whose driveway I checked before I barged in without knocking.

The others weren't here yet. I bypassed the living room for the kitchen. "Ally! I'm nuking my coffee!"

"Thank you for announcing that!"

"You're welcome!"

The kitchen was catching the sun's first desultory rays, weak things that made no halos as they bounced off old chrome appliances. Ally's dad owned a grocery store. Her mom owned a dance studio. They left the house at five a.m. and came home around ten at night. Ally saw her mom at ballet class and her dad at his store, where she cashiered part-time. He'd written her up twice for chronic lateness. It was a problem at school, too. That's why we met here every day, to keep Ally on time. It was my idea freshman year, after she graduated from middle school with one of the highest GPAs and the worst tardiness record in our class.

I hit the microwave's MINUTE button and heard the front door. "I'm just saying," Ty was saying, "it's not as weird as the one I had where we were anime characters on a pirate ship. Remember? Ally made me walk the plank?"

Heather came in the kitchen with Ty right behind her.

"Do tell," I said.

"Brad Pitt had a motorcycle accident outside my house," Heather said. "I nursed him back to health and birthed his love child." Heather'd known she was a lesbian since she was six, but lately she'd been having these very lifelike hetero dreams, and they were wigging her out big-time. She beseeched me: "Did you dream anything freaky?"

"Rainy never dreams," Ty said before I could.

When Ally wasn't out with seven minutes to go, I used my last-ditch ploy and convened everybody outside for a smoke. Heather and I were a quarter of the way to our filters when Ally exited her back door and locked it, joining us. Not because she couldn't resist a cigarette, but because she couldn't resist giving us flak for smoking.

"How is it?" she asked. "How's it feel, coating your respiratory system in pesticides?"

"Tingles," I said. "Tells me it's doing more."

Ty took a baggie of sliced veggies from her backpack. "I don't get how you can drink a big coffee and smoke every day. The one time I tried it, I was bouncing off the ceiling." She chomped into a carrot. "I mean, Rainy, your mom. Wouldn't she kill you?"

I'd told them plenty about my mother. Cancer nurse at Mayo, had an apartment in Rochester, did the drive back and forth. She was superbusy and distracted but a really good person, a great mom. I'd patterned her on Nurse Hathaway from *ER*. Julianna Margulies struck me as tough but fair.

"She'd ground me for life." I pinched the ash and pocketed the butt. "Good to go?"

We got moving. I was jittery, my mind going too fast. It'd calm down in an hour or so, but that hour would be brutal. As if she sensed my sensory overload, Heather didn't talk to me. We were trailing Ty and Ally, who crunched celery sticks and bantered about their calorie allowances for the day—a discussion that boded well, since I never risked my sticky fingers in the cafeteria and they gave me the components of their lunches they considered too fat-dense.

The droves were flooding Dewey's main entrance. The Goths and their black everything. The preps and their pastel everything. Artsy types in self-aware grunge, and the college-obsessed with their ferrety panic. We didn't fit with any of them. Ty did, kind of. She was our outlier. Her parents were okay, just old. The rest of us needed out of here. The details varied, but we'd raised ourselves. We weren't outcasts exactly. We were more like floaters.

I'd thought about it a lot, because somebody like me, who came from what I came from, I should have been on my second pregnancy, addicted to crystal meth, losing the last of my teeth. And the reason I wasn't—for real, I mean it; this is the only reason—was because I found a handful of people who believed my lies. I put on an identity and stuck to it. I hadn't realized why I created a persona at the time. I just knew, starting middle school, that I was entering a deep pool of new people who didn't remember Rainy Cain's scandal from fifth grade.

Therefore: My mom's a cancer nurse at Mayo. She works all the time. I get mad guilt points in the form of a daily coffee allowance and a blank permission slip to do whatever I want. She trusts me. She tells me at least twice a week, on our nightly phone calls, that I'm the best thing she's ever done and I'd better live up to that.

Heather, Ally, and Ty believed it, every word. That gave me something to live up to.

We joined the crowd at the very back, its mass filling four tiers of dull-brown brick. School should've been a respite for me, but it was just a different gauntlet. I'd rigged it that way accidentally/on purpose, maxing my APs and piling on extracurriculars—debate team, track and cross-country, two choirs. I excelled quietly, not begging attention the way real overachievers did. I hadn't started a single college application, and most deadlines were a month away. I pushed myself because I was scared of what would happen if I didn't. What I'd become. It was also great cover. People favored a simple character calculus. Daughters of cancer nurses got A's and won ribbons. Daughters of crazy women got knocked up and drug-addicted.

All of which is to say, I can't remember any specifics about what was to be my last day of high school. A full docket of grueling academics plus two concert practices with memorized repertoire would blur nine hours for anybody. I think I got my AP History report on imperial versus senatorial rule returned with a big red A on it. I seem to recall lunch was hilarious—Ally was ragging, so she was hangry, and the line was long, and Heather and I egged her on by talking about the delectable smells until she blasted us. Our mixed ensemble's concert rehearsal had one of those moments where seventy voices somehow found that dimension of ecstasy and we were one.

I hope all of it was real and all of it was on that dumb nothing Thursday, because what a way to go out. But I might be taking good things from lots of days, to counter the myriad bad that came after. I'm still not sure.

I know for sure Heather and I clashed on what drills to do that afternoon.

"Track's wet, dude." Heather's tell for a shortening fuse was when she addressed me as "dude." "I'm not breaking my leg. Call me a pussy."

"Well, you are what you eat. I'm sorry. I'm so sorry."

She chased me. My legs shot out, knees fluid, gait relaxed. Coaches had been telling me since I was twelve that I ran like it was more natural than standing still. Heather couldn't catch up without cutting a corner, and that would mean muddy grass, where she actually would slip. I let her get me when we'd run two miles.

After, we made for the parking lot—mostly empty now, and dark. Her green Gremlin could've passed for a coffin on wheels. "Coming over for dinner?" she asked.

Years of my refusals had taught her what I'd say if she offered me a ride home. If I assented to dinner at her house, I'd insist on walking afterward or I'd wind up staying over. I'd never told any of my friends my address. I found ways around it, narrowed it to a neighborhood, described features of the exterior that were so general they applied to most houses. I had a horror of hearing a knock on the door, watching Mom go answer and Heather saying, "Is Rainy here?" Mom saying, "Who?"

Or her losing it. All-out losing it, this time for keeps, for public consumption, in any of the million ways I'd watched her lose it in the concealed confines of our house: cleaning jags that lasted for thirty-six hours, where she moved every single piece of furniture on the main floor and put the medicine closet in alphabetical order; what I thought of as "emergency preparedness," when she ran to the basement and stayed for days, using a bucket for a toilet and eating stockpiled nonperishables. I couldn't handle her basement episodes. The house got way too quiet and way too smelly. I'd stick a spare wifebeater in my bag and rent a hotel downtown for a few nights. Dominate a TV, order room service.

"I'm cooking. Surprise." Heather's voice came out even. Her long fingers were flipping through her keys. I wondered sometimes how much she suspected.

I patted my backpack. "I've got a fuck-ton. Thanks, though."

"So do I. We'll cram."

We got to the Gremlin, and she unlocked it, slinging her bag into the passenger seat. I was this close to caving, going with her.

"Enjoy the SpaghettiOs," I said.

"Shows what you know. It's Velveeta Shells and Cheese."

"Mmm." No kidding. Mmm. "See you tomorrow."

I waved when she drove past me. I lit a cigarette. Second-best inhale of the day, the one after a long slog of obligations. My stomach growled, and I remembered I was out of cash. I had been since Monday, when our AP English teacher gave us a surprise assignment that required buying two hard-cover books.

So I'd be going out for supper tonight.

I put my backpack frontways and unzipped the smallest pocket. It took a dozen bobby pins to get my hey-look-at-me hair secured. My wig was shoulder-length and dark brown with thick bangs. The bangs annoyed my eyes; they also hid them. I stole the narrow black apron from Ty's house last time I stayed there—her sister was a waitress at Chili's. The finishing touch was a thick slather of maroon lipstick. My bearing had been northeast this whole time, and now downtown stretched in front of me, the glass-enclosed foot-bridges of the Skyway like tubes in a hamster's cage.

I got a free day pass at a gym and went to their locker room. I shrugged on a white button-down shirt I kept wrinkle-free in a freezer bag and stowed my backpack. The Skyway map was framed on a wall close-by, but I didn't need one; the network's bends and loops and intersections were branded on my long-term memory. Aboveground mole holes connecting theaters, concert halls, museums, sports arenas, restaurants, six-figure apartments, luxury hotels, little stores, and massive multidepartment monstrosities. The tunnels themselves overlooked the streets, so the cars passed underneath you in a tide. Seeing those millions of streetlights and headlights and shop lights in straight lines, beckoning, still choked me up when I was hormonal.

The Skyway was unusually busy for a Thursday. I trailed a knot of women and girls who all had the same long brown hair. They talked in such quick succession I felt like I was in a *Gilmore Girls* episode. They peeled off and went to an escalator. I hit the door at Fourth Ave, hopped down the dull stairs, tied on my apron, and waited around the corner from City on Tap's hostess station, examining my nails.

A party of four came in, business-casual. They were trading polite laughter at a joke that had been delivered outside. They passed me, disappeared.

"Four please. Nonsmoking."

The plunk of menus and a tinkly hostess voice: "Right this way."

I went in.

The secret is posture. If you stand up straight, everybody thinks you belong there, wherever you are—as long as you look the part, and I did. A trifle young, maybe, but the tables at City on Tap were low and candlelit, putting a helpful distance between the diners and me.

Lots of awkward dates going on. My favorite. Women never cleaned their plates on dates, but a surprising number of dudes didn't, either. I found a Brooks Brother and a native of Banana Republic in a corner booth. She was talking with her hands while he nodded and sipped an inch of liquor. He'd left two sliders; she'd hardly touched her—what were those? Wontons?

"All finished?" I said.

"Yes," the woman said, not looking at me. "It's breathtaking," she continued. "I've spent my whole life in ignorance of what an interior designer can bring to a room, and now I'm converted."

I turned. It wasn't just any turn; waitresses do a kind of ballet. As I curved around another booth, a hand rose out of it. "Miss?"

"Yes, sir."

"We'd like our check. We've been waiting ten minutes."

"Right away, sir. Just let me set these down and I'll be right back with that."

The busing station was adjacent to the kitchen but not in the kitchen, which was another reason this place ranked high in my marks. I took a paper sack from the ten or so folded in my apron, snapped it open, and tipped the leftovers in with a trio of fluid motions. They were tucked away when another busser approached with a brimming tub. We did a two-step around each other, and I cruised right for the front, untying the apron and tucking it under my shirt.

"Thanks," I said to the hostess.

"Have a great night," she said.

I mounted the stairs, banding the wig back into a ponytail. I unbuttoned my blouse, rolled up the sleeves, wiped off as much lipstick as I could. I found a bench with a view of Marquette Street and opened the bag.

They were wontons. Fried, crab. Not bad. The sliders were greasy, juicy, bacon-y handheld heaven. After that, I wanted something sweet. And a beverage, other than water-fountain water. I didn't like pulling the waitress schtick more than once a night, so I backtracked to my backpack, carefully folded and ziplocked my button-down, left my apron, and coded the locker shut.

The Barnes & Noble Café was crammed. I got some E. E. Cummings and claimed a seat. In less than an hour, I'd collected three two-thirds-eaten pieces of cheesecake, various flavors, which translated to one whole piece of cheesecake, or, as I preferred to think of it, a cheesecake sampler platter. All it involved was watchful observation and table-hopping. When I was done, the barista called out a hot chocolate that nobody claimed for a full two minutes. It was fate.

So, exiting onto the street at six thirty, backpack situated firmly on my shoulders, I felt almost uncomfortably full. It'd gotten chillier while I was inside. Not some wimpy five-degree dip, either—my sweater might as well have been made of mesh. The sky above me was clear, spookily so. No clouds, no stars. Flat black. People were still out in force. Minnesotans hold on to their warm days with a denial that's almost admirable.

I took the ponytail out, but I left the wig on. I had another hour before my house was feasible, and I liked to pad it, give her an extra twenty minutes for the pills to kick in.

Tomorrow was Friday. It'd be smart to get cash for the weekend. I didn't want to; I never wanted to. I tried to think of ways around it, but I failed.

Most of downtown was pretty open, not a lot of alleys. The exception was an area around Target headquarters, where the retail chain had elbowed its way into an already dense crop of luxe restaurants and bars with kitschy drink names—those places you gotta go when your life is nine hours in a box and two more each way in another box, eat, bed, get up and do it again.

A handful of corporate buyers were huddled at the bus stop, checking their watches. A guy in his early thirties—pudgy, geek glasses—was trying to crowd a few women farther under the overhang. He was catching runoff from the stop's plexiglass roof. He could've avoided it by staying to the side, but clearly it was the principle of the thing.

"Ex*cuse* me," he said, and turned to see who'd bumped him.

"Sorry," I said, and raised both my hands. Empty. "I'm so sorry," I said, pouting my contrition. There's really no such thing as laying it on too thick.

He got an eyeful of me. This delightful moment of incredulous blinking, his long, tedious day a dissolved cloud. He took a wide step, holding an arm out to indicate where he'd been standing a second ago. "I insist," he said.

I went where he pointed. The women had witnessed all this and had formed an opinion of me that was as negative as his was positive. Two crossed their arms. A third's smile said, "If murder were legal, I'd stab you in the throat with my pen. Oh, yes I would."

"Long day?" the man said.

"Very," I said sweetly.

"At least the weather's holding."

"Yes, it's nice."

The third woman piped up. "It's supposed to snow a foot tonight."

The man said, "Maybe a miracle will happen and it'll pass us."

"Christmas miracle," I said, intent on the sidewalk.

Men love women who hate themselves. And most women do. We're taught to from the age of nine or ten: you bleed, you're weak, ick, ack, you're disgusting. A great many women fight their self-hate, though, by hating other women more. Particularly women they're jealous of. I had ample experience with this. I had, after all, lived through junior high.

But men? They're scared shitless of us. And not because of any complicated Freudian business where they think our wombs are going to open wide and swallow them, negating the existences we have the power to create—but because they want to fuck us, always, and these days they have to ask our permission unless they want to face about a 2 percent chance they'll get jail time.

I was a virgin, obviously.

"Finally," someone said, and I knew the 7 was close.

"Could I—" The man took out his phone, a Nokia so new it didn't have a flip feature. "I'd really like to call you sometime."

I mumbled nine digits. He asked me to repeat them, and I waited for the bus's loud rush of air. He'd think he typed it wrong. He'd think: Wasn't meant to be.

"Go ahead," he told me.

"I'm waiting for the 9."

"Oh." He waggled his phone.

"You should hurry," I said, grinning. A flattered damsel.

He climbed on, the doors closed, and the bus gusted away.

I stayed alone at the stop until it swung right, then I took an alley. I pulled his wallet out of my sweater cuff, pushing against remorse at his dorky driver's license photo. Ignored the name, counted the cash: eighty, all twenties. I stuffed it in my pocket. I took off the wig and unpinned my hair. When I emerged on Tenth, I tossed the wallet in a trash can and reluctantly aimed my legs toward the house.

It was getting cold. The temp had dropped an easy twenty degrees since Heather and I ran our laps. I doubted it was much above freezing now. The uppermost Midwest loves its dirty tricks. This one time in the 1800s, there was a crazy drop in temperature, and the teachers at the one-room schoolhouses told their kids to hurry now, it might really be blowing soon. The storm hit minutes later. Some of the children's bodies weren't found until spring, when the snow melted.

I thought about what I'd do if that same thing happened tonight. Idiotic question, because I was surrounded by houses, shops, cars. I probed the idea anyway. It was a quasi-grown-up version of What If. My first-grade teacher had taught us that game, and I was class champ.

What if a blizzard hits right now while you're out in the open?

I'd knock on the nearest door.

What if it's locked?

I'd bust a basement window.

What if this is the 1800s—no houses, no stores, just land and fences and cows?

I'd find a pasture, slit a cow's throat, cut open its belly, crawl inside, and dig out every few hours to see if visibility had improved.

That was why I became class champ in first grade. That was also why my teacher retired the game as a fun activity. At age seven, I offered answers like "Cut open a cow," and it gave my classmates the willies. I'd taught my mom the rules so we could play at home: No spaceships, no Uzis, no fairy godmothers. Just you. You and the problem. She was beyond awful at solutions, but she was incredible at coming up with problems.

What if a stranger drove up to you in a van and told you to get in?

What if he had a gun?

What if he chased you?

What if he caught you?

She elaborated on the stranger in the van a lot. Every strategy I had, she'd counter with a variation of "What if that doesn't work, Rainy?"

My life would've been a very different story if she'd been wacko from the beginning. But she was a wonderful mother in my earliest memories, despite pronounced quirks, which, back then, I never associated with a larger, time-bomb-type problem. Why would I? The person or people you're born to become your baseline. They're reality. Her rules were my rules. Her ethos of "No shoes in the house, they're full of bacteria" and "The neighbors are always watching us, so we close the blinds at night" and "It's fun to dress up and play pretend, but it's a secret; it's a secret that we do it"—none of it registered as warning signs. I guess I questioned the instances where she told me to pretend we needed to leave the house forever and we only had five minutes. I vaguely remember thinking, "Oookaaay," as I packed my favorite Barbies, wondering if every other kid on the block endured similar scary games.

I mulled it over every night when I went back to her. So annoying—you'd think I'd give up. Part of it was necessity. Depending on how many lies I had to tell on any given day about my mom the cancer nurse at Mayo, I sometimes started to believe the charade. I had to sort of reset. I picked through mind-movies of the real her: playing badminton with the sprinkler going in summer; shared afternoon snacks of nachos or buttered Saltines, with a knife down the middle of the plate so we knew which were whose; old movies on the couch with greasy popcorn and Mom mouthing Audrey's lines; watching her make dinner while "Landslide" spun on the old record player. She'd lift the needle every time it ended, move it back to the beginning. *Rumours* was her favorite album, but "Landslide" was her favorite song.

Annually, at the end of May, when the crab apple tree in our backyard exploded bright pink, she used to take the cooler to the picnic table on our patio, fill it with Popsicles, and connect the record player by extension cord. "And now," she'd say, coming from the house with a huge pitcher of what looked like plain water, "the moment you've all been waiting for." She'd pour it into our birdbath. She said it was a magic potion, and I believed her.

Normal birds came. So did hummingbirds. They were fairy-size, and I asked if they were fairies. Mom said yes, they were my guardian fairies and she'd brought them here to say hello.

What if you thought your mother was an angel, or a sorceress from another world, a better world?

What if you didn't know her sanity was as thin and fragile as a cat's whisker?

What if you tugged it?

This was the hazard of trying to build a bridge between now and then—the gulf between them was too wide. I wound up swimming in it, every time, and it was dense, dirty, self-pity water. I had no use for it. It got me nowhere.

My street was glowing windows and smells of roasting meat. I passed the Porters' house. They were in the dining room. Their youngest was still in a high chair, his mouth creamed with baby food. Jana and Cole were jabbering; I could hear it from the sidewalk. The wreath on their door was traditional red and green.

Ours wasn't; it was purple, to match the door. I was dreading our door so much that I slouched over my feet, watching the blue letter *N*s on the sides of my running shoes catch light, their iridescence the last sensible thing, the last shine of balanced reason as I got to the middle of our lawn and stopped dead.

All the blinds were wide-open.

TWO

Hard, sharp edges of our naked windows. I blinked over and over, to soften them. There were no lights on inside.

I divided. One half of me invented reasons Mom might leave the blinds open after dark: she overslept, she's sick, she forgot, she fell, she had a car accident coming back from the grocery store.

The other half heard familiar horns and strings. They were kicking up to a crescendo. The music was muted by distance, by the door. What was she doing in there? What kind of total breakdown had her violating the number one house rule?

I considered going to the neighbors, telling them my seemingly sweet mother was actually batshit nuts and asking if I could use their phone. It would've been second nature to think up a lie, but I was smack-dab in first nature, my true nature, the nature she'd nurtured, whose number one rule was: It's a secret. Never tell.

Willing myself to the front door, I lifted the knocker and let it fall. Nobody answered. I was going for my key, but I stopped and tried the knob. It turned. Air went stale in my lungs as I held a breath, pushing the door wide. I walked into my house like I was underwater.

The music was so loud. Celine Dion. Her best-of CD. Mom found it under the Christmas tree last year, a gift from me. She loved *Titanic*. She played this track every night when she was in the bathtub.

Though never this loud. Never with the bathroom door open.

That hall branched to my left. Her bedroom was at the very end, her bathroom the last door on the right. The darkness there was flickering, candlelit. Shadows danced on the wall, out of time with the song. Even Celine's pianissimo was ear-shattering.

Behind me, I felt a cold breeze. I'd left the front door open. I'd put my backpack against it, to hold it open. I didn't remember doing that, but I was glad I had. I could finally see the grandfather clock in the hallway. The pendulum had gone still, either by itself, or she'd opened the glass door and stopped it. The hands were frozen at 9:27.

Someone had turned on my autopilot function, which was something I rarely had use for. I have no other explanation for why I walked up that hallway and stepped into a gentle orange glow. The open door sat flush to the bathtub. I lost time but not much. Celine was in full forte when my mind unfroze and brain feedback let me process what was in front of me.

My initial thought, hand to God: I tried to decide what color the bathwater was. I couldn't call it "red" or "pink," since it was in-between. It was a gorgeous color. Like a rose, but not a rose raised in a hothouse. A rose on a bush on a well-loved lawn, opening at the tail end of summer, saying hello and goodbye in the same bold blush. In the tub, my mother's head and knees stuck out, the rest of her was sunken in rose water. A razor glinted, floating beside her knee. Six prescription bottles lined the rim of the tub, their caps set beside them. I leaned closer, to read their names, and as I did, their mechanisms of action and side effects and chemical structures—mnemonically stored for the AP Psych final last year—crowded my head.

"Mom?" I said, then remembered that hadn't worked when she'd been alive.

People wax poetic about how a dead body looks so different from a live one, how a spark is missing. I disagreed. She just looked bored. I had a sudden, overwhelming mental image of her reaching out of the water and grabbing my neck. I straightened and blundered on wobbly knees.

I turned. The girl in the mirror told me, "Calm down."

My reflection nodded. She was so white. As white as her exsanguinated mother, who would not sit up, who would not reach with another blade and slice my Achilles from behind.

What do I do?

"Call the police," I said. "You prepared for this. Not for this, but same—" Same what? "Go ahead. Call."

My reflection nodded again—yes, yes. But we went farther into the room. The candle on the counter was one of those enormities with three wicks that can burn for twenty hours straight. It was more than a third gone. It smelled like clean laundry. I looked in the trash can and spied a Yankee Candle Company label. I was close; the scent was Fresh Laundry. A cup of tea rested by her makeup mirror, and I bent to read the tag: green, Lipton. The cup was full. A wheel of lemon floated in it.

I sat on her makeup bench. She'd done her makeup. Her lashes were combed to eradicate mascara clumps. Did she use waterproof? The idea almost made me laugh, and I clapped a hand over my mouth. Tears welled, as if the laugh had liquefied but still needed a way out. I couldn't do this. I couldn't do this, could I?

"You're doing it," I said, and tore some toilet paper. "You're doing it," I said again, "You're doing this."

So. So, okay. I could just leave. Blow out the candle, shut off the music, and leave.

Instead, I went to her bedroom. Her comforter was perfect. Her green housedress was laid atop it, white pumps on the floor underneath. She didn't get dressed this morning. The clock there was also stopped: 9:27. Two hours after I left for school. Maybe she finished her coffee. It probably took her the entirety of *The Today Show*. She drank a whole pot by herself.

I wanted to close her blinds, but that would be tampering with a crime scene. Suicides were crimes, technically. Perp and victim were the same person. Strange.

I wanted to do something strange. I went back in her bathroom—she was the same, *of course she's the same*. I considered putting on makeup. She used to make me over all the time when I was little. She got dresses and heels in my size. She bleached my hair a couple of times. I didn't know it was weird for a mother to do that. Not until my fourth-grade teacher asked me if I got in trouble for bleaching my hair and I told her my mother did it.

I was in the kitchen, holding the phone. It was squawking at me: "Are you there? 9-1-1, what is your emergency? Hello?"

The words dropped into my mouth, so welcome: "My mother killed herself. Please send someone."

"Are you alone?"

"Please send someone."

"I'm sending someone right now. Are you sure [illegible]e's dead?"

"Yes."

"Did you check for a pulse?"

This croaky *awk* sound I emitted sub[illegible] for "No, but the water is colored like a rose."

"Miss?"

I put the phone on the counter. It kept talking while I was walking toward the front door. I glanced in the living room, duded-up for Christmas. Our tree was fake, but a good fake. Fake pine with fake frosting, like somebody'd gone ape on it with liquid paper. There were presents underneath, the same empty boxes Mom set out every year. She rewrapped them every year. She took a whole day to do it. I went and plugged in the Christmas lights.

I meant to go outside and wait. I was going, but my feet were moving like they were in quicksand. Why do we call it quicksand when it slows us down?—because you sink so quick, dummy. On our lawn, snowflakes fell to the dead grass. The snow was sticking. That meant it'd get bad soon.

"You're doing this," I said, and went outside and sat on the stoop, pawing for my Marlboro pack. I did a drag that probably put lung cancer in my toenails. Blowing out the poison took most of my terror along with it. I chain-lit, which I never do.

I had one Red left. I had eleven matches.

The world around me was a shaken-up snow globe, and not [illegible] a good way.

"C[illegible] down. You've got eighty bucks. You could get more and get [illegible]el. A nice one if you want, downtown and ritzy if you wa[illegible] [illegible]der room service, have a hot b— Have a hot shower. Get [illegible] tails with ton[illegible]sleep and pick up the plan where it dove-[illegible]"

Tomorrow. I was abuzz with the luxury of tomorrow. How I had one, now that she didn't.

I got up and tamped my cigarette in the fallow dirt of her planter, ready to blow this Popsicle stand. Except I set one foot on the snowy grass and saw a police cruiser doing about fifteen per, slowing for my driveway.

It moseyed right up to our garage door and parked. The engine cut. A cop got out. He wore a uniform, no hat. The closer he got to me, the more I could tell my appearance had conferred its usual set of advantages and disadvantages: adult male meets adolescent girl with big lips and a lot of hair and is titillated, so he'll be nice out of shame but he'll also fight a flare of anger, sweetmeat he knows he won't get to taste. Guys in my age group did the same thing once they found out I had intelligence and self-respect and didn't need their attention in order to feel validated, making it unlikely they'd get to stick their dick in my pie just for telling me I had pretty eyes.

He was a few inches taller than me. Six feet. His brow wanted to furrow. "Why aren't you crying?" it said.

"You make the call?" His vowels were funny. Not Minnesota-funny: we talk like toddlers experimenting with beginner-level phonics. This guy sounded—I don't know. Pissed.

"Yeah," I said.

"You move her at all?"

I shook my head.

"Stay here," he told me, starting inside. He rocked back on the foot that hadn't moved. "You can get in my car. It's warmer."

"I'm fine."

This time, he stopped before he'd fully bent his knee. "You're all right here? By yourself?"

"I'm good, yeah." But he wasn't looking at me. He was inside the house, looking at the dark hall ahead. I didn't believe in auras, but this guy's anxiety was palpable. "Straight ahead," I said. "Right at the stairs. You'll see it."

His Adam's apple bobbed. He went in. When he turned the corner, I folded my arms and legs, going pencil-thin, holding my heat. I took out my matches, counted them. There were still eleven. I frowned at the stairs as the cop reappeared beside them. "How'd you get here so fast?" I said around a filter. I popped a match, but an icy breeze blew it out.

His shoulders settled lower as he crossed the threshold outside. "You old enough to be smoking?"

I threw my last Red to the ground.

"I was kidding," he said.

"No, you weren't."

He leaned opposite me, back propped in the doorway. I took a good look at him and . . . Nothing to really hang your hat on. No gap in his front teeth or ears that stuck out or a hank of hair that went all Alfalfa in back. This cop was what my friends and I called "blandsome."

"I am now," he said. "Have at 'em. Really."

I squatted and retrieved the cigarette. I licked my lips at it, but the filter was wet and muddy.

"I meant a fresh one," he said.

I crumpled my pack to demonstrate its emptiness. "You should be more specific with your instructions, Officer."

"Blaine."

"What?"

"Not 'Officer,' not 'Sergeant.' Just Blaine." He nodded at the Collins house, next door, with its gaudy, blazing display of Christmas lights. "They ever get cited for the wattage they're using?"

"They've got a dimmer. They throw it whenever the cops come, then turn the lights back up once you're gone."

He was staring.

"Yes?" I said.

Blaine didn't seem bothered. In fact, I thought he might be fighting a smile. "You got a name?"

"Rainy Katherine Holly Cain."

"Two middles or two lasts?"

"Just Rainy." I'd been chewing on a hangnail and right then peeled the wedge of skin free. It started to bleed. "Great."

"You need a Band-Aid?"

"I need a cigarette."

He sighed. It made a cloud. He patted his breast pocket and hip pocket, held out two items: a half-empty pack of

Parliaments and a gold lighter. I glared at his offerings like they were a mean joke.

"Go ahead." He shook them at me. I didn't take them. His hands fell to his sides. "Think fast!"

I reached on a reflex and caught the pack. He threw the lighter a second later; I let it drop. It landed in a tuft of snow by my right sneaker. Blaine didn't pick it up, and neither did I.

I used a match, successfully this time.

"You and your mom didn't get along." Not a question. Blaine pointed at his own cigarettes, asking to bum one.

"I've got an alibi," I said. "I was in prison."

Blaine picked his lighter from the ground and used it. Waited.

"High school."

He inhaled wrong and coughed.

I was proud—he didn't strike me as an easy laugh. My mother's dead body sat thirty feet away, but I couldn't scrounge up the right response; there were too many to choose from. I couldn't fathom what the correct act might be, so I wasn't acting. It was frightening and exhilarating, and adding those to my neurochemical gumbo only got it spicier. Spinnier. I was getting dizzy.

"Are we waiting for something?" I said.

"Detectives."

"Why detectives?"

"CYA," he said. "You got any family we can call?"

"Nope."

He dropped his filter and ground it with a shiny black shoe. I pinched and pocketed mine for a puff later. I chewed on my fingers some more, though my chattering teeth complicated the process.

Blaine peeled his back off the wall and leaned forward, almost bowing. "Listen, we can wait in my cruiser."

I shook my head.

He hopped off the stoop, beelining for his car. I didn't want to get in there; I didn't want to sit in the back, where purse snatchers and serial killers had left their purse-snatcher and serial-killer germs. The dome light lit Blaine rooting around in his glove compartment. I guessed he was going for cuffs. He'd cuff me, put me in the back. I'd resist—I'd go to prison for resisting arrest.

When he slammed the door and I saw a box of Band-Aids in his hand, anger stuck in my brain like a long, sharp pin. I wanted to hit him. More than that. I wanted to beat him up, beat him until he was a stain on the sidewalk. It was alarming how bad I wanted it, but it was also outright comical. He had fifty pounds on me. And he was getting me Band-Aids because my finger was bleeding.

"You're doing this—"

"What?" Blaine said.

But was I? Was I really doing anything, or was I sitting in a seat, on a roller coaster, screaming for somebody to stop the ride and let me off?

“What’d you say?” he said, close now.

I needed to move. I went inside. I was gagging, my tears mixing with snow. I kept my eyes open wide. This wasn’t the time to cry. Though why this wasn’t the time, I had no idea. I only knew it would be a failure.

The front door closed. Celine wasn’t singing anymore.

“You killed the groovy tunes,” I said.

“One suicide’s enough.”

I laughed. It was like a rocket blast in the silence. “Want the grand tour?” I hit the living room light. Passing the tree, the purple sofa, I hung a right to the dining room table. I hit that light, too, and the table big enough for four bragged its one chair. High knobs of dark wood she polished every Monday.

“Want a snack?” I said, hitting the light for the kitchen, going to the fridge.

“Wait, that’s—” He went silent when I tugged on the fridge handle and the padlock caught. I yanked on the freezer, and that lock caught. I pulled a few padlocked cabinets, to stick with the theme.

“Wanna see my room?” I was on a roll. I ran up the stairs, to my door. I dug down the neck of my shirt and took out the key that hung from a shoelace, unlocked my dead bolt. When I pushed inside and turned on the light, a voice in my head asked very politely what the hell I was doing.

“Holy.” Blaine didn’t mean the mess. That was at about a category 2: clothes in senseless piles, books arranged in stacks by library due date, the mattress on the floor only semimade. He meant the walls. I'd covered every square inch, ceiling and closet doors included, with photographs of the ocean at sunset. It'd taken me three years of slicing pages from the travel mags at the library. My rules were: there couldn't be any people in the pictures, and there couldn't be anything man-made.

Good rules. Specific.

My blinds were open. Red and blue lights revolved out there, whirling. I noticed with detached interest that I was close to passing out.

"Took 'em long enough," Blaine said. "Wait here."

I followed, of course. We passed the guest bathroom. What had she believed about the monster or poltergeist who showered there? What had made her decide her daughter wasn't real? I almost stepped on his heels. Blaine turned and saw me following, and that's why he caught me when all sensation left my body. "Whoa. Whoa, easy."

My deadweight slid to the floor, with its natty indoor-outdoor carpet. Mom redid downstairs to soft plush, but she'd left this. Nobody ever came up here. Because of the locked room, where some wicked thing lived. The thing that used to pilfer from the kitchen, until she locked the kitchen up.

Sometimes, in the night, she came and checked on the monster. If it dropped something, or if it had music on. I'd be on my mattress surrounded by homework. I'd hear her approach on creaky stairs, watch her arrive in the shadow under my door. Sometimes, she'd lie flat to the floor to look under the gap.

What did she see? A demon where I sat? Objects in space, moving of their own accord? Could she discern the photos on every wall?

"It's Rainy, right? Hey, Rainy, come on back."

Is that why I put them there? To assure myself whenever I walked in that I was a real person? That I existed?

THREE

Oxygen tastes gross. Counterintuitive, but there you go.

"Deep breaths. Try and relax." The paramedic hovered. He'd secured the oxygen mask's band around the back of my head. It contained the plastic stink of bygone vomit and sterilizing alcohol, and I'd have been rabidly uncomfortable if I didn't remember Blaine carrying me out the front door, his voice custom-made for ripping this guy and his partner about seven new sphincters each. "What part of 'I need a medic' don't you understand? Shut your fucking mouth and help me get her on the stretcher."

It was cruel of me to be delighted by this, but I was. I could still hear him a ways off. His specific words were mush, but the cadence of them, the bent, angry staccato—it stuck out from other sounds. Sounds of more vehicles arriving. Sounds of men. Men tasked with knowing what to do, or at least knowing how to pretend they knew what to do.

Sounds of women. "Is everything all right?"

Yes. Yes, everything's stellar, because that's when you call the cops and the paramedics and the coroner's van.

"Relax," the paramedic told me. "Your pulse is jumping. Just try and relax."

"Jer," a man said. "We're gonna need your help inside."

The paramedic put my arm down. He climbed out of the rig, and I was left to count how many compartments an ambulance had. Next would be a hospital, and I didn't want to go to the hospital. I hated the smells.

I slid the mask off, inhaling the clean scent of winter, seeing that my neighbors were maintaining what I'm sure they thought was a polite distance. The crowd's nucleus was five women in homey wool, clasping each other's plump fingers for mutual support. They were the neighborhood's knitting circle. They invited my mom to join them every couple of years. She'd plead hopelessness with a needle, watch them leave through a gap in the blinds. I pegged the "Is everything all right?" inquiry as having come from that group, specifically from the woman in the middle. Sheila Knell. The lenses of her square witch glasses shone at me.

Another guy was making a circular gesture that encompassed my house, explaining something to his wife. He was a compulsive explainer. Last summer, I'd been reading

Einstein's Dreams on my lawn while he was walking their collie, and he'd stopped and launched into a forty-minute explanation of thermodynamics.

I knew eight other people by sight. They congregated in a messy mass, forming twosomes and threesomes, breaking up again. A cop stood in front of them. As near as I could tell, his purpose was to keep the rabble on the sidewalk, but he was busy watching my house, same as the crowd he was supposed to control.

My legs weren't quite roadworthy yet, so I knee-walked out of the ambulance. I paid close attention to moving steadily as I sat on the rear bumper. I took out the Parliaments and struck a match, smiled at the gathering. Silent gasps washed over me. Sheila hissed at her knitting groupies. I couldn't hear her, but I could guess the content: "How can she smile at a time like this?"

I chain-lit, remembering Ally's kitchen at sunup. Maybe school wouldn't hear about it right away and I could tell the girls goodbye. I checked left. Two boy shapes were at the Krenelkas' b-ball hoop. Meaning Kyle would hear, meaning Kyle would talk, meaning the news would have permeated Dewey High as fast as poison gas by first period.

A shadow cut the streetlight and stood over me. "Really?" Blaine meant the cigarette.

I'd made eye contact with Sheila. She took the challenge and squinted. I let her scrutiny break around, flow past. I was a stone.

At the edge of my vision, Blaine turned from me to the crowd and back. His voice hit that extra-pissed timbre I found so oddly tranquil: "Burke, c'mon!"

The crowd controller jumped.

"I want everybody behind the sidewalk." Blaine waved his hands, shooing them. I wondered where he'd put his coat, then realized I was wearing it. "No more blocking the street. Have some respect, back up."

Sheila said, "We have a constitutional right to assemble—"

"Here's my badge number." Blaine tilted it into the streetlamp. She actually took a pen from her purse and started writing it on her palm. "Sergeant Blaine Clay, Fourth Precinct, under John Kunz. You file a complaint, tell him your constitutional rights." Blaine paused, waiting for her to finish, then took a step back and swept everybody with a very police-y glare. "Listen up. I want you all to try something. I want you to try and put yourself in someone else's shoes. If you do that and you're not ashamed of yourselves for standing here like this is a goddamn football game, try again." A few people split off from the crowd. "Very good. How's it going for the rest of you? Still feeling all right about yourselves, standing here?"

The center began to give.

"I will make that complaint." Sheila's group proceeded south, toward cider and trash talk.

"Can't wait," Blaine said, and said to the other cop, "Think you got this now, Burke? Think you can manage?"

Burke nodded, his face red.

Blaine marched to me, pointed at his cigs in my hand. I held out the pack. He took a seat and lit up with that gold lighter. Fury made him stiff, deliberate.

I should've been afraid of him. "Are they getting her out of the tub?"

"Yeah, they are." He set his head against the ambulance's tall frame. "You wanna wait for her or leave now?"

"Where'd you get your accent?"

"Brooklyn," he said without hesitation. "My parents moved to Minneapolis when I was twelve, but it never went away."

"How old are you?"

"How old are you?" he said.

"Eighteen in February."

Blaine blurted a word, a startle-whispered "Jesus."

I'd have offered to show him my license, but which one? Did I want to be nineteen, twenty-two, or twenty-six? I didn't even have one with my real info on it. Priorities. "You look twenty-five," I said. "Max."

"I'm twenty-seven. Why's it matter?" The snow was coming down in enormous feathers, laying a down blanket on the dirt. "We can wait in my car. The van's blocking me, but once—"

Once your mother's loaded in like a high-class dessert tray, we can paint the town.

"Let's go," he said.

"I'm fine."

"You're shivering."

"I'm fine."

"You're—"

Crying. He left the accusation unfinished.

My tears rolled down in perfect silence. I wiped my nose on Blaine's coat, until his fist appeared holding a bouquet of tissues.

I'd once asked in History, "So there's the year 1 BC and the year 1 AD, but what do we call the year between them? Zero?" Must've been strange to live in Year Zero and not know it was Year Zero. The thing that divided time for the rest of recorded time wasn't felt everywhere, not by a long shot. It was this quiet event in a stinky hog shed.

Living in Year Zero was nonliving. Limbo living.

Was I alive? You can see me, right?

Blaine got my hair out of the way. Dinner came up in an acidy puree, onto the snow, making it steam. My trajectory carried me off the bumper. When I was done, I put my forehead on the ambulance's dirty license plate. "Do you have a mint?"

"Yeah. Wait—hang on."

Puking has such a sedative effect. Almost makes you understand the appeal of bulimia.

"Here." Gum. Cinnamon. Blaine's hand trembled holding it out.

A clatter came from the direction of my front door. Hydraulics smacked. Wheels squeaked on slick concrete, and Mom commenced her last gallivant down the driveway. I thought of her in the sun, waving at little Louie Schweitzer going by on his bike. She strolled to the mailboxes, met the mailman. She commented on the weather, her voice singsong and banal. Sounding of sweetness, not psychosis.

A dull thud—they were loading her. My eyes were clamped so tightly shut that the muscles there hurt. It was interesting, pure viscerality. I observed it, the whimpering noise I made when the two doors closed. My hands slapping over my ears when the engine started. A deep-down drill sergeant shouted at me to shape up, bear up, man up—but something automatic and autonomic and subatomic told it, "Fuck you, leave me alone, she was crazy but she was all I had."

"C'mon. I gotcha. C'mon, up we go." I heard a car door creak open, and I gave some weak resistance. He cupped the top of my head like they do on TV. "It's okay. Trust me, it's okay." I fell into a seat. I had my ears in my hands like they'd molt if I let go. I couldn't focus. It was as if I were trying to make sense of a picture that's made up of a million smaller pictures.

I see this large picture of my pretty, pretty mom. Zoom in, and here's her taking a tenderizing hammer to the phonograph one sunny afternoon for no particular reason, or maybe because I was singing along to "Songbird" and she thought the evil spirits dug the melody. Chunks of record and record player shooting in different directions. Shrapnel. Her face feral.

Here's her in the tub. Bored. She'd never again look anything but bored, 'til the skin tanned and tightened-back in her coffin, exposing a helpless smile.

I opened the car door and dove sideways, just missing the seat. This time was more effortful. Less to chuck up.

"Epic," I told my sad pool of bile. Blaine had put me in the passenger's side. "Thank him," I said, mental-noting. "Remember to thank him."

The coroner's van beeped, reversed. Its headlights were a bright, painful surprise. I contorted for a few handfuls of snow and gargled. Blaine came around the car in the middle of this attractive process. He approached like he wanted to help.

I held up a hand. "I got it."

"Sure?"

"Yeah."

I looked a second later, and he was gone. I nuzzled the door's armrest. "Thank him a lot."

I rocked back into my seat, shut the door, cranked the rearview, and attacked my blotchy pallor with wet tissues. I wanted to hunt for more gum, but rifling through a police cruiser didn't seem like the best idea. Blaine was on the lawn, talking to three other uniforms and a guy in a suit. The suit asked something, and Blaine checked his watch before replying, tipping his hand back and forth to show approximation. He pointed at the car and stepped toward it.

I stared at the dashboard clock. The driver's side opened, closed. The car started. I'd arrived home less than an hour ago.

Blaine's hand waved over the numbers. He'd said something, but I'd missed it.

"Sure," I said.

"Or we can go straight there."

"No, it's fine."

"You're positive?" he said.

"Positive."

I played a game, guessing what I'd agreed to: Pit stop for cigarettes? Nude modeling? Ritual goat sacrifice? My house disappeared and reappeared on my right.

"Do you miss where you're from?" I said.

"I'm from here."

"Where you grew up, though."

"I grew up here. You can smoke if you want. Crack the window first."

"I'm fine," I said. The Minneapolis skyline took over the windshield. Traffic had gone from nonexistent to nuts in a few quick turns, and horns sounded around us. Gotcha-blizzards reliably turned rush hour into rush three-hours, as the IQs of otherwise functional drivers liked to sink along with the temperature. Blaine surprised me by taking the highway. We saw three accidents in eight miles. All had police on scene already, taking statements and assessing damage, trying not to get run over. Gusts tore drapes of snow into horizontal funnel clouds. The roads only got more treacherous, but Blaine kept up a casual stream of questions: Any college plans? Got an idea of a career yet? Do you play sports? I said I was on the fence about more school and what came after, told him about track and cross-country. That last question I could bandy back; I asked what sports he played in high school.

"All of 'em," he said, and signaled our exit at one of 35W's worst cloverleafs. He hugged the inside of the ramp, calm, like outside was sunny and sixty-five.

"You're a good driver," I said.

"Thanks. I do EVOC every other weekend."

"I don't know what that is."

"Emergency Vehicle Operations Course. I teach cops not to crash cars."

"Life skill."

"Right," he said. "How's Denny's?"

"Have you ever crashed?"

"Not yet."

"Not once?" Apparently, what I'd agreed to earlier had been food. My stomach was not any species of up to that. "Never?"

"Nope. My dad taught me to drive on the EVOC track."

"Your dad was a cop, too."

"His dad, too. Irish New Yorkers, so. What's your dad do?"

"Died," I said. "Before I was born."

"Sorry."

"It's fine. I never met him."

"That's why I'm sorry."

We exited less than a mile before Bloomington, where the airport and Mall of America shone their promises. The Denny's vow was much humbler: Grand Slam $7.99! Employees' cars clustered by the Dumpster. We were the only other vehicle. The KFC and the Aéropostale and the Taco Bell across the street were these tiny lighthouses, warning people away. It looked like the end of the world.

Blaine blew into his cupped hands as we crossed the lot. His coat encased my shoulders, warm as a big bag of yak fur. "Here," I said, pulling my arm from a sleeve.

"You're keeping it."

"I run warm."

"You weigh what, one-twenty?"

One-fifteen, fuck-bucket.

Blaine hurried ahead and got the door. "I'm insulated. Keep it."

I smelled meat and butter and forgot my acrobatic vomiting from a half hour ago. Kylie Minogue sang "Santa Baby" on the Muzak with this goo-goo-ga-ga elocution, and it was just *death.* The hostess's voice matched it perfectly. "Hi there," she said. Her nails were red talons. I pictured her swooping down on Blaine from above—*cawww!*—and carrying him to her nest.

"Hi, yourself," Blaine said. He was smiling this smile that made him look like a game show host. "Two, please. Smoking. I don't suppose there's a wait, huh?"

Oh man. This poor fortysomething with her '80s eyeliner.

"If I made you wait, would you arrest me?"

"Nah," Blaine said. "Citation only."

She led us to a booth. "Coffee?"

Blaine replied, "Only if it's hot," and she rushed off to fetch.

I tented my menu, hiding laughter behind food-porn pancakes and omelets. I lit a cigarette.

"How long you been hooked?" he asked. "Cigs."

"As opposed to my heroin habit."

"As opposed to that, yeah."

I shut my menu and laid it flat. "How long have you been practicing that George Clooney bit you were doing a minute ago?" The only sexy I could pull off was the ironic kind, and I went full throttle on it now. I channeled Sharon Stone in *Basic Instinct,* pouting my lips, letting smoke mist my face.

Blaine nabbed the Parliaments. A grin escaped his first inhale. Sly. At most, amused. Nowhere near happy.

She was back. "Piping hot."

"Thanks," Blaine said.

"I brought cream, too. And extra sugar. In case you like it sweet."

"Thank you. We're ready to order."

I felt bad for her. She was flummoxed. She scribbled my pancakes and turned to him, excited. He grunted all caveman, ordering his Grand Slam. "We're gonna need some time," he said. "Leave the pot. No refills or anything."

I thought that was a bit much.

"Better?" he asked me. He slid a steaming mug across the table.

I dumped cream to make it pale tan and pulled my knees up under my chin, turning to look out the window. "Why are we here?"

"I figured you were hungry."

"Why are we really here?"

"Did I tick you off somehow?" he said.

"What a coincidence. She's thinking the same thing."

"Who?"

I sipped. Heaven. Out the window looked as beautiful and boring as heaven. A van slunk into the parking lot. Snow striped its black panels. Its bumper had a sticker that urged me to free Tibet. It went around the back of the Dumpster to the lot's other side. I hoped whoever was in the van didn't get seated near us, but a couple of minutes passed and no one came in.

"I'm lost, Rainy. You want me to be mean to her, or you want me to be nice to her?"

I looked at him like: Well, there you are.

Blaine went, *"Chuh!"* and shook his head. I read someplace that blue-eyed men are consistently rated by women to be the most attractive and the least trustworthy. I'm watching Blaine, and suddenly, I get it. That clear, cool color let me observe the lies as he formed them and set them aside, landing on the truth.

"CPS is slow." He shifted in the booth's bench, caging his elbows around his mug. "Child Protection Services. I got a contact there I called. She said December's the worst for finding beds, so it'd take a few hours." He shrugged. "Only places to wait at the station are interrogation rooms, cells, or the pit. Desk pit—you'll see it. I thought you'd be more comfortable here."

"Oh." The Jackson 5 were singing "Santa Claus Is Coming to Town." I thought of asking Blaine to please, please shoot the speakers. "I started when I was eleven. Cigarettes."

He undid his silverware and laid the napkin in his lap. I was about to mimic him when I heard, "Pancakes?"

I about bit into the plate. They were good. Once I doused them in syrup and butter, they were better. People bash Denny's, and I don't understand. It's food. It's edible. Anybody who had to bathe his palate in truffle oil in order to not bitch about a meal was warped.

I set the dish aside, took a long pull of coffee. Reaching for the carafe, I saw Blaine staring. His Grand Slam still steamed in front of him. I'd forgotten to slow down and hoovered the whole stack in a minute.

He pushed his plate to me.

"No, thanks," I said.

"I'm grown," Blaine said. "I don't need it."

Shame is warm, sticky. His cakes' syrup called to me, assuring me I'd never see him again. That my present humiliation was already a memory. Mariah Carey started singing "All I Want for Christmas Is You" while I ate.

"When I was a kid," Blaine said, "we lived in this walk-up on Union. That doesn't mean anything to you, but back then, it wasn't a very good neighborhood. Is now, or it's getting there. You can tell if you count the Starbucks in a five-block radius, right?"

A corner of my mouth rose, totally on its own, because: "Right."

"There was this alley between our building and the Vietnamese restaurant next door, and they threw out a bunch of fish every night. I'm not exaggerating, Rainy—had to be at least two hundred cats living there. In a space maybe a quarter of this dining room."

All I had was hash browns left. I picked for the crispy ones.

"My bedroom was fourth floor, right above that alley. I got the fish smell, I got woke up by meows and hisses, even in winter. But summertime? When they were in heat?"

Blaine winced and pointed to the ceiling. Just as Mariah hit her high note.

Caught off guard, I did this hot coughing fit, spitting into my napkin. Blaine laughed, too, and pushed a glass of ice water so all I had to do was bend down and suck the straw.

I put my head on my arms on the table. It was cathartic. Deeply not cute.

The waitress asked Blaine if that was everything, and he asked for pie—whatever kind, surprise him. She brought two pieces of cherry, plus the check. Blaine gave me his slice, and I didn't argue. I'd wolfed it down before he'd managed to slip her a twenty.

"Change?" She batted spidery lashes.

"No. Thanks, everything was great."

Why'd his dismissal shrink her proportions, slump her back? Why'd chicks do this to themselves, prostrate themselves, simplify themselves to a shorthand of willingness for guys to accept or reject? Why couldn't I do it, what stopped me? My first and only date when I was fifteen, this senior I knew from track—we went to a scary movie, and he asked, at the scariest part, if he could hold my hand. And I'm ensconced in the movie, I'm way into the movie, so I shake him off. When we go to the parking lot, I say I'll take the bus. I figure he'll try and kiss me, but he just gets in his car and goes. The next day, he told the entire school I was a lesbian. I clocked a lot of friend time with a lesbian; it was an easy sell. I acted like it bugged me, but it simplified my life quite beautifully. I hated that whole game. How girls were destined to lose.

Blaine topped off our mugs. He sipped, staring at me.

"What?" I said.

"Do you wanna talk about it?"

"About what?"

"Most important part of being a cop is knowing how to listen. I'll listen."

I couldn't believe his nerve. I was furious, out-of-this-world furious. Because now I owed him, and he knew that. And he was using it. The kicker was, I understood. I'd have been intrigued if we were the other way around. Locked-up kitchen. Dry-eyed daughter suffering momentary stabs of grief she recovers from. Caffeine and a big meal were duking it out for control of my brain, energy shutter-clicking my thoughts, lethargy gumming them up. Yet I stayed steady, gave no indication of the chaos inside.

"Look," Blaine said. "People are mostly doing the best they can—"

"Don't do that. Don't platitude me. People are mostly doing the best they're willing to do, not the best they can. A person's actual best is pretty damn good, but it's a lot of work. So most people find the maximum amount of work they're willing to do and then they call that their best." It came out in a rush. I'd never had that particular thought before. I loved it instantly, its mercilessness.

This might be fun.

I sneered, and I hoped it made me ugly. "What do you want to know?"

"Nothing." He slid sideways. "Nothing, let's go."

"You ever play What If as a kid? What if your mom picked you up from school every day but this one afternoon she was really late? What would you do?"

Blaine resettled, literally on the edge of his seat. "How far is it?"

"Two miles."

"Winter?"

"Spring."

"I'd walk." He was keyed, his fingers white around his cup.

"'Kay, awesome. You walk. You get home and there's a key rock. You use the key. You go in and you cue up some *Super Mario*."

I was in my house. My living room. I was eleven. I was beating a level I'd never beaten before, pumped about it. Watching Mario stomp on a winged turtle in midair, getting coins. Ding! Ding-ding! "The door opens. She comes in. She takes the video game console and throws it. It hits the lamp right next to me. She screams that she was running around, asking everyone if they'd seen me—secretaries, teachers. She tells me it was embarrassing. It was embarrassing for her. I'm on the floor and she's over me, and she's slapping me, saying, 'I was so embarrassed' again and again, and her hand comes across on the 'bar' in 'embarrassed.' Her hand's really strong from cooking and dusting and folding towels and making beds. You wouldn't think that makes you strong, but it does."

I left out that the slaps had actually started coming on the word "hate" instead. As in "I hate you, I hate you." Blaine might have interrupted, told me she didn't mean it. She did mean it. Mom had blue eyes, too. Lightning had seemed to flash inside them, to travel out along with her hand, stinging my left cheek, getting it soft and tender. Something she planned to cook later.

"And I'm taking it like usual." And I know I'm screwing this up. How do you explain the thing that defines you? The thing that'll always define you, no matter what else happens. The thing that cracked the lens you see yourself through. "Only, I'm getting mad. She's the one who was late. I'm thinking, 'Yeah that's why she's so mad, that's why it's got to be on me, because it can't be on her.' She has to put it away from her, that she messed up. Projection—except I hadn't studied psych yet. I didn't know the term, but I knew that's what it was. My first adult thought, I think. And I kicked out."

My stomach contracted. Gorge backflooded my pipes. I swallowed, and: "I kicked her. Not that hard. I kicked her in the knee. She made this—it was a *guh* sound. She sat back on her butt, and it was right then, on the impact: a light went out. I watched it happen. I'd learn—I didn't know then, but I'd learn—psychotic breaks can be triggered by anything."

"Okay," Blaine said. "Okay, that's—"

"So your next question is, 'Well, when did she lock up the food'? You're skipping ahead, but that's fine. The food was my fault, too. I gave her the idea. I put a dead bolt on my bedroom door. She kept taking my stuff—furniture, clothes, toys, all of it—and setting it out on the curb for trash pickup.

I was really lucky I beat the garbageman that first day. The first day I went back to school after—y'know, after."

He raised both his hands, the international sign for "stop." "Hey, Rainy? You can—"

"No, I can't." I'd been watching it this whole time. A highlights reel behind my eyelids. It was such a strange movie, my life. If I could have walked out, I would have. "Your next question is, 'Why'd she lock up the food?' And the answer is, I don't know. Interesting, why don't I know? Because she wouldn't talk to me. She never talked to me again. She hasn't spoken to me in over six years. She ignored me to the point that it seemed like she couldn't see me, couldn't hear me. If I dropped something, if my steps echoed on the floor, those things she could hear, and they terrified her. If I touched her, it terrified her. 'Fascinating, Rainy, why didn't you tell somebody?' I did. My fifth-grade teacher, Mrs. Scott. It took me a while, because Mom'd had episodes like this before, one or two days at most, and she always told me afterwards, 'Mommy's a little crazy, but that's our secret, isn't it?' I liked that. 'Our secret.' I thought that's what this was, and it'd be over soon. I was waiting, thinking she'd come out of it. Then this one day, at school, I got caught stealing from another girl's lunch. I was so hungry. I saw the oatmeal pie peeking out of the sack, I took it. Mrs. Scott asked why I would do that, and I told. I about had a panic attack, but I told her. Mrs. Scott told the principal. Principal calls my mom, Mom comes in. Your next question is, 'How could a schizoaffective anxious-depressive convince everyone around her she's sane?'"

"Because she wore a nice dress," Blaine said.

"You don't have to pretend," I said. "I wouldn't believe me, either."

"She wore a nice dress and nice shoes, and she said, 'How about this weather.'"

"Don't pretend."

"She pinned it on you. Didn't she?"

I was stumped. How'd he know? How was he guessing right?

Don't fall for it, I thought. He's playing you, he's laughing inside.

"Very good," I said. "But I don't blame them. She was a phenomenal liar. Better than you. Even better than me. So your next question is, 'Why didn't you run away?' Answer: Because the principal talked with me after his conference with my mom. And he said—I'm quoting—'Do you know what happens to little girls who steal and tell lies and run away? They go to juvenile hall. Do you know what that is, Rainy? It's prison for children.'"

I scoffed, remembering the fear I'd felt at the time. If they could see me now. "After that, I adapted. It wasn't so different from a video game. Figure out the boundaries and stay inside them. Boundary one: don't get caught stealing. Boundary two: don't tell; they won't believe you. You need mushrooms and flowers to eat so you can grow. You need coins for extra lives."

Blaine began to sag on his side of the booth, shoulders folding in.

"You're not buying it, right? That an eleven-year-old could do it on her own? It wasn't instantaneous. It was trial and error, with plenty of error. My lies were too big at first. The best lies are simple. Something you can stick with that still gives you mobility. My cred was shot by the time I worked that out, so I had to change school districts. That's why I'm at Dewey."

"A parent's gotta petition for that, don't they?"

"I sign her name better than mine, dude. Plan was, I'd stick around 'til I turned eighteen. Maybe finish high school, maybe not. It wasn't that bad once I got used to it—she was basically a crappy roommate—and I figured, after I'm eighteen, I'm not police jurisdiction. Can't call me a runaway then. If I graduate, even better. Everybody loses track of everybody in college. And when I've got just a few months to go, she pulls this."

Conventional wisdom states that spilling your guts makes you feel five pounds lighter. I'm like: Well, yeah, your guts are on the floor.

"If the truth is weird enough, people think you're telling a story. Fine, tell a story, one people can feel comfortable with. They'll decide it's the truth. It fits better. It fits this." I waved generally: Denny's, street, city, country. Blaine. "You'll go home tonight, and tomorrow you'll tell your buddies about this whopper you heard. This grand epic—a mother ices her daughter out for six years, yeah right. They'll laugh and laugh, and you'll laugh right with them."

Blaine revived, sitting up, his nostrils two delightful black holes of rage-flare. Nobody likes being seen through. They blame the seer.

"Or you'll tsk-tsk about kids today. These rotten, shallow, lying little narcissists that make it so much harder for hard-working men like you to pretend they're doing their phony-ass best."

They revile her, and if she's smart, she learns to love their hate. She masters the fine art of throwing kerosene on the kitchen fire.

"You go ahead, man. Go right ahead. And fuck you very much for supper."

FOUR

The plows had done their first pass on the main arteries. Our tires gripped through three inches instead of a foot. Blaine brooded. He excelled here, much as he excelled at driving. When he did both at once, they fed each other. Symbiotic skills. He glared at the road like he had a grudge against it, and it answered by becoming magically navigable, afraid of him, as I still should have been.

Instead, I found the journey exotic—not the landscape, white and flat, but the novel circumstance of sitting beside a human being who knew . . . who *knew.* I'd told Blaine the outline; I could fill it in. I could tell him I knew what grass tasted like: about how you'd expect—the greener, the better—though you forage mostly at night, so it's hard to be fussy about color. You get annoyed how much you have to eat in order to feel full, so you move on to neighbors' garbage. Scouting in the wee hours, a bipedal raccoon. I knew what it was like to surprise a raccoon and go running for my life across way too many backyards. To move on to restaurant Dumpsters. And it's while you're noshing through the mother lode of Red Robin fries one night that you realize it'd be more high-risk (getting-caught-wise) but less high-risk (getting–*E. coli*–wise) to infiltrate the restaurants themselves. Don't steal fresh meals from the kitchens; steal leftovers from the patrons. Nothing goes missing. Nothing gets missed. Become a bipedal garbage disposal. But how? Then working out the how, and how it isn't impossible, it's not even difficult. Favor low light and busy hours. Learn the restaurants that are friendliest to your MO. It's masterful, if you do think so yourself. Fourteen years old, lipstick and a wig, you'd say you were a gymnast if anyone asked—"I was a gymnast, 'til I got too tall"—so that your slight frame made sense.

I told him nothing. What would it get me? What had it gotten me so far, other than a terse 'C'mon' back at Denny's, and silence?

We split off the interstate, took a few turns, and came to a building that could have been a DMV or a community arts center. There was a decal on the glowing front entrance, a shield with FOURTH PRECINCT stamped in the middle. I wondered how criminals felt when they saw it. I saw it and felt like a criminal.

Blaine read my mind while we drove down the ramp of a parking garage. "No reason for you to be scared."

"I'm not."

"Good. No reason to be."

The sublevel was wall-to-wall cop cars. The only empty space was marked CAR 75. Blaine parked, we got out, and our shadows merged, shortening and lengthening again with each brazen halogen. A pretty, petite woman waited at a desk ahead of us, a camera above her head. There was a door to her right labeled EMPLOYEES ONLY.

"Some weather," she said to Blaine. Her tone was glacial.

He took a pen that was chained to the desk and filled out a line on a clipboard. "How've you been?" he said while finishing his signature. He waved as we went, as if she'd replied, and opened a door that gave on a tunnel and up some stairs to a maze of halls, where the occasional uniform passed us. Labels like INTERROGATION, EVIDENCE, VENDING: I couldn't muster any interest in them. I was occupied by the great wall of noise we'd be hitting any second. Whenever I thought we must be close, another turn gave on another hall.

"You all right?" Blaine said, growling.

"Fine."

"You love that word, don't you? 'Fine.'"

"Yep. Good word."

He hooked left. Finally, here was the noise I'd been waiting for. Fifty or more desks were packed together in a mammoth space. A cop at every one—and often two cops, dialing landlines while telling cells to hold, shoving sandwiches in their maws, chicken-scratching, and setting paper in trays. The ceiling was so high I expected basketball hoops to come down and a game to get going, but this illusion was dispelled by a staircase rising on either side, to offices a tier above. Those doors were closed, their windows dark.

"Is it shift change?" I half yelled.

Blaine's voice, however, was made for this. "No. The storm. Every car's got ten accident reports to fill out." He pointed. "We're headed for that guy."

I had no clue who he meant, but I started walking. Blaine reached to set a hand on my shoulder and steer me, then thought better of it, settling on a process that was more usher-like. He created a buffer zone between me and the cop mob—a border of arms that much bigger men respected as they made plays for the coffeemaker, copy machine, or any of the hallways that wheel-spoked from the center. I wondered if they were inventing excuses to cross our path, since each of them seemed to need to tell Blaine hello.

Blaine didn't speak. He nodded where appropriate, while I focused on the progress, the directionality, the man under the office overhang, watching us approach. An office beside him had CAPTAIN JOHN KUNZ stenciled on the glass.

I thought Blaine would introduce me, but he herded me into the office, where he could say with normal decibels, "Wait here. Soft couch." I processed the couch, and bookshelves, and a desk with ten trees' worth of paper hiding its whole surface. A fish tank in the corner, nothing demonstrably alive in it. There were windows all around, which would have been terrif had it not been for men passing, staring in at me. A freak guppy alone in my roomy bowl.

I groped for the door as Blaine pulled it shut. “Could I wait at your desk?”

“It’s kind of in the middle of everything.”

“That’s good. That’s better.”

He led the way. I didn’t follow immediately. I looked at Kunz, and that was a mistake. I was so amped—I’m talking out-of-this-dimension stress overload—and whenever that happened, my paranoia-penchanted DNA kicked in. I had this ridiculous momentary intuition that Kunz knew me from somewhere. He raised his cup, indicating I should tag along with Blaine. I did, happily, because I hated feeling like that. It always made me wonder if I was one bad episode away from going permanently bugfuck, same as her.

“It’s this one. Have a seat.” Blaine knelt, running a hand over his hair, flattening a buzz cut that was flat to begin with. He ripped a drawer open, handed me a bottle of Evian—“Drink that”—and left.

Phones jangled. Paper fluttered. Shoes squeaked.

His desk was immaculate. I picked up the lone picture frame, the only personal thing on Blaine’s desk. I brought it close, confirming it was indeed a photo of a car and only a car. Candy-apple red, the crossed-flags hood ornament centered perfectly. I set the photo down and picked up a paperweight, leaning back in the chair, turning the circle between my hands. It was a stone. There were three of them. I grabbed the other two, compared sizes. They were the smooth, ovular rocks people took from the lakes up north while on family vacations.

Every other desk in the place was a mess. Brass badges twinkled on a shocking number of flabby man boobs and a sad minority of fit pecs. Fierce male voices, fierce male smells.

I set the rocks down and used my toe to turn the chair.

In Kunz's office, Blaine was speaking with the verve of a lawyer pleading a case. The captain interrupted. When Kunz quit talking, Blaine delivered a parting comment and turned his back. As he exited the office and came my way, I understood how badly I needed sleep. I was wired-tired, caffeine bridging the gap between my willed vigilance and a crash I could see ahead. A bad one.

"Ready to get outta here?" He got on a knee, tearing his bottom desk drawer open. He took out a cop hat and put it on.

We did our journey in reverse. The parking garage lady made no attempt at conversation, and it spoke volumes, as did Blaine's tight smile at her. He went loose behind the wheel, at home there. We were the only car on the road. Plows were out, but they'd moved on to highways. Their attack formation stormed the ramps to I-94 and 35W. The rest of the city was a starched white shirt. Nobody wanted to wrinkle it.

“I tried. I really did.” Blaine threw his hat on the dash. “CPS doesn’t have a housing situation for you. A lot of fosters return kids around the holidays. Overflow goes to children’s centers, so they don’t have any beds. You’re seventeen. Powers that be decided either an open cell in lockup or a halfway house. I didn’t want you in the clink for the night. Tomorrow, I’m giving it both barrels. I’ll find you a decent spot if I’ve gotta cry blood. Okay? My word, okay?”

The police car console had a lot of tech built in. I found the regular radio and flipped it on, hitting presets ’til I heard an oldie. The Mamas and the Papas. “Monday, Monday.” Jaunty major key, basic rhythm.

Blaine’s undertone contained a hum of unsaid, subliminal bull, further assurances he’d figure it out tomorrow. ‘It’ being me. It was going to prison. It was fine. I was fine.

I was fine until the sweet resolution of that song melted into fingerpicked acoustic. Stevie Nicks took her love and she took it down. I don’t know what happened. It wasn’t a weeping fit; that would have been infinitely preferable. I discovered I’d curled up in my seat, as best I could with the seat belt to negotiate. I was rocking, and I was holding my hands near my ears but not on them, like I was trying to catch the music and keep it there. Blaine pulled over, saying my name, like it meant jack-all to me when Stevie’d been afraid of changing because she’d had somebody to build her life around.

“Just drive,” I shouted. “Just go, just take me there, I don’t care, it’s nothing, I’m fine, go, drive—” and so on, until the tires sloughed back into a lane. A radio ad screamed about a holiday sale. I made an effort to sit up, my cheek flat against the ice-cold window, dry heat blasting my face. Blaine took a ramp.

"It's south?" I said.

"Scenic route. Here."

A weight settled on my knee. I'd seen one before, but only on TV. "I don't know how to use it."

Blaine showed me, twirling a thumb around the iPod's dial. Not once did he look away from the highway—freshly cleared and sanded, it stretched under a bright half-or-more moon that was parting the clouds. We crossed the 35W bridge, the Mississippi black and churning below us while every building and lot and house glowed wicked, freaky white. Christmas lights blinked, doing little to alter the monochrome of a city buried in powder. It was like driving through an old photograph.

He exited onto County Road 42 while I found my way to *Rumours*. It didn't surprise me he had it. I hoped he wasn't one of those posers who'd found Fleetwood Mac all of four years ago, when *The Dance* came out. I'd been thirteen at the time and I was like, I've loved them my whole life, buttheads! The iPod let me pick which tracks I wanted to hear. This seemed a sacrilege to an album crafted for vinyl, when the order of the songs as a whole mattered as much as each on its own. I hit "Second Hand News," set it to play in sequence, and watched that white world. Water towers with whited-out town names I could name anyway: Rosemount, Apple Valley, Burnsville.

"You ever climb one?" he said, pointing at another water tower, this one for the thriving metropolis of Savage, Minnesota.

"Isn't that illegal?"

"Yeah, it is. Teenagers do it all the time, though."

"Did you?" I said.

"Sure. Prom. You go to prom?"

He would not get another recital from me. Not a single number, not a note.

"Prom night," Blaine said, "you go to the dance, then you do something stupid. We climbed up there and drank scotch." He laughed fakely. "It was warm for May. Only reason I'm here to tell you about it." There was a U-y ramp that civilians weren't supposed to use, but Blaine slowed onto it and turned us north. "You should climb one sometime."

"Why?" I said.

Blaine fiddled with dials. The wipers quickened, and the radio's bass thickened.

"Could we climb one now?"

"Little cold for that," he said. "And slippery. You wipe out off a water tower, it's no joke."

I repeated "Go Your Own Way." "Why'd you guys go up there on prom night? Didn't you have an after-party?"

"They didn't do those yet. You know why they do after-parties, right?"

"So we don't go climbing water towers."

"Exactly."

"Better to keep us in one place."

"Yep."

"Keep the cattle penned." I rerepeated "Go Your Own Way."

"This your favorite?" he said, drumming the beat on the steering wheel. He got on 55, then took the exit at Lake.

"How long were you guys up there?"

"All night. 'Til the sun came up." Blaine braked gently, his face souring. I looked out my window.

"Wow." I said it with reverence. Most buildings this butt-ass had been torn down out of a sense of civic duty. This one sat between Lake and Twenty-Eighth, west of 35W, set back from the street. A strip mall with a Blockbuster, a Panera, and three empty suites hid this eyesore from view. Pastel tiles in random clusters failed spectacularly at breaking up the uniform depressive gray, succeeding instead at highlighting how this was a jail, a whole jail, and nothing but a jail.

Blaine skirted the empty parking lot, searching for an ideal space in the twenty dozen available. "It's one night, Rainy. You've got my word. One night."

We went by a long line of windows up front. It was a smoking room. The chairs were cheery colors, but a lot of the cushions were ripped. A woman in scrubs with a brown mullet was walking around. She had a tray laden with paper pill cups. People were packed together, sucking tobacco. Each one of them was a "too." Too thin, too fat, too inked, too pale, too young to look that old, too old to look that young. This guy with several rings in his lower lip watched us pass. He puckered up and kissed at me.

"I wonder how many times I can get raped in one night," I said. "I'll let you know. I'll keep a count."

Blaine braked.

"I'm kidding." I was not kidding.

Blaine was an athlete, but so was I. He knew this part of town, but so did I, and I knew it on foot. I undid my seat belt and reached for the door handle, ready to run. I opened it to a shock of cold.

Cat-quick, Blaine lunged. He caught the door and yanked it shut. He put the transmission in drive, turning at the halfway house's entrance.

"Belt up," he said, and kept going.

"What?"

"Put on your seat belt."

He gassed it into a turn, the foul edifice shrinking behind us. The tinkly intro to "Songbird" was playing, but I skipped it. Blaine's profile was a Mount Rushmore of tension, ideally suited to the thump and wail of "The Chain." He made a left, and another left, into a McDonald's drive-thru. "What do you want?"

"Nothing," I said.

He got me two cheeseburgers, fries, an apple pie, and a shake. We parked and snarfed. I had no idea what was going on, but as long as I wasn't at this present moment being checked into that hellhole, I didn't care. So much the better that he was wolfing a supersize #1. I'd outrun him easy when we went back.

I nudged the volume a tad higher on "You Make Loving Fun."

"Favorite band?" he said.

"The last great band."

"Why's that?"

I crumpled my Mickey D's into a ball.

Blaine said, "Done?" He got out of the car, went to a trash tub by the pickup window. A vehicle abruptly separated us. A tall van, its black side panels resolving into messy, snow-blown zebra print. It moved slowly, even for this weather, flashing a mountain sunrise on its bumper. FREE TIBET, the sticker said.

"What I'm about to suggest . . ." Blaine's voice broke my concentration. A thought had quarter formed in my head, something important. It was dissolving. "You can say no, okay?"

I quirked around in my seat. The van slo-mo'd left and was gone.

"Rainy?"

"What if I say no?"

"Do you ever just cooperate?"

"Fine. Suggest."

"You can stay at my house tonight if you want."

My eyebrows went up like a flag.

"I'm not leaving you there," he said, squirming a little. "I don't know what else to do."

"Won't that get you in, like . . . massive trouble?"

"Let me worry about it."

"Okay," I said. "Your house." I sounded light. My misgivings were diffuse, and my answers to them were wildly unfamiliar: So what if he does? What if I want him to?

We glided past the golden arches, and soon, we were getting on Cedar again, then turning off at Thirty-Ninth.

"Are we going to my house?" I said.

"I live six blocks from you. It's okay, we won't pass your place."

"I'd be fine if we did."

"Shocker." Blaine hit a button on his visor, and an average two-story on the average street cracked its garage. Pulling in was a tight fit. The space was meant for two cars, but two narrow cars—not a wide police cruiser and the tarped thing on our left. A low line of red peeked from under the canvas. The tires had that crossed-flags insignia on their hubs.

The engine cut. My bravado sank. Fresh, clear, energetic fear took its place. It was as if I'd taken a power nap, or my instincts had, and they were waking up, sniffing the air. All they smelled was December and the tang of gasoline.

Inside the house, the kitchen led to a dining area, to a living room. A few stairs went down, and a longer set went up. Upstairs was a hall of doors, down was a den. I could see books in the den, hundreds, in shelves lining the walls. In the living room, dead ahead, there were shelves of movies on VHS, dozens, and I went to those. I digested the titles. They were mostly old. Betty Grable and Fred Astaire and Clark Gable and Lana Turner. I spotted *Breakfast at Tiffany's* and stroked the spine.

"Find one you like?" Blaine was in the kitchen, scooping grounds into a coffeemaker.

I needed him to make sense to me, right now. The layout was very open, but his house did not square. I'd predicted a full-size man cave—chairs with beers in the armrests, a gaming system and the latest joystick controllers. I wondered if he'd had an immediately clear understanding of me when he'd walked through my house. If he got me, just like that, and what I had to do or give or learn to have that skill.

"Breakfast at Tiffany's." I said it much too loudly. I listened in disbelief as my mouth ran away. "The movie's based on a novella by Capote, but they massacred it. She's supposed to get on the plane to Brazil and Fred never sees her again. He sees her in a photo—she's riding a horse or something in South America. He recognizes her, but he doesn't, because she's not the same person. That's the ending."

Blaine shuffled through a newspaper. "That's a downer."

"That's the real ending."

He picked two mugs off a mug tree, and offered one by raising it. "It's decaf."

I shook my head.

"Those are my mom's," he said, tilting his cup at the movies. "I never watch 'em."

I folded my arms, gave my diaphragm a squeeze. It wasn't a big house. No one had come to meet us, greet us, so I'm all: You live with your mom? She's where exactly?

Blaine held my eyes while pouring. "I need you to be straight with me. Do you want out of here?"

I tried to call up some more savvy teen-snark, but I had none left. I dug in my pocket and held up his cigarettes.

"Down in the den," he said. "Open the storm door first."

I went. The stairs felt perfunctory, shallow. The books were history, history, and military history. I grabbed the storm door and pulled. The glass slid on its track, detonating a blast of single-digit Fahrenheit. I sat, weak. Three Parliaments left in the pack.

Leave me alone, leave me alone: a litany I sent to him as I found an ashtray at the bottom of the nearest shelf. Blaine appeared at the top of the stairs.

"I'm not having sex with you," I said, searching for that light tone again and achieving the polar opposite. "Kinda saving that for a special occasion. Leap year, maybe."

"That's not why I brought you here." He sat on the top stair, his legs bent extreme for how short the risers were.

"But you're that guy," I said. "You're the guy at the bar, the guy at the party, the guy at the wedding. You never bring a date, but you always leave with one. You're Joey on *Friends*, except a cop and not dumb."

He laughed quietly.

I didn't like that. It was a dismissal. "You're a riddle, a sphinx," I said. "You're a blank. You're whatever they want. Guys love that in other guys. Girls love it in guys. Guys and girls both hate it in girls. It's the double slut standard."

Blaine's cheeks went bright pink. "Little tip, Rainy? If I was a statutory-raping piece of shit, pissing me off wouldn't be your best bet here."

"But you're always pissed off. I'd rather you try it now, if you're going to, than attack while I'm sleeping—"

"Okay." He sat up, gesturing "safe" with his hands. "Okay, stop. Stop. Time-out." He made an arm T. "How about you? What girl are you?"

"I'm the girl who gets on the plane to Brazil and Fred never sees her again."

"That's bullshit."

"I knew it," I said. "I knew you didn't believe me."

"Not that. Not the diner. I'm talking about right now. You pretending you get my whole deal."

"Then tell me your deal."

He picked up his coffee cup and sipped. "My old man would've called you a spitfire."

"That's a term guys use when they think a girl's a cunt but they want to fuck her anyway."

He surprised me again, nodding. "I just wanted to ask about how you handled yourself. How you kept it together tonight."

"Yeah, real funny. I fainted and threw up on my driveway."

The heat kicked on. Blaine said, "I punched out an EMT and had to be sedated."

I thought he meant tonight, that he'd punched out an EMT while he was yelling at them on my lawn. But "sedated" made no sense. "When?"

Blaine spun his cup by the rim, watching whatever liquid was left swirl in circles. "I was fourteen. She did it in the garage."

FIVE

It reminded me of choir. The Christmas concert we'd been rehearsing. Sopranos got this astonishing key change at the end. I swear we grew wings. I floated out of myself. It was scary, exhilarating, transcendent.

"She had music going, too," Blaine said. "The radio was on."

"What song?"

"'Hey Jude.'" He smiled. "I fucking hate that song."

It's a miracle I didn't wet my jeans. If he was saying what I thought he was saying—

"I got out early from practice." Blaine scratched his jaw. "Football. It was November. Come in the front door and I hear it right away. It was at the *na-na-na* part. I figured my dad was home." Blaine broke off. His head lolled forward. "Sorry. I don't talk about this."

I thought that meant he was done. Disappointment crushed me. "It's okay."

"I went to the kitchen, poured some milk. I don't know. I don't know why I went out to the garage. He worked on the car all the time with the radio going, so it wasn't weird the engine was on. I just went, I guess to say hi. See if he wanted a hand." Blaine's brow puckered. "No, that's not it, either. He wouldn't let me near that fucking thing. Said I'd scratch it.

"There's these holes." His hands moved, to cover the holes. "You see it in witnesses all the time, these disparities. I remember going to the door. I remember that almost too well—like I'm trying to make up for the rest. Because here's the thing: I don't know what happened to my glass of milk."

Blaine held out his coffee cup. "I'm holding it, and I open the door, and there she is in the 'Vette with the top down, and her skin's blue, and that fucking song is going *na-na-na*. I must've dropped it."

He dropped the cup. It fell to the stair beneath his feet but didn't break.

"So it must've broke. Unless I set it down somewhere after I hit the button for the garage door and ran to her. I don't remember doing that. Or dragging her out to the driveway, starting CPR. My dad asked me later why I didn't call an ambulance, and I go, 'Didn't I?' My neighbors called. One of the EMTs tried to pull me off her, and I swung around and hit him."

Blaine made a fist. He pointed at the middle knuckle on his right hand. "See that scar?"

I nodded, though I was too far away.

"That's the next thing I remember, breaking my hand. Never break your hand, there's no pain like it." He set his fist in his lap and examined it. "I talked to them later. Dad made me. I said I was sorry, and they said it was all right, no problem. They're looking at me with this pity, thinking I lost my mind. But I didn't. Not then. There was a logic. I thought if they went away, it wouldn't have happened. She wouldn't be lying there in the snow."

He looked up. I had a hard time recognizing him, because the blandsomeness was all gone. Blaine had animated. I didn't like it.

"When I got the call for your house, they gave me the specifics—a girl found her mom suicided. I didn't want to go. Then I think, 'No, go. Go and do it right.' I wouldn't let anyone stare at you. No drugs, no sedatives, even if you were hysterical. I wasn't going to take you out of there 'til you wanted to leave, and after we left, I'd tell you: 'It doesn't get better. People are gonna say that, but don't listen to them. It doesn't get better. It just gets less.'"

He scooted closer, forgetting he was on stairs. He teetered, and inched back, bent practically to ninety degrees. "I was going to tell you, at first she's all you see. You come to, you see her every few seconds, these flashes—but that's only a couple hours. Then it's every few minutes. That part's hard, that's the worst. It lasts about a week, week and a half. Then you're over the hill. You can go twenty minutes. Thirty, forty. Took me months to make it an hour. I know a trick, though."

He smiled a terrible smile. "You make it an appointment. You set up a time, every day, and you think about it. Think about it any way you want, whatever works. And you don't skip, not one day, or it's worse when you remember again. That's what you do."

Blaine left me an opening. I didn't take it.

"Except you're not doing any of that. You're not going to need any of that, are you?"

I folded into the corner. Crumpled the Parliament pack.

He got up, jumped the stairs, went to the desk at the end of the bookshelves, and pulled a drawer. He tore cellophane, threw underhand. Fresh cigarettes landed by my heel, followed by his gold lighter. He sat on the floor so I could look at him levelly.

And I did. Blaine wasn't enjoying this at all. His skin was stretched too tight, like he wanted to jump out of it and run. Yet he'd sit here until the end of the world—letting me watch a parade of old nightmares that was flattening him—to hear why I wasn't doped in a hospital room. He wanted to know what my secret was.

I wished it were something that would help. "I do that already," I said. "The day I kicked her, that's my appointment.

Every day when I walk home." I lit up and corrected myself: "The day I broke her."

Blaine didn't argue.

"You played baseball," I said.

"Second baseman. I was better at football."

"You liked baseball better."

He grinned, catching the pack when I threw it. "Now why's that?" I pointed at a signed baseball two shelves over, a glove right above me, a framed trio of player cards on the desk behind him.

"My dad's," Blaine said. "His house. His shit."

"Where's . . . ?"

"He stopped a speeder and got clipped by a semi." Blaine took an envelope off the desk, tapping ash into it. "He stepped out on my mom every chance he got. That's why we moved. She kept bumping into his girlfriends in New York. She thought we'd come here and he'd shape up. We come here, and all it does is give him more space. She got depressed—I'm no shrink, but I'll go out on a limb and say sleeping twenty hours a day qualifies as depression. My dad thinks it's not. He thinks it's her wanting attention. And he gives it to her, yelling at her, telling her the house is going to hell, where's his dinner. Here's the real kicker, is he was maybe right, because she yells back and that's about the only time I saw her anything but miserable." Blaine shrugged. "I took over the cooking and cleaning. I couldn't handle those fights. Her last shot at getting what she needed, and I fucked it up for her."

Here's where I was supposed to disagree. "Not your fault," "she was sick," bleh-bleh-bleh. I wouldn't insult him like that, because he hadn't insulted me like that.

Blaine nodded at my silence. Our atmosphere changed. Which came first—his respect increasing or my nerves decreasing? His uniform seemed irrelevant now. And none of the ages on my fake driver's licenses felt old enough.

"Does it help?" I said. "Going out, bringing a girl home?"

"I never bring 'em here."

I thought: Well, what the hell. And aped a Vickie's Secret model. Slight sulk to my heavy lips, begging, but not for a kiss. I couldn't tell how serious I actually was. It wound up not mattering.

"I'm not having sex with you," Blaine said.

I laughed so hard my throat hurt.

"Save it for leap year," he said, and I was useless for about five minutes.

"I'm serious," I said, when I almost was. My head felt heavy. My night had been . . taxing. "Does it help?"

"For a little while. Then it's worse, but that's not for long, either. I hate sleeping alone. I wake up early without trying, so it's easy to get out of there." He flicked his badge. "Say I gotta get to work, and it's almost never a lie."

I stood up and turned to peruse books, to stay awake, but I did it too fast. My vision blurred over names of eminent dead men. Seneca, Cicero, two kinds of Pliny. I prattled, forgetting to frame my references. "My teacher's awesome. He said he might be hurting our AP scores, but we were going to spend two months on the period. The parallels are incredible. When the seat of power's too far removed from industry and resources, it always breeds discontent."

"Hey—"

"Marcus Aurelius was full of it, though. Stoicism's a total rich boy's religion."

"Hey, you're swaying on your feet. I'll show you your room."

I didn't walk; I floated. Up the stairs, and more stairs. And I saw a bed and I went to it and fell on it, and there was Blaine in the hall.

"This locks from your side. I'll lock it behind me, okay? You're safe here."

My eyes were buttoning. Sinking into a never-seen abyss of sleep, I barely heard him say: "If I'd have known she was dead in there, I'd have shot you before I let you go inside."

Bedroom door shutting, his steps down the steps. Beeps of an alarm system, and my own alarm system ringing a warning I didn't understand. It demanded connections before vital input got lost. Two words.

FREE TIBET.

SIX

3:35 a.m.

I sensed yesterday at my back, but I couldn't look. I lay there, thinking about how I wasn't thinking about it. The clock refused to speed up, so I got out of bed, examining the room for signs Blaine had been in here, even benignly. The door was shut. Sliding glass to my left gave on a snowy deck, its patio furniture lumped white.

My heartbeat was feathery. I was picturing Blaine on the other side of the door, psyching himself up, gathering the nerve to come inside.

I went to the door, put my ear to it, and looked for the shadows of his feet in the bar of dull light at the bottom. I unlocked and opened it, thinking how funny rape-fear is, how rampant, because if you're a girl who's ever been to a public swimming pool, you've felt the stare of that stranger. He's always there, and he changes faces, and he dreams it's night and you're by yourself. Loads of rapists only do it in their minds. They never bump into the perfect opportunity, but they imagine that opportunity tirelessly. I'd been aware of predators since my earliest memories. I wondered why, what special equipment I had.

The house was a jungle gym of shadows as I moved down the upstairs landing, passing a linen closet, a tiny room with a writing table, a bathroom after that. I eyed the shut door at the landing's far end. Blaine was asleep behind it. I could hear him. He didn't exactly snore, but he was way under, greedy for air.

Exploring his house was too tempting to pass up. Besides, it was only fair. He'd gotten to go through all my stuff while I'd chillaxed in the back of an ambulance. I went downstairs.

The kitchen counter was empty. I opened his fridge. I'd assumed pizza, Chinese food, more pizza. The containers threw me. I opened the freezer, found the same. Tupperware were dated, with a COOKED line and a TOSS BY line. At once impressed and bummed, I closed the doors. No way I could sneak food without him knowing.

I wandered to the living room, its window that gave on his street. I searched for hints of my street, pinpointing where it was by the Collins house, glowing like a fallen star. The police must have left. I turned and sat on the window's narrow sill, taking in Blaine's house from a new angle. Nothing reflected him. The carpet was ratty shag, clean but frayed, in need of replacing. The lamps and light fixtures were pretty Tiffany-style pieces with dangly crystals. I shopped his mom's videos again. Hollywood's golden age.

I thought of Blaine opening a drawer in the desk for his cigarettes. Or his fridge, a Dewey decimal system of premade meals. He fit himself into nooks and crannies. All righty, then. At the bottom of the video shelves were five cabinets. I pulled one open.

And found porn. A *lot* of porn. I had my middle-school giggly reaction and stamped it: He's human, it's normal, grow up.

I went downstairs to the den, seeking refuge in a gentler medium. I rode my languor to the desk chair and sat, sagging my skull backward to the ergonomic cushion. The desktop was pin neat. Fifteen pigeonholes waited for correspondence. I reached into each of them expecting nothing. When I touched something, I knew before I pulled my hand out that I was holding money. Still, the denominations were a surprise. They were hundreds, a fat fold of them in a blue rubber band. I counted what I had. It was $3,100. The paper was crispy; the cash had been there awhile. Did he even know about it?

I bent over the money, breathing hard. It filled the spaces between the bills, made them breathe with me. They whispered, "We belong together, Rainy."

I hunched over the desk. My hand fell deep into its recesses, where I touched metal. Until then, some small part of me believed he was lying, that his parents live in

Florida, they golf every day, he's just a lazy schmuck about redecorating. But the eight-by-ten photo shot those doubts to smithereens. Blaine looked maybe five. He was on his mom's lap. She had Farrah hair. Her smile was like she was being scalded and trying not to scream. Dad had a hand on his wife's shoulder, but he was seducing the living Toledo out of the camera. And Blaine, so heartbreakingly happy. Too young to be anything but oblivious.

I put the picture back.

I folded the money and put that back, too.

I turned the chair. Which of us had it right? Blaine, who'd kept this house an altar to their toxic self-absorption? Who lived surrounded by the evidence, examining it for clues, hoping one day he'd figure it out. He'd devoted himself completely to building a tired, unoriginal, chauvinistic exterior—or, I strongly suspected, that exterior had been forced upon him. His interior was this packed, cluttered museum of guilt and regret. Did he really think a woman couldn't see it? When he went up to her in a bar, said 'Can I buy you a drink,' did he honestly believe what she liked about him was his remoteness, his inability to truthfully engage? No. What she liked was the idea she could tease the decent man out from behind his douchebag pretense.

So was it I who had it right? Eager enough to leave it all behind that I'd almost robbed the very rare human who could understand. If you're raised by someone who basically lives two lives, you become awful in a way, because you're always ready for anyone you meet to change. You gut-deep know that inside a person is the truth of that person, and the more they deny the truth of who they are, the darker and uglier that truth gets. You become determined to invert the paradigm, wear the worst of yourself on the outside, carry the best of yourself way down inside like a secret.

Then I decide—or some knee-jerk imperative in me decides—to plunge my hand back into the desk's hidey-hole, cram the cash in my pocket. And bust balls for upstairs and up more stairs and left and five feet, and there's his door. And I'm huffing and puffing at it, like I want to blow it down. I'm seeing it happen as I stand still: going in, he's on his back, so bland handsome, so asleep, and I pull my jeans off to give him less reaction time before straddling his lap.

It hurts, right? The hymen snaps. What's up with that, biology? Why make every girl's first time into an endurance test for pain? Fuckever, my endurance was awesome. I was a distance runner. I'd ride him right past the pain.

I sat down outside the door. I more oozed down—like that liquid bad guy in the second *Terminator* movie. Good movie; bad guy had an incredible ass. I put both hands over my mouth, eyes welling. I wanted that other life, the one where nobody knew where I came from. The one by the shore with so many footprints it looked like there weren't any. If anyone made note of me at all, it'd be for a song I sang from a perch where they couldn't see me, in an apartment where there was nothing to unpack.

I listened to him sleeping. If I woke him, if I told him everything I wanted, down to that last detail—the space that had somewhere to rest, somewhere to read, and something to cook in—would he get it?

I went to my room. I opened the closet and the dresser drawers and the drawers in the bathroom. They were all empty. They had smooth, stainless contact paper, waiting for contact with something. The shower smelled like lavender-scented ammonia, and both sinks' fixtures shone.

I wanted to go to Blaine's door, open it, get under the covers with him, and beg. Plead for him to take it, take it from me, and tomorrow I'll leave and you'll never see me again. I promise. Please.

Instead, I slid between the cozy sheets. My mom tried. She tried for a really long time. But, my God, I could feel it: the effort, the fatigue, the thin threads fraying. I wanted to tell her to quit, ease up, save herself. I didn't have the words. They wouldn't have mattered anyway. Nobody takes a five-year-old seriously.

Nobody takes a seventeen-year-old seriously.

SEVEN

"Come on," Blaine said, giving the horn a tap. He embarked on a complex circuit of turns, alleyways, and underpasses that shorted rush hour. The old Pillsbury factory and the sculpture gardens and the Loft passed in a whacked, unheard-of order. I got the sense he was showing off. "They'll call this afternoon. I wanna say noon and not be lying, but I'd be lying."

"Okay."

"Someone from Child Protection Services will be waiting in the office after seventh period. They'll escort you to a car."

"'Kay."

"I'm overseeing the situation. It'll be a good place." He waited for another syllable. At my silence, he turned down "Jungleland"—Blaine had picked the music this morning. "Why are you so quiet all of a sudden?"

I chose a genuine concern. "Will you get in trouble? For harboring a fugitive last night?"

"No."

"Are you lying?"

"No, Rainy. I'm not. I say the right lines to the right people, and they assume your paperwork got lost."

"Kunz won't."

"No. Kunz won't."

I grinned at people in the passing yards, bright-coated kids holding moms' manicured hands. The Nokomis housewives, all highlights and bangles and Uggs. "Could you let me out here?"

Blaine pulled over, tires bouncing onto plowed snow. "Hang on," he said. He took a block of rubber-banded cards from his pocket and slid one free. "This is me. Cell's on the back. You need anything, call. I mean it, okay? Call collect."

"Thanks." I put it in my back pocket. "Bye."

"I'll check up on y—"

I slammed the door. Climbing the drift, my running shoes punched through the crispy skin, into tender snowmeat. Blaine's cruiser had similar trouble but lots more weight to work with. It preceded me up the street and away.

The air smelled of ashes. It made me want a cigarette badly enough that I'd chewed two fingers to bleeding by the time I turned the corner. Dewey High shouldered above its veiny trees and a wide stream of cars. The clock above the main entrance showed four minutes 'til the bell.

I went south to a coffeehouse on Franklin that did amazing things with cinnamon rolls, meaning they used way more icing than necessary. I chose a cushy seat by the fireplace and drank my coffee, debating my best route to the bus station and wondering how much the schedule had changed.

But the thought of traveling wore me out—preemptively, like I'd already done it. Crossed a thousand-thousand miles and stayed awake the whole time.

I took out his card. *Sergeant Blaine Clay, Minneapolis Police Department*, a work number. *Cell* in scribbly blue pen at the bottom with an arrow. I memorized the digits on the back and had a healthy laugh at my own expense.

You want to call him, huh? Great. That's great. And say what? "Blaine, what's up? It's been minutes. I swiped three large from your dad's antique desk, but let's chew the fat."

I put the card away, hunting for a distraction. The café had a newspaper bin, but as I stood and moved toward it, my entire body buttonhooked as if vetoing a terrible idea.

Five seconds later, I was outside, walking downtown's roomy grid—thinking, looking in store windows, fingering the cash in my pocket. I wanted that gray wool peacoat. I wanted this bedspread with the little blue flowers. I watched my shoes, in order to not watch the windows, and that was the wrong thing to do, because I needed new shoes.

The notion of spending his money felt like some uncrossable Rubicon of sin. I couldn't, I wouldn't. I'd return it. I'd go to his precinct right now and—

And? Slip it in his desk with a few dozen cops watching? Get an envelope, write his name on it, leave it with a secretary like the most backward Christmas present ever?

I veered toward Central Library. I'd read awhile, mull it over. It's not like I was on a time limit here. Nobody knew where I was; nobody cared. I could drop off the face of the earth and nobody would care. I found, as I neared Central's layer-cake design, that I was almost running.

Once inside, I went upstairs to the 900s, picking a bunch of titles I remembered from Blaine's dad's den. Sitting on the floor, making a nest. *Alaric and the Visigoths.* Kick-ass band name. I opened the book, and it instantly worked. Words took me far away.

I didn't look up until my stomach growled. The clock was doing vertical splits. It was dark outside.

He was probably still at work. Not home by now, not yet. In between, driving? Don't call him while he's driving—he can just not answer, relax. I'd call him and I'd ask if he ever thought, driving home, that his dead mother would be there when he arrived. I absolutely needed to ask him if that's why he kept the house.

I went downstairs and passed the library's information desk, where a beige woman was scanning bar codes. "You have a jacket, don't you?" she said. "It's supposed to get to twenty below tonight."

I didn't answer, except to put my sweater on. A bare second later, cold bit me like a pit viper. I doubted the phone booth would be warm; it wasn't. Picking up the receiver, it dawned on me that although I had over $3,000, none of it was change. I watched my scabby fingers dial 1-800-COLLECT. A nice robot lady asked my name, and I told her.

"Rainy?" He sounded— Well, Blaine always sounded like that. "Are you there?"

"Yeah. Yes." I floundered and fell on etiquette. "Hi."

"Where are you?"

"I'm—" I'm at the corner of Can't Believe I Called and Crap I Take It Back. "I'm sorry. Sorry. I don't know why I did this."

"Do *not* hang up!"

"What's wrong?" I looked outside at Fifth and Hennepin, I guess hoping Blaine would materialize out of thin air.

"Listen to me. Did you cut school today?"

I said nothing.

"It's okay if you did, but you need to tell me. Tell me right now."

My throat was corked. Why'd he care?

"Did you cut school, yes or no!"

"Yes! Yes, I fucking did—I'm not going into the system so Chester the Molester can hump me 'til I'm legal in seven fucking weeks!"

"Rainy."

"You buy me some fucking pancakes and you think you're my friend? Fuck you! I'm gonna forget she ever existed! I'm gonna go so fucking far away, you're gonna forget—"

"Rainy."

"—I ever existed!"

"Stay where you are. Stay right there."

"What?"

Hennepin is a mess in the best of times. Most of downtown's one-ways feed into it. The two patrol cars headed for my corner were having a bear of a time making progress. One was southbound. The other came west. No whirly lights, no sirens. Stealthy.

"Stay there, Rainy," Blaine said.

Another male voice, faint: "They see her."

I dropped the phone and ran. The crosswalk sign on Fifth advised DON'T WALK; I didn't listen. A grille slammed to a stop inches from my legs, but by then I was already past it, into another near collision with a driver's side and an openmouthed man making a careful left turn. He sat there stunned while I climbed over his hood. A pair of voices behind me cried, "Hey!" and "Stop!" with such rigid authority that I almost obeyed. Downtown's grid tattooed itself on my brain. If I made it to Seventh, I could use the Marriott.

"Rainy Cain!" one of them hollered.

A line on the sidewalk, people waiting for Mongolian stir-fry. "'Scuse me," I called, and cut the gap they made, listening for the cops to call the same thing. They did as I shot left and saw the Marriott flags. I lucked out at the parking garage—no oncoming—and threw my shoulder into the nearest entryway door.

The lobby was a shock of marble. I passed two worried maître d's. I glanced back, watched the policemen plow into the foyer. Both were chubby-ish. One was on his radio.

But I was at the door I needed. I opened it and took the stairs toward the Skyway.

I forced my legs to slow. The place was nuts, like Woodstock with Christmas carols. I split the tide of shoppers, peeling off my sweater as I went and tossing it in a trash can. I was down to a white tank top, which was strange but not that strange: this many people and the walkways became a sauna. Plenty of kids and a few of the adults had outer layers wrapped around their waists, coats stuffed in bags or left in the car. None of them had long white hair.

I crossed the nearest footbridge. Ahead was the rotunda by the Radisson. Kitty-corner was a souvenir shop, where Vikings merchandise, including a rack of gold-and-purple stocking caps, took up most of the display window.

The store was mobbed. I put my hair in a twist and mashed it under the cap. The tag snapped right off. Out the window, in the holiday chaos, a new cop—who was unbelievably tall—poked from the top of the masses. His head moved side to side, slow and thorough. I joined the checkout line as he passed. Once he had, I counted to five and left the store. Hands in pockets, head down. The black bubbles in the ceiling's corners hid Cyclops eyes, transmitting to a surveillance room somewhere. MPD could commandeer it any minute and comb the footage. I went straight for the hotel.

Checking in without a credit card takes some finesse. Luckily, I'd had practice. I accepted my card keys with extremely bogus calm.

"I wonder what's going on out there," the desk lady said.

I said, "Shoplifter, maybe," and thanked her, went to the elevator, found my room, got in, shut the door. I slid to the floor as my legs gave out.

You're done, you did it, take five, you deserve a fiver.

The room was nothing special. It had put a significant dent in Blaine's stash, but my guilt had gone the way of the dodo. All this for $3,000? Fine, I was a punk for stealing it, but tracing my call, going all Big Brother on me? Overreact much?

I crawled on all fours to a chair by the window, envisioning the streets of Minneapolis disco-lit with police lights. I was chuckling as I crabbed onto the seat and put my chin to the sill, because that was such a charmingly egocentric image. Like they'd—

They had. Only, double what I'd imagined, maybe triple. I started counting the cherry tops. I quit at a dozen, my head getting light.

"Not for you," I said, turning to face a bed that faced a flat-screen. "It's not about you, Miss Universe, forget it."

My suspicious side said differently, but I'd ignored her enough that tuning her out was easy. I went through a few what-ifs: . . they find you on the security tapes and track you here; . . . they show your photo at the check-in desk; . . . they kick down the door and storm in.

"Can't control any of that," I said. "Sorry."

So I chose denial. I shut the curtains, hung the DO NOT DISTURB sign on the door. Got naked and donned a fluffy white robe, hopped into bed. For once, I had the remote control. I planned to imbibe a dumb action movie, but when I tripped over a documentary about Chernobyl, that sealed my fate for a long, rapt evening.

The camera crew was one of the first to enter Pripyat since the meltdown. They were British scientists. They wore radiation suits, took Geiger counter readings, walked the abandoned city. Over the last aerial shot of the hot zone and its tranquil emptiness, its absolutely normal-seeming topography, a classy English voice-over reminded me that Pripyat wouldn't be habitable for another ten thousand years.

I hit the power button and went to the bathroom, absentmindedly turning on the jets in the tub, reassured that if they were going to find me, they would be here by now. I was testing the temperature of the water when I thought of a tub with no jets but with a pleasant rosy coloring, set off by candlelight.

You say to yourself, "She'll do it, and then it will be over." But then she does it, and the fallout keeps falling.

You tell yourself it isn't complicated. But family is. It's limitless love. It's godlike power attached to someone human. And you can know you mean nothing to her, and she can throw you away like a bag of garbage. Then she can split her wrists open and it's still a meltdown.

You can't get into a tub, but you do. Your tears blend with your bathwater.

You think about all the things in the world that go wrong. You think about how everything dies. You mentally watch it all happen. You picture the poisoned streets of Pripyat, how life there has come to a complete and utter stop. And you realize that none of that matters to you, that you just don't care.

You say to yourself, You're being kind of an insensitive prick here, Rainy.

Except your childhood's a wasteland, a ghost city. You don't want to think of her as the reactor, with lights still on in the building because people dropped everything and ran. You don't want to be doing this, weeping uncontrollably in a bathtub. But nobody's here, no one's listening, you're all alone, it's fine. Walk Pripyat's vacant streets. Hear the squeak of doors left open. Hear them blow shut on a breeze rich in strontium-90. Look in the windows, many of them broken. Look at the spaces looted of valuables, scattered in trinkets. Toy dolls. Toxic mattresses. Paperwork. Cheap chairs. Look at what gets left behind.

And know, beyond a shadow of a doubt, that you will not be one of these things. You will not allow it. Instead, it will be you who leaves everything behind. You will never quit; you will always be in motion. You'll step out of your own bones if you have to, and keep going, and you'll be nothing but formless slime, but that is acceptable. That is a price you are willing to pay. You'll pay more. You'll give anything.

I grabbed a bar of soap and scrubbed. Imagining I was on an empty sidewalk, flanked by shops announcing their wares in Cyrillic. I saw my mom. She was wearing the green housedress she'd laid out yesterday morning. She wanted to take me to the amusement park, buy me a ride on the carousel. I informed her I was grown up. She was too late.

I'd leave Sunday. I might take the train this time, spring for a sleeper car. I could sleep the whole way there. Maybe I'd dream of being a kid again, swinging in one of those swings where the seat looks like a diaper, pleading with my mom to push me higher. Hearing the laughter of other children sharing the sandbox or clinging to the merry-go-round or pumping their legs to move the teeter-totter. And nearby, the fat concrete bellies of the corrupted plant, where the chain reaction can't be stopped.

Limitless power. Human error. The sirens start to scream.

EIGHT

The next day dawned charcoal—the shade of a hotel room with its curtains closed tight. I padded to the windows. Fresh, mean white was everywhere. Even the air. It was a level of snowiness that hung the stuff suspended. Not a blizzard but right on the cusp.

I took out two crisp twenties, ordered crab cakes Benedict. I'd do nothing today. That was my ambition, and it fulfilled a bunch of smart directives. Lie low, let the snow blow over. Then tomorrow, when everyone and their mother is traveling, go be one more face. I couldn't admit my other reasons. How drained I was. How a patch of the bed was tear-soaked. I had no idea if or how much I'd slept. The whole night was a bad dream.

I made the whole day a swirl of escape. Leaving the curtains shut, ordering plates of salt and fat. Eating by the glow of movies, TV dramas, and sitcoms I flipped among and fell into. I'd fall out, fall asleep, crawl back to consciousness. I woke to the *Friends* theme alerting me what time it was. That's when I got up, pulled back the shades, and looked outside.

A stormy sea of traffic. A half-moon on the rise.

I was putting on clothes before I knew why. The resolution for a walk, for a stiff hit of life, had taken me over. I knew if I stayed here, I'd call him. I wanted to ask him . . . anything, nothing in particular. The bills folded beautifully, fitting against my thigh like they were missing parts of each other.

I needed a coat. I took the Skyway to Marshall Field's, intent on buying one, but the crowd was even thicker than it had been last night, and the memory of that phone call with Blaine still lingered: "Stay right there."

I shuddered, detouring to the customer service office. The guy at the desk was wearing a name tag, and I read it to forget it. He had a bow tie printed with tiny snowmen, along with an expression that suggested he'd been standing at this spot since Black Friday.

"Hi," I said, making my voice chipper.

"How can I help you?"

"So the other night? When it was warm out? I was trying on jeans, and I left my coat in the dressing room." I tapped my Vikes cap. "Remembered the hat, brilliantly." He scooped under the counter and opened a cabinet. "What's it look like?"

Play the odds. "Black. Basic." And you need: "A hood."

"Lift pass on the zipper?"

"Yes!"

He evaluated me, some sudden burst of professional responsibility. "Where's the lift pass to?"

Man, fuck your mother. "I'm not sure where we went last. Either Buck Hill or Hyland."

He handed it over. Long and thick, Columbia brand. "Thanks a million," I said.

I went through housewares, to a street exit. Ten below doesn't feel that different than zero. By then, it's just cold. Long johns would've been wise, and I did ponder getting some, but my coat went most of the way past my knees, cutting the wind. I walked south, leaving downtown. Snow-wraiths dragged shrouds down the centerline; they were my only company. My house was several miles to the right. I went left.

To Powderhorn Park, the lake bathed in light. Southeast, where houses strained the term "houses," bragging pillars and pricey brick, triple garages, rounded windows. Most of them were dark. I thought how my neighborhood was dinky by comparison—and I shouldn't have thought that, because then I got curious. Whether my house was different, whether you could tell. I wanted to see if my front door wore a sash of police tape. I guessed the blinds were still open. Did they unplug our tree? *Really* shouldn't have thought that, because that made it a fire safety issue, and I was going due west with no further argument.

The route was quiet. Houses, houses, grocery stores and gas stations that served the houses. I hadn't smoked since last night. Now I could kill off a pack. I had my eye on a mini-mart to buy some when I realized it was on Blaine's street.

Spontaneously, my hood went up. I'd check if he was home. I bet he was, since I'd been walking at least an hour. My legs were going rigid with cold, although it wasn't time to freak out yet. When it was, I'd hit a McDonald's. Or my house—jimmy one of the windows whose fastenings I kept loose. It appealed to my masochistic side. I'd have to visit her bathroom, make sure they drained the water. I could clean the tub; she'd like that.

This daydream consumed me. The sight of Blaine's house was a blip as I continued on my way to macabre chores.

I stopped in the middle of the sidewalk. The shoveled, sanded, salted sidewalk.

Blaine's wasn't cleared.

He either hadn't been home since yesterday morning or he was dead. Nobody leaves a foot plus, especially not on their sidewalk. That's grounds for shunning. It's the uppermost Midwest's most basic, informal, inviolable law.

I heard his garage grunt. The door opened a few inches. I ran to the house opposite his and hugged the edge. The cruiser floated inside. Blaine got out. He was in uniform again. His posture wilted when he looked at his driveway, and he trudged to where a shovel hung on the wall. We were fifty feet apart.

I told my body to turn around, and it did. This house's backyard was unfenced. It was exhausting stomping through snow that cupped my knees, but I went at it with fervor, with passion. I got to the next street and used yards again. I did that for six blocks, ignoring pins and needles in my shins, ignoring shivers. I couldn't feel my feet as I stepped onto my driveway.

All the tracks from last night were gone. It looked like nothing had happened. Except the blinds were still open, and there was a garish cross of CAUTION: CRIME SCENE on the door. I sat on the stoop, reminiscing. Before I'd learned to rig our windows, I was stuck outside an entire summer night. She'd changed the locks. I was twelve or thirteen at the time. It wasn't that bad, just boring. I doubted I'd make it very long in subzero temperatures, but I was thinking why not try, when my lizard brain ordered me: Look up.

A black van was parked two doors down, to the right.

FREE TIBET, the sticker said.

My legs snuck from under the coat as I panned the other way, pretending nonchalance. Pretending it was time to go. I was a few feet from the corner of my house when the van's rear door slid open and a bald man sprang out. He ran straight for me.

Different from last night. Different from the cops. He was faster. Guys that huge were supposed to be slow, but he could move. But I could *move*. I was in my backyard, getting distance, when he yelled, "Kat!" right behind me.

I felt a hold on my coat. The zipper screamed, and it ripped apart. My arms swept out of the sleeves. Red-hot cold hit my skin. I was wearing a tank top in ten below. Up the hill and over it, my legs pumping through the powder like it wasn't even there. I followed my own tracks, chopping their strides in half. The cuffs of my jeans were pasted in snow. My feet weren't there. My legs weren't there.

He was still there, still coming, but I was *going*, and euphoric. Rationality couldn't catch me. Logic ate my snowdust. I was so fast and so free, and so was he. "Kat!" Then I found a vein of energy deep and buried; I tapped it. He fell behind, but not far.

I could hear a shovel. I didn't have the air to say his name. I couldn't seem to slow.

"Oof!" Clatter-thwack. Shovel down. "Rainy? Rainy!"

I clawed at coat. Shoulder of a good, warm coat. Letters I could read: *MPD*. My knees smacked driveway.

"Rainy, what the hell's—" A holster unsnapped, unburdened of a gun. "Freeze," Blaine shouted. "Freeze, Sam!"

I had a grip on Blaine's pant leg. His other leg jerked to give chase, but I grabbed it and tried to say a good, pathetic, "Please."

"You're okay." He whispered it, moving me. His coat went around me. "You're here. Stay calm."

Suddenly, I was soooo calm.

"I'm gonna pick you up now. Okay? Stay awake. That's the important part, stay awake."

Progression of sights and sounds that I knew from being through them once before. I gave up and shut my eyes.

"Don't do that! Wide-awake now! Right now!"

Blaine's neck was at the tip of my nose. I smelled him—good cologne. He was pounding up the stairs. My back pressed into softness. He tried to peel my fingers from his bicep. His cheeks were streaked as if with pink paint. He took his cell phone from a pocket, and it flashed when he flipped it open. I grabbed it, threw it. I heard it hit the master bathroom's tile and slide. Blaine went to go get it, but I wrapped around him.

"Rai— You need a doctor!"

I didn't answer, except to scream a bunch of things I'd never said out loud, to anybody. "I'm real, right? You can see me, right? I'm not dead, I'm not a ghost, I'm not a devil or anything, am I? She hated me, she hated me, she was sick, but she hated me, too. Was she right? Was she right to?"

"Everything's okay," he said. "Everything's okay, stop. You can stop." Blaine rocked back and forth. "You're okay. Everything stops now."

He was so warm. I tried to crawl into him. He was a sleeping bag, and I'd find the flap. I found his back—good enough—and latched my fingers there.

His tone changed, though the words were almost the same: "Okay?"

"No."

"Okay." His whisper oceanic in my ears. "It's okay."

Blaine's breath was sharp cinnamon, covering coffee. There wasn't a light on in the whole house—he'd been in too big a hurry to get me under blankets. Blaine was building an igloo around me out of the comforter. He got into a crouch. "Where have you been?"

I didn't see the point of lying. "The Radisson."

There was a moment of quiet. Then Blaine laughed. Not the kind of laughter you join, more the kind you break out the backward coats for. He was swiping his eyes with his wrists, settling his hands on his half inch of hair and regarding me with a level of exhaustion that can't be faked. "Do you have any clue what the past thirty-six hours have been like for me? Any fucking idea? No? Lemme give you a hint: I show up at your school when the bell rings. I'm in civvies, so you're not embarrassed—"

"You didn't say you'd be there."

"Well, I was. And you weren't. You were in your penthouse suite while I'm thinking you're—" He cut himself off. Started to stand. "I gotta go make about ten phone calls."

I finagled my arm free and caught his. "Sorry about the money."

"What money?"

"Nothing. It's—I found a twenty behind the nightstand last night and I took it."

Blaine waved off my apology. He went to the bathroom and hit the light, got his phone.

"Who's Sam?" I asked. How had it taken me this long to ask?

"Right now I need you to stay here."

"Fine."

"I want your word."

"I said, 'Fine.'"

"I want you to tell me, 'Blaine, I'll stay right here, you have my word.' Say that."

"You're gonna go set the alarm. You'd know if I left."

"But now I've seen you run."

I dug out of my blanket and began untying my shoes. "You have my word I will not leave your house, and you can have my shoes as collateral."

"Keep 'em," he said, going to the door.

"Why?"

"Because if you fuck me over and bolt, I don't want you losing toes." He left the room and headed down the stairs. The alarm beeped. He came back up. A door shut.

I retied my sneaks, offended. Like I'd run again with a criminal landmass after me. And honestly? Couldn't even go there.

My legs were stiff. Standing required an assist from the bed. Blaine's voice rumbled in his office, enough to mask my creeping down the stairs. I was going to put the cash back—what remained of it anyway. I was wondering where his laundry stuff was as I passed the living room, thinking how great it'd be to put my clothes in the dryer. Ten minutes and they'd be toasty. But I couldn't come up with a way to do it that wouldn't make me feel like the sex objects in his DVD collection.

Peeking toward his porn cabinets, that's when I saw the file. Alone on his coffee table was a cream-colored folder. It caught my attention because it was so thick, the width of two phone books stacked together. Hundreds of individual papers were warping the sturdy manila they'd been wrapped in, and this problem was exacerbated by the rubber band straining to keep the pile collated, like a Sunday *Tribune* overloaded with circulars. The file's label tab was sideways. I tilted my head going by, to read it.

CAIN, SAM.

I looped the couch. The door to Blaine's office was still closed. Beeps in there—he was dialing.

I got the rubber band off and took a corner of the folder in two fingers, reverently. On top of the whole mess was a black-and-white photograph. Ten people, sitting by a tree. On the tree, some of them, since it was a weeping willow, and a branch near the ground did that thing where it split sideways, made a bench.

I'm thinking: See? This has nothing to do with you.

But I'm also bringing the paper to the tip of my nose. There's two girls making out in the middle. There's a guy with a ZZ Top beard and sunglasses glaring at them, a homely chick hanging on his arm. There's a man wearing a dress, bottom center, getting a kiss on either cheek from two more girls. A fat guy falling out of frame.

Maybe I saved them for last on purpose. At the far right was my mom. I hardly recognized her. She looked happy. She was sitting in some thin grass, her legs stretched ahead, tangling with the legs of the man behind her. His arms were a cage she was elated to live in. He was the bald man, only he wasn't bald. He had hair to his shoulders. His body was normal in the photo—actually, he was on the scrawny side. He was holding two fingers aloft, showing a sweat stain under one armpit.

I plunked my ass to the floor, pushed backward with my heels, to a corner. Blaine's scared bark of "Rainy!" couldn't reach me here.

I kept staring at the photo as his steps thudded down to me. He asked, "Water?"

I didn't answer. Blaine ran to his kitchen. I folded the picture into crisp quarters and slid it in my back pocket. He made one attempt to take my hands and put them around a glass, but I jerked backward, cracking into the shelves. "My dad is outside," I said.

"Yeah. Somewhere."

"You knew."

"Not 'til yesterday. Not 'til after I dropped you off at school."

"Are you lying?"

Blaine put his fingers in a V under his eyes, to draw mine there. "Am I?"

"What's going on?"

He got the file, shuffled paper. He dropped a stack of sheets, and they scattered. "Wednesday night, my precinct got a call from the feds. You following?"

I made a noise.

"From the FBI, okay? FBI says to put a unit on your house. The day before your mom— Three days ago. Kunz gave me the assignment. He gives me most of those, he knows I'm not a talker. He tells me I'm watching for this guy." Blaine held up the bald man's mug shot. It had a plaque at the bottom: CAIN, SAM, then codes and numbers I didn't understand. "They didn't tell me who lived at your house. They didn't tell me what this guy did. I saw you leave for school. I was sitting there all day, you come home, I get the call, and . . . And you have to believe me—I didn't know. We didn't know she'd react that way."

"What? What way?"

"They called her. The bureau called her that morning. They told her he'd escaped."

"Prison," I said.

"Yes."

"My dad escaped from prison."

"Yes." The rim of the water glass floated by my chin. "Drink this."

My nerveless hands were no help. Blaine tipped it into my mouth like he was bottle-feeding a baby. I got greedy. "Slow down," Blaine said. "There's more, take it slow."

He went to go get more. I stayed on the floor, surrounded by forms, reports, statements. My eyes landed on another black-and-white photo. A house on dirt. One bony, sick tree in the foreground. A tire swing strung from a thin branch.

"Here." He'd added ice. "I get to work yesterday morning, right? Kunz calls me into his office first thing. There's these two suits who haven't smiled since fucking *Laugh-In,* and they want me in interrogation. Kunz tells them, 'Hell, no.' Remember how I said nobody'd care if you didn't check in at the halfway house? Guess not. They're threatening me with prison time if I dropped you off at a friend's or paid a late call to CPS. I checked with Child Protection Services right away—remember me saying that? These guys intercepted. They wanted you at that halfway house because it's got security guards, locks, surveillance. So I'm thinking, 'Well, this cop thing's been fun. Probably be a security guard myself next month.' And I fess up and tell them you were here. Then comes the scary part: they calm right down. They look at each other like, 'Thank God this uni from Podunk did something smart by accident.' And they start firing questions at me. Firing them on full automatic: how you seemed, what we talked about, whether you were in a hurry to get out of here. I go, 'Hold on, hold on. How about I ask a few?'"

Blaine laughed without humor. "Try that on the FBI sometime—it's real effective. I know Kunz can be . . . 'intimidating' is a good way to put it, but he's a great man. I've known him most of my life; he lives the job. And when he says, 'Y'know, Blaine, maybe an interrogation room would be best for this,' I'm ready to shit I'm so surprised. But I've played poker with him. I've learned the expensive way how to tell he's got the cards. I spent three hours with those guys. Three hours saying, 'I got her some food. We drove to my house. She went to sleep. We didn't talk.' Meantime, Kunz went through the briefcase one of the agents left behind and copied your dad's federal file. Him and me took a long lunch, went through it front to back. When we were done, we knew the FBI wasn't going anywhere. I cooperated. I didn't have a choice. But even if they hadn't been standing over my shoulder when you called me, I'd have come after you on my own. Understand? This scamming a night at a hotel, this going it alone—that's over. You need our protection."

He took my empty glass, went and filled it again, came back and gave it to me, and began sweeping papers, knocking stacks together on the coffee table. I sat dumbstruck. I'd learned everything and nothing. "What did he do?"

"I'm gonna walk you through that. Right now, we need to go. There's some important people waiting on us. And you got here twenty minutes ago, not two hours. Right?"

Not a problem. It felt like twenty minutes. Felt like five.

"You still with me?" he said.

"I need a cigarette."

"There isn't—"

"One cigarette."

Blaine's head fell forward. In exasperation, but also in a subtle check of what he was leaving me with. He went downstairs, and I heard the desk drawer. I grabbed the picture of the house. It reminded me of the Depression, what I thought a house in the Depression would look like. Concrete blocks for a foundation, overlapping boards as crooked as bad teeth. There was the end of a clothesline peeking from a backyard that could only be called a "yard" if you forgave it for having no grass.

Blaine sat beside me, bumped one out of the pack. I lit the cigarette, though the tip and my hands both jiggled.

"Where is this?"

"Nebraska." Blaine opened the window behind us. "That's the farm where he grew up."

I glanced at the collage of images on the floor. I leaned over and picked another. They were on the porch, in two lines—three boys and four girls. The mom wore a done dress, the dad a brimmed hat and coveralls. "When is this?"

"Late sixties." Blaine pointed. "That's him."

Sam was a string bean, fair-haired. His face couldn't have been more different from the smiley photo hidden in my back pocket. The whole clan wore expressions that hinted that this picture-taking business was a chore, but nothing in their lives had ever been anything else.

Blaine took the photos from me, put them with the rest, and wrapped them in their folder.

"Why'd you label the file?" I said.

"Hmm?" He goosed the rubber band around, trying not to snap it.

"If it was so top secret to copy a federal file, why'd you label it?"

Blaine stared at the name on the tab. "Habit."

"You could take me to the train station."

"I can't do that."

"You could. You could say I got away from you. I jumped out of the car at a red light. I'm fast, like you said. I'll vanish. I swear, he won't find me."

Blaine picked up the water glass and gave it to me. I passed it over my lap, placed it on the shelf. "Please?" I said.

A warm mitten wrapped my left hand. It squeezed. "I'm with you on this. Every step of the way. I promise." It pulled. "We gotta go. Come on, come with me."

I went straight for the garage, thinking: Blaine's the Pied Piper, and I'm a rat trailing his magic flute to the river.

He opened the cruiser door for me. "It's okay," he said. "It's okay."

When the car started, "The Chain" came blasting out of the speakers. Blaine turned it down.

"Who's your favorite?" I said.

"My favorite what?"

The car slanted into the street. I pointed at the radio.

"Stevie," he said. I looked over at him. The van's lights were off. But it was growing—its grille of twinkly teeth chomping for the driver's side, where Blaine was saying, "Who else? I thought she was everyone's—"

I must have reacted. Blaine floored it, and the cruiser roared backward. My head wrenched and hit a hard pillow. A mix of sounds louder than loud, but "The Chain" cut silent. I checked out for a few seconds, until the pillow went softer and my neck had to hold me up again. The cruiser's hood was narrower with a high hump in the middle. The windshield had shattered. White balloon in front of me, deflating to the dash. Another one in Blaine's steering wheel.

Airbags. Those are airbags.

Blaine shook his head and put a hand to the temple I couldn't see. His fingers came back bloody. He glared in wonderment at the van standing over his TKO'd cop car. A voice speared out from it. "Get in, Kat. Your friend will be just fine."

A house would open. Somebody would come. For sure they'd called the police.

"Run," Blaine said. His hand was wandering–

"On the wheel. Both of them."

Blaine obeyed.

"Face the windshield."

Blaine didn't. "Run," he told me. "Fast as you can."

"Kat? I'm counting to ten. Get in. The cop will be fine."

Adrenaline isn't exactly a clear-thinking elixir. Strange, then, that I didn't consider running. Not for a second. I wasn't confused enough to miss the insinuation: if you don't get in the van, the cop will not be fine.

I could see the slice upside Blaine's head now–a fang from his window hung from the cut. "Go, Rainy," he said. "Run, get out of here."

The street was so quiet I hardly had to raise my voice. "I'm coming out." My door made a noise like a belch as I opened it. Blaine grabbed my arm.

"Let her go, Officer Friendly." I heard a click, or thought I did.

Blaine said: "Don't piss him off."

I was still mostly convinced I'd fallen asleep. I was asleep upstairs. I'd wake in the morning to the smell of pancakes, bacon, strong coffee. It would take a valiant exercise of will not to tell him about this freaky dream, but I wouldn't tell him. Nobody likes hearing about dreams.

I flattened a foot onto the sidewalk and held on to the cruiser for balance, feeling my way around the back.

"That's right. Come on."

Never mind. Forget it, I'd cave. I'd say: "I had the strangest dream, Blaine." And when I got to this part: "I turned and saw you bleeding. That whole side of your head and neck was bright red. You were watching me walk away, and all I could think was that you were fire, you were full of fire. I was scared of you and scared for you. I wasn't scared for me—it was like I wasn't there. Because I wasn't. Because it was all a dream."

"Hop in back, honey."

I slid open the van's side door. Inside was too dark to see. I heard very faint lo-fi radio. Guitar getting stomped by a brash, froggy croak that was somehow more sweet than sour. God, how we love the dead girls. How closely we listen once they can only speak in the past tense.

Freedom's just another word.

I stepped inside.

II

KAT

NINE

When we learned about the sympathetic nervous system during junior year, I thought that was a dumb thing to call it. What did fight or flight have to do with sympathy?

Answer: If you're, say, sitting in a dark van, and the reassurance that none of this is happening has finally worn away, and there's a circus strongman in the passenger seat and another guy driving, and neither of them talk to you for miles and miles as you take one highway after another, pointing the van's busted pug nose west, its cracked lights cutting into farm country after about a half hour, and your spine is to the seam of the big doors, knobs of vertebrae right in the center, and you're prepared any second to be murdered, your nervous system's "sympathy" takes effect and pretty much erases the mental marker-board.

Mind triage: The music's good.

I cleaved to that, to lyrics so familiar my mouth sang silently along without any conscious effort. "Light My Fire," "Blowin' in the Wind," "Layla." There were no seats where I was sitting. Dark synthetic carpeting was littered with road food wrappers, cigarette butts, partially filled water bottles. Outside, the close, clawed trees alternated with pastureland and glinty barbed wire, snow and snowy mud.

Inside, the bald man's chrome dome reflected the dashboard light, his breadth blotting the outline of the seat he sat in. I tried to catch sight of his face in the rearview mirror, but all I could see there was the driver, who I caught staring back at me so often I wondered how we were staying on the road. I didn't know where we were, which told me a lot. I'd gone most directions out of the Cities by main highways. So I figured we were on a state highway, and I watched for a number. Eventually, enough moon leaked through the trees that a sign shouted its 12 at me. I nodded, for some reason reassured.

In my favorite hypothetical, the highway patrol stopped us on an APB. They wouldn't, of course. Not out here. But I had no doubt there was an APB. Blaine had put one out; it's what he would do. I was sure he was fine. He was giving his vocal cords a workout on everybody whose job it'd been to corral—

My dad.

I looked again at the massive shape in front of me. I wanted to think "ogre," but I kept thinking "butterfly." A butterfly with its wings spread. Unlike the driver, he didn't smoke. He worked at a bottle of Dr Pepper for more than an hour, still didn't finish it. Every so often, he put on a set of headphones with a loopy cord stretching toward the floor and listened, then took them off and muttered to the driver, who did nothing but steer and eat a sunflower seed every couple of hours from a huge bag on the dash.

"He passed away," is what Mom had told me, any and every time I asked about my father. The first time I asked I was three, and wanted to know why other kids had daddies and I didn't. I didn't understand what "passed away" meant, but Mom walked away after she said it, so I thought it meant my dad walked past us one day and kept going by mistake. I asked her that night why we didn't talk to some people in the neighborhood, see if they'd seen him, and she sat me on her lap in the rocking chair and explained: "No, 'passed away' means 'dead.'"

I still didn't get why she'd used a code. My mom was dead; she didn't "pass away." She ventilated her veins and swallowed fifty pills and, somewhere in that shatter-wreck of a head, she knew I'd be the one to find her. And she also knew these guys would come find me.

"There," Sam said.

The van made a sedate right onto frozen mud, with deep tire ruts that the van sloughed through. The church at the end of the road was a lonely holy ghost, white clapboard, completely secluded. I could always run, and there were woods to hide in. But I'd already done the hypothermia bit once tonight.

The church's driveway wasn't plowed, so the driver didn't attempt it. Instead, he stopped beside a placard with broken glass, got out, and went around the front of the van. He didn't have a coat. He was bone-skinny. I felt a jolt of pity for him, but it evaporated fast. There was a pale-blue short bus parked flush with the church's south wall. On its side was a painting of five children, all races and all smiles, with the legend under them in flowery cursive: *Let the little children come to me, Matthew 19:14.*

Something hit my shoe, and I jumped back, my legs shooting forward at the same time. My foot kicked a bottle of water, which pinballed to Sam. He put his hands up like, Don't shoot, Officer.

He picked up the water. "I thought you might be thirsty. I rolled it to you. I should have said something first. I apologize."

The mix of midnight and headlight kept Sam a shape, a big bad shadow. His voice was firm yet gentle, seeming to listen even as it spoke. "Could I roll you another one?" He set an Evian sideways on the floor and pushed it toward me.

It stopped a yard away. I left it there.

"We're not going to hurt you. We need to switch cars." He turned to the windshield. The driver had the bus's hood up, his toes on the front fender. His whole wiry torso was inside the engine compartment, and he slid around with purpose.

"If only we didn't have to steal a 2001 Ford Irony, huh?" Sam said.

Outside, the guy slammed the hood and showed a thumbs-up. Sam returned it. "I didn't want it to be like this. I didn't know Harmony would . . ." He put his head in his paw and rubbed.

It was disturbing, hearing my mother referred to by her first name. Nobody called her that. Nobody really called her anything. Except kids—then she was Mrs. Cain.

Sam moved behind the van's wheel. It wasn't easy; his girth made the process a squat-and-shuffle. He put on his seat belt and reversed. We parked at the start of the trees. The bus passed us, stopped, and idled, the red of its brake lights coloring our thin woods. Sam got out, went around, and reached for the van's side door. He slid it sideways and backed up.

"It's going to be fine, Kat."

I hurried out, too chicken to look at him, and went toward the bus. The emergency exit at the rear was open. I climbed in and dropped into the farthest-back bench. The door closed behind me.

Sam got the black box with the headphones and deposited it on the bus's front bench. He made another trip for a pair of paper grocery bags and chucked them onto the floor by the bus driver's seat. Then he went back one last time, put the van in neutral, and rolled it down a steep ditch.

Sam got in and put on his headphones. The driver turned us back on the road, flicked on the bus's radio, and settled on an oldies station.

My fear was getting loose, a tight shirt I'd squirmed around in until the material began to stretch. I almost relaxed as minutes stacked into hours, as the roads we were on rolled by farms and tiny hamlets. We merged onto 94, and from Minnesota's rich variety of water and plants and dips and rises, we crossed the line to Fargo, North Dakota, where God took a hydraulic press, fed a pancake through it, and called it good. The driver took the first exit. I thought our destination might be one of the miserable houses I could see slumped behind tiny yards, but he parked at a curb, got out, and ran to a poorly lit driveway. Sam didn't say a word. In no time flat, the driver returned from the house, evading streetlamps. In his hand, license plates flashed. Quick with a screwdriver, he got back behind the wheel, dropping our Minnesota plates to the floor. We didn't pass a single soul as we returned to the highway, leaving Fargo dead-asleep behind us. Sam fell into a doze not long after the interstate became a drab, infinite plain.

"Don't piss him off." Translation: "Don't light the fuse."

I'd been inspecting Sam closely, and there'd been no strong indication whether he had a long fuse or a short fuse. What buoyed me, though, was that he gave every indication of having a sane fuse. If someone is able to sit still, it's an excellent sign.

I moved to the bench on the right side of the aisle. Ever since Sam had fallen asleep, the driver'd revived his one-sided staring contest in the rearview mirror. He moved the mirror to follow me. I gave him an eye roll and kept my eyes rolling, to a billboard for a restaurant called Ground Round in Bismarck, North Dakota. Eighteen miles. Applebee's, Cracker Barrel, and Perkins signs counted the distance down, until we crested a barely-there incline and the horizon glittered with light. Bismarck's outer fringes included a terraced white building that resembled an Aztec temple. I wondered what it was. We passed hotels for eighty bucks a night and a steak dinner special for $12.99. Under three overpasses, and we were entering Mandan: WHERE THE WEST BEGINS. A cemetery lazed off an exit. My ability to see it notified me that the sky was going gray with dawn.

The horizon behind us turned vivid. Its color soaked the bus and the ice and the black pavement. The sun poked its head up. I squinted and turned back around.

From the front, Sam was smiling at me, sort of shyly. I answered in kind, thinking only afterward, Smile the same way back at him. Smile shy.

He stood. He didn't have to bend much—he wasn't that tall, just muscle-massive. He negotiated space as if there were a man of average stature inside navigating, and his packed-on poundage was this constant, happy surprise. My best math put him over forty, but his skin was lineless, palest pale, almost waxy. His features were outsized: eyes, mouth, nose, name it. It made him look weird. Engineered.

He sat down on the bench one row up and across. Sideways, his back to the window. The sunrise found his bald head and grooved there. "Hi," he said.

You're humbled, I thought. Only, I was, was the thing. I went with it. I waved.

"My name is Sam. I'm your dad."

I tried to say, "I know." Tried twice, but I couldn't shake my enthrallment with his scalp, how the sun was making it shine.

"Yes," Sam said. "Mr. Clean. I started losing it ten years ago." He rubbed his head. "I decided, why fight it?"

I'd never done theater, but I guessed this was what stage fright felt like. "I—" I took a piece of my hair that had curled. It did that sometimes if I sweated during the night. "I screwed up bleaching it. Left it in too long, so now it's—"

White? Do I say it's white?

He was waiting.

"Ridiculous."

"It's gorgeous," Sam said. "You're gorgeous. I knew you had my eyes, but it's—it's remarkable."

He was right. Our eyes were an odd muddy moss green I'd only ever seen in a mirror.

"How'd you know what I looked like?" I said.

"Harmony sent your school picture. Every year."

I'd been throwing away my school picture proofs since sixth grade. "Did she write you?"

Sam shook his head. "I worried. About you with her. How bad was it?"

"Not too bad," I said, and locked my jaw shut.

Sam shifted his line of sight to the scenery. He let me stare, take him in. Maybe hoping it'd normalize him for me. Exactly the opposite was happening. I looked outside and searched for a handhold, a way to take control.

"We came here in seventh grade," I said, sounding all kinds of laid-back. "That billboard? Medora? It's this trip my junior high did, a welcome for the incoming class. The teachers participated, so for phys ed we rode horses, for bio we dug fossils. There's fossils in the Badlands."

"Badlands?"

"You'll see them. Orange brown, pretty funky. It was a fun trip."

Playing minigolf with our geometry teacher. Taking a tour of Teddy Roosevelt's cabin for history class. I went on and on about meeting my best friends, Heather, Ally, and Ty. We got assigned the same hotel room. We stayed up all night talking. I rooted in memories of them, in the version of me they'd believed and befriended. "We were comatose on the ride back. I mean, passed out, just—" I pulled a face, letting my tongue loll.

Sam laughed like a shout.

I reacted as if he'd shouted at me; I flinched. In the long silence that followed, I traced cracks on dry seat leather with a fingertip.

"Kat?"

"Rainy," I said. "It was raining when she had me. She hadn't thought of a name. She looked outside and said the first thing she saw, and they wrote it down." I looked outside. First thing I saw was a dead rabbit on the shoulder. Could've been worse.

"Katherine was my grandmother," Sam said. "I loved her very much. She once scared a grizzly bear off our porch by banging a soup pot with a ladle." He laughed a lot more quietly. "She loved the Mormons who'd come around. They were the only ones who ever did. We didn't get much company." The motor filled a few heavy seconds. "She died when I was six."

"Sorry," I said.

"Thank you." His hands folded. He shook them at me in what looked like supplication. "I didn't want it to happen this way. I need you to understand that. We got to Minneapolis on Thursday night. I saw you sitting on the back of an ambulance, your house full of police. When I found out what she did—" His mouth worked around the soundlessness of shock. He waved vaguely toward the driver. "That's Johnny Blue. He's a good friend of mine."

I glanced to stick a name to the face, forgetting he was the creep in the mirror.

"We followed you." Sam's tone lowered further, to confidential. "That policeman you stayed with, was he at all inappropriate?"

I shook my head no.

"Good. I was concerned. That wasn't professional of him. It's far from standard procedure, so I was—concerned. I said that already."

I made a T with my arms.

"Absolutely," Sam said. "Time-out. Take as long as you need."

Sam's head was turned. He was giving the headphones a longing look. Sparing me his scrutiny, as I'd requested. Up to now, he'd mostly done what I'd requested. Would he answer if I simply asked what he wanted? Probably, but how true would the answer be?

He should be covered in tattoos. He should have a gold tooth, brass knuckles, and ritual scarification denoting how many inmates he'd murdered while incarcerated. He had on blue jeans and a white T-shirt. His flesh was unmarked, as flawless as the sky outside. He was peeling off the tip of his middle fingernail with his teeth.

I remembered his file. "You grew up on a farm, right?"

Sam turned back to me, smiled. "I did," he said. "Not much to tell. Chores and more chores."

I lit my last Parliament, nodding. A blur of red ran behind him. I traced it, or tried—it was too fast. A red car, passing us and vrooming ahead to a pinpoint. Our driver leaned way over the wheel and shook his head—I doubted in disapproval of its speed.

Blaine and his classic Corvette: he got on the highway right after the hospital released him, and there he goes—he's chasing us; he'll save me, my hero.

Sure. Yeah, he hopped in the family suicidemobile and drove all night. Blaine and his concussion. Blaine and his head wound. Blaine bleeding, offering me one last piece of counsel. Which I now drop-kicked. "You could have killed him."

"Who?" Sam said. "The policeman? That was an accident."

"No, it wasn't."

"I told Johnny to dent the front. We hit a patch of ice, honey. We couldn't slow down."

"You said you'd hurt him."

"I said no such thing. I said he'd be fine. And I'm sure he is." Sam sat tall when I didn't pander to this, as I'd been instructed to do. He swelled; his clothes strained to contain him. Color should have filled his cheeks, but years of lacking sun must have caused his epidermis to forget it had rosy possibilities. What he said next was so mismatched to his foreboding physicality that he had to be kidding. "Would you like to call him?"

I didn't laugh. It wasn't funny.

Sam leaned over to put his arms on his thighs, making himself smaller. I looked at him and thought: Know who you're up against, man. I play this every day, I'm a pro.

But what if he was sincere?

Did I want to call Blaine? I used a motion I could disavow. I dipped my head once.

Sam erupted from his seat, and my musculature tightened, all of it—it was like my vagina did a sit-up or something. He blew straight to the front. His legs were underdeveloped compared to the top of him, and his ungainliness got worse when he moved fast, very Tasmanian Devil. He plopped beside Johnny Blue, pulled a spiral-bound book from one of the paper bags. It was a road atlas. He showed Johnny a page, pointing. He put the headphones on and peeked back at me. Gave me a thumbs-up.

I entered a perfect, refined present. It was wonderful.

"Ten minutes, Kat." Sam set the headphones back on the floor. "That cool?"

"Cool," I said. Because it was cool. I'd call Blaine, say 'sup: "'Sup, Blaine? I'm feeling an Egg McMuffin, wish you were here."

A blue SERVICES sign announced fast food and gas ahead. The level plain couldn't hide anything. To our right was a ramp. We took the exit and passed a gas station. Fifty yards more, and the van pulled over.

Sam turned around. "Do you need any money?"

"For what?"

"For the call." Sam made a phone of his hand and put it to his ear.

"No."

"Use the back door," he said. "This one sticks."

I went to the door, pulled the emergency lever, jumped down, and watched the bus roll away. I was on the side of a wide road, approaching a Texaco station. I sensed someone watching me, millions of someones. Or just him, but he'd left. I was alone.

I turned and walked backward. The bus wasn't on the road. I shaded my eyes to see the fast-food places, check the drive-thrus. Maybe they were getting breakfast? Couldn't tell. Too far.

It struck me I should run, but when I turned around, I'd arrived. I went inside. The clerk was watching a tiny TV. He wore a red Texaco hat. The bell had rung when I'd entered, but he didn't look away from his talk show. If he had, he'd have seen a young girl shocked out of her better judgment, hair gone white, wearing a cop coat and gawking around like she'd never seen a convenience store before.

The pay phone was on a far wall, between the restrooms. I picked up the receiver, dialed collect, and waited all of five seconds.

"Are you okay?" Blaine said.

"Yeah, are you?"

"Is he right there? Is Sam right there with you?"

"No."

"Tell me where you are. Right now."

"I don't know."

"Ask someone."

"Where am I?" I yelled at the clerk.

"Beach," he said. He picked up a Coke can and spat in it.

"Beach," I said. "He's lying. It's land."

"Beach, North Dakota? I'm turning around. I'm turning around right now."

"Did you go to the doctor? Do you have a concussion?"

"I'm on Ninety-Four. I'm in my car, do you understand? I'm less than fifty miles from you. Listen, Rainy, really try and listen. Has he hurt you? Has he hit you, is that why you sound so out of it?"

"No."

"How'd you get away from—Never mind, never mind. Did Sam switch cars?"

"Yes."

"To what?"

"Blue bus."

"What?" Blaine said. "Light blue?"

"Yes."

"Kids painted on the side?"

"Yes."

Blaine swore fluently. It was impressive.

"I'm tired," I said. "I'm really tired."

"I know. I know you are."

Motion at the store windows. I hoped for a bright-red Corvette—but bright-red Corvettes didn't galumph. That's what Sam did, he galumphed.

"Here's what you do," Blaine said. "Hang up and call 9-1—"

"Too late."

"Why?"

The door dinged. Sam smiled at me pleasantly. He paused at a display of gummy snacks and took a bag of worms. He waggled them, like, Am I right or am I right?

"Rainy," Blaine was saying, "hide. He doesn't like it when people get away from him. Hang up the phone and hide."

"Blaine," I said, "are you sure you're okay?"

Sam opened the bag and ate a handful.

"Are you sure? Are you sure?"

Sam signaled to give him the phone. "You're frightening my daughter," he said into the receiver. Listened. "That's quite a threat, Officer Friendly. I don't appreciate it. Almost as much as I don't appreciate your interest in my seventeen-year-old." Listened. "Your language is quite colorful. You should do stand-up comedy."

He hung up—"Sit, Kat"—and reached out to assist, like I was going to fall. I got to the floor and put my head between my knees without his help. Sam folded my hand around a Powerade. "Here, drink this."

"Hey," the clerk said. It sounds idiotic when Midwesterners speak sharply. Like a three-year-old with a stuffy nose trying to impart discipline. "You're paying for that, hope you know."

Sam went toward the counter. "I apologize. My daughter needed sugar. She's a type 1 diabetic."

The clerk turned in his chair. He pointed the brim of his hat back. "Oh, hey. Hey, sorry." He stood to get a clear bead on me. "You drink up there, hon. Take what you need."

"Thank you for that," Sam said. "Do you rodeo?"

"Oh, you betcha. How'd ya know?"

"Your hands. I have a good friend with hands like that. He can tell a man anything he wants to hear about rodeo and about a hundred things he doesn't."

The clerk spat into his Coke can and smiled brownly. "Where's your buddy ride?"

"Upstate New York. Used to." Sam picked up a Bic lighter out of a display, began bouncing and catching it. "Some fat cats had him fix a few races and he got five years. Guess what the fat cats got?"

"I'm gonna guess they got zero to no years." The clerk drooped onto the register. "See that camera there? My boss put it there to catch whoever's been picking out of the till. He's got a house in Dickinson I could put twenty of my trailer in."

"I'm Sam. I haven't shaken with a rodeo grip in too long."

"Harvey. Harvey Meyer. I tell ya what, most of what I get in here's a buncha jerks treat me like the help, know what I mean? I'm their cleaning lady and their butler and their goddamn chef." He tapped a case of pretzels turning on hooks.

"I hear you," Sam said. "A man can't even protect himself anymore. A man needs a permit to keep his family safe."

Harvey nodded vigorously. Sam lifted the back of his shirt and reached to the waistband of his jeans, pulling a giant gun out by its wooden butt. Harvey's neck quit moving the second he saw it.

Sam set it on the counter. "That's a .44 Magnum. That's a Dirty Harry gun. That's a man's gun right there."

"Oh, yeah, you got that right. But, you know—my boss, he don't allow any guns in here. We got that sign there in the window."

"That's what I'm talking about," Sam said, his hand not on the gun but right above it. "That's what I mean. Your boss with his mansion—he doesn't understand. He's not like us, Harvey. He's got servants to defend his property, servants like you. He's got you sitting here watching Povitch all day, making his money."

Harvey blew out a sigh and hunched over farther. "Yeah, you got it. He's a real piece of s-h-i-t all right. But that's how it goes."

"Hey, Harv. What if that wasn't how it went? What if we turned it around on him?"

"Well, heck, how do we do that?"

"How many other cameras does he have in here?"

"Just this one." Harvey reached up and flicked its underside. "Corporate's got a couple out front, though."

"They all closed-circuit?"

"Yeah." The word angled up, a question.

"Give me the tape. Say I robbed you." Sam tapped his gun's silver nose. "Put all the cash from the drawer in a bag, and we'll split it. I'll leave your half under the freezer outside."

For no clear reason, I deemed this the moment to stand. I got a grip on the pay phone and jostled something, snapping Harvey and Sam out of a shared trance.

Sam peeked sideways at me. He winked.

Harvey took off his hat and fanned himself, laughing. "Ho there, you got me. You got me, Sam, I hafta give it to ya."

"What would be the harm?"

"C'mon now."

"I could tie you up. I could blindfold you. You could say you didn't get that good of a look at me. At her." He stuck a thumb over his shoulder, where I was holding the pay phone like a life ring. "How much is in the drawer right now, Harv?"

"Been a pretty busy morning. Four hundred, give or take."

"And what could you do with two hundred bucks? Take your girl out? You've got a girl, right?" Sam eased the gun off the counter, pointed the barrel toward the ceiling. "Tell them I pulled a piece on you. It's the truth."

Harvey darted his eyes from Sam's to the gun a few times. He went "Hah!" and clapped his hands. "Jeez Louise, can't believe I'm pullin' this, but what'll they do? Fire me for getting robbed?" He opened the till and flapped open a paper sack.

"Wouldn't make your boss too popular around here," Sam said. "You could get the town to boycott him 'til he gave you your job back."

"Hah!" Harvey glanced out the window, raised the cash tray, and took out two hundreds from underneath. "I want the Benjamins for my half. Make sure and weigh them down." He took a handful of lighters off the Bic display. "Use these."

"What do we tie you with?" Sam accepted a bag full of small bills. "Kat, lock the front door."

“That’s good thinking,” Harvey said. “Turn off the ‘Open’ sign, too, hon. It’s got a switch right on top.” He beckoned Sam with a wrist. “The VCR’s in the office. Come on and we’ll grab that tape.”

“Lead the way.”

They went through a door between the counter and a nacho nook, Sam stowing the gun in the back of his pants, Harvey crowing about what his girlfriend would do for a pretty necklace. Me standing with a bag of gummy worms, unsure when Sam had given them to me. I went to the door, thumbed the bolt, shut off the sign. I was breathing this wild hummed allegro as they came back in. Harvey was blindfolded with a hankie. A roll of duct tape looped his wrist like a bracelet. Sam held his shoulders from behind, guiding him. “Two steps to the right. There it is—have a seat.”

Harvey submerged behind the register. “Hey, should we tape my mouth? It’d give you a better head start.”

Sam pulled a hank of tape free. “No, it hurts like you wouldn’t believe to pull it off. I’ll go over your sleeves so it doesn’t get any arm hair. But, don’t worry, you couldn’t get out of it if you tried.”

“Oh jeez. You’re not kidding there, are ya?”

Sam slapped the roll of tape onto the counter. “Now, are we cool? I can untie you and we can forget the whole idea if that’s what you want.”

A release of air, a gasket letting off steam. Then: "Sam, you take your pretty little daughter and get on out of here. I barely saw ya."

Sam came around to the aisles, saw me, and stopped. "Kat, relax. Whatever you think is happening, that is not what's happening." He pointed at the Powerade, abandoned on the floor by the phone. "Did you drink any of that?"

"Nnn . . . no."

"Yo, Harvey?" Sam called.

"Yo."

"Is it cool if we grab some stuff to go?"

"Help yourselves."

Sam took a shopping basket off a stack and gave it to me—"Here"—and beat it for the back room again. "Harv, you comfortable?"

"Oh, yeah, don't worry about me."

My sneaker unsealed from the sticky tile. I began to browse. Doughnuts first, the white ones. I got some of the chocolate glazed, too. There was the Powerade I didn't drink; I screwed the cap back on and took that. I took some toiletries. Box of cleansing wipes, jar of moisturizer.

Sam still wasn't back. I headed for where he'd gone. There were those sexy nachos posing on the cheese dispenser.

"Is it okay if I take some nachos?"

"You go ahead, hon," Harvey said. "You take a hot dog, too. On the house."

I went and selected a plastic container of chips. I hit the CHEESE button, that unnatural fluorescence coming out in a cascade.

"Tell ya what, you've got a heck of a dad there. You make sure and say thank you to him for taking care of you like he does."

I carefully avoided looking at the bound and blindfolded Harvey as I went behind the register and took two packs of Marlboro Reds.

Clodding steps. "Kat, you ready?" Sam steered me. The door we exited gave on the north side of the building. "Would you help me?" Sam led me by the hand.

As we rounded the front of the store, a car came off the ramp so fast its tires jounced. It wasn't a Corvette, wasn't a cop car. It sped by.

Sam squatted in front of the ice case. He took the two hundreds from the bag and a bunch of Bics. "These won't do it. Do you want one?" He put a lighter in my hand.

He still had the duct tape. He tore off two tiny pieces, sticking them to his jeans, and picked a pair of small rocks from the parking lot. "Gets windy here," he said, taping a hundred dollar bill to each rock. "So they don't blow to Winnipeg. How 'bout that?" He placed them under the ice chest and stood. He took my basket, held out his hand. "Mademoiselle."

My mouth was watering. All I wanted were these fucking nachos. He led me around the building's side to a brown station wagon with Johnny Blue at the wheel. Sam opened a door, and I scooted onto the middle seat. He got in next to me.

Johnny put the car in drive. I looked back as we left the station, sure there'd be some dead giveaway. But it was merely closed for business. Up ahead, I-94 was, too—Highway Patrol had checkpoints going east and west. We took a leisurely right and went north, toward the burger joints and humble houses. They were chaos. Police vehicles of every persuasion had the town surrounded. People were running out of the perimeter, hands on their heads. Big men in heavy gear were getting ready outside the circle, FBI and US MARSHAL in yellow print on their bulky coats or vests. I searched for the epicenter of all this, the focus of their attention. It helped that I knew what color it was.

Our bus sat parked at Arby's. In the last space of the lot.

Next I searched for Blaine. I couldn't find him, or more like I found forty of him. When I was about to quit, I found what I should have been hunting all along. The Corvette looked exactly as it had in the photo on his desk. Cherry red, boxy yet somehow sleek, it was parked askew by a playground. Two Highway Patrol cars and an unmarked sedan were nearby. The sedan was the one I'd seen catch some air coming off the ramp, though now it had a red light on its roof. I remembered how those spinning lights had made me dizzy only days ago. Now they looked like the still point of a spinning universe. And before I knew it, they were gone.

TEN

We drove north until we came to a set of railroad tracks. Across the ties was an intersection with another unending two-lane. We took it west. The road was fuzzed on either side by high grass, and its lack of variety made the stray rock seem exciting. Sam kept to the far side of the seat. The shopping basket was between us. I felt him reach inside, and he showed me the chocolate doughnuts. "May I?"

I was awakening, feeling monumentally stupid. Going: No, literally they should build a monument to how stupid I was back there.

I counted should-haves, one each for the hay bales in the fields all around us.

"Hey," Sam said.

I turned to him, expectant. Excited for an opening that might lead somewhere.

"Hey," he said again, and pointed outside. "Hey."

There was nothing new. A few low terraces of rock. Those and—I got it.

So bad. "Hey," I said, pointing at a bale.

"Hey." Sam pointed, pointed. "Hay, hay."

Johnny moved the mirror. His brow was puzzled.

"Hey!" Sam told him, waving merrily.

Johnny ate a sunflower seed. It might've been my imagination, but I thought he did it moodily. My hands sank to my lap, laughter cut off.

"He's nothing to be scared of," Sam said. "Know what he went in for? Car theft. His brother owned a chop shop in Jersey. The good cars are in Manhattan—that made it a federal charge when Johnny got caught. FBI wanted him to rat out his brother, and Johnny wouldn't, so he got ten to fifteen, when most GTAs get a year or two."

I tried to sound casual. "What did you do?"

"You just saw what I did." Sam reached around his back, holding his other palm out to indicate how not a big deal it was when the gun reappeared. "These are never dangerous in the hands of someone who knows what he's doing." He snapped out the wheel or whatever—where the bullets went—and spun it. Loaded. "I don't shoot people. That's not who I am."

What was I supposed to say: Yeah, wow, nice gun, Dad?

Sam slapped the revolver back together, put it away. He was a little shamefaced, as if he'd gone in front of the class for show-and-tell and nobody'd applauded. I did a survey of the car, trying to find a topic. The headphones and the box they sat on had a place of honor in the passenger seat. "What's that?" I said, pointing at it.

"That's a police scanner." Nothing else.

Behind us, in the far rear seat, Colonel Sanders smiled sketchily on a plastic bag. I could smell it now—fried chicken. My craving for a tummyful nearly made me miss the FOR SALE sign buried under the food. The back windshield was dusty, so there was a clean rectangle in the bottom corner where the sign had been.

The highway's tongue split, and we veered right. A squat building sat next to a picnic area. No other cars in the modest lot. We stopped perpendicular to the parking spots, idling. Sam got out, came around, opened my door, and played footman. "Milady." I accepted his hand, and he leaned around me into to the backseat, snagging the KFC bag.

I'd done plenty of rest stops. You got your indoor plumbing, you got your vending machines—and you got your pay phones. "I'm just gonna wash up."

Sam slapped the roof twice. "Sounds good."

Johnny drove off, rejoining the flow of the road. I walked toward the building's bright door, in whose reflectiveness Sam was methodically unpacking containers, taking no interest in me whatsoever. I pulled the door open. Inside were Funyuns and Ring Dings, Coke and Pepsi. And a phone.

Sam was removing lids, putting sporks in each tub, separating plates from napkins, making stacks. Setting the table. He could look up any second.

I went into the ladies' room. There was a row of sinks and another of stalls. The light was disturbing. Most of the fluorescents had burned out, so midmorning snuck through a line of high windows, making the room inappropriately intimate. Part of me just wanted to lie down. I was starving, and the last decent night's sleep I'd gotten was at Blaine's. Every one of those forty-some hours since was bagged under my eyes, growth rings on a really old tree.

A giggle came bubbling from the stalls.

I jumped. "Hello?"

Same giggle, youthful soprano. Someone else shushed. Tight acoustics rebounded the sounds. I ambled down the row of toilets, hesitating when the very last stall hinted movement. I saw a pale, skinny arm and went the rest of the way, curious.

The girls were college-age. The one on the left had a beer bottle by the neck, holding the base at me as if it were jagged and broken, deadly. But she'd forgotten to break it. She had light-brown curls in tight, wild springs and freckles on her nose. She was in serious contention for the least threatening human I'd ever seen. "Gimme your wallet," she said.

"I don't have one."

"Oh." The bottle fell and rolled with a scraping noise on the cement floor. It bumped into many, many others. "Never mind."

The other girl giggled. A stud sparkled in her nostril. Her crop top showed a flat stomach, and her cutoffs barely covered her ass. Her legs were even longer than mine. She had to be freezing. "Who did that to your hair?" she said.

"I did."

"On purpose?"

"Sort of."

"Could you, like"—Curly seemed to search for the right words—"screw off? This is a private party."

The idea of prevailing upon them for help surged into my mind, but I knew it was ridiculous. "Stay here, okay?"

In the vending area again, with the archaic pay phone, I went through the mental motions of what I'd be screaming at me to do if I were watching all this instead of living it: pick it up, dial 911, let the receiver hang, hope for the best.

Sam squinted in, holding a drumstick. The sun on the door had been blinding when I'd first come in. Could he see?

As I walked into pleasant midforties, a breeze brushed my hair to a side. Sam held out a clean plate. I took it, began filling it to the point that it needed my whole hand underneath or it'd collapse.

"When did they change the gravy?" he said.

"Couple years ago. And they got rid of their fries. Total crime. They went great with the gravy."

"I miss the lumps."

I nodded at him emphatically. He'd made one of those everything sandwiches, where you pile the meat and the sides inside the biscuit, and every bite you take dribbles everywhere. We were stuffed in five minutes. There was a lot left. I matched lids to bowls, to keep bugs out and warmth in. "Driver's coming back?"

"He is," Sam said, "but Johnny doesn't eat much, just sunflower seeds. His stomach bothers him. I tell him it's the chain-smoking. He tells me he smokes to settle his stomach." Sam moved to sit on the table, putting his feet on the bench. His back went straight and tall. "I'm proud of you, you know. Most girls would be having hysterics. I knew you weren't most girls, but all the same, I'm impressed. You're levelheaded enough to appreciate that I'm not a threat. I'm grateful for that, more than I can say."

"Is this cool with you?" I showed him my cigarettes.

"No, but it's a little late for me to disapprove." Sam took the lighter from my fingers, clicked it, and held the flame out for me.

I blew my exhale away from him. "Back there, with Harvey—that's really all you did?"

"Yes, ma'am."

"You got eighteen years for that?"

"No, I got twenty-five to forty. But I did it a lot. Too much." Sam turned in either direction, spiraling his back, popping it. He heard my mute question and sighed. "One hundred fifty-seven robberies in twelve states."

I laughed, very kinda.

"I know, I know," Sam said. "You have to understand it was a different time. We were young. We were invincible. We were high."

I laughed, loudly this time—and this one was pure, this one was begging for mercy. I had to get up. I tossed my plate in the trash. "Blaine told me—"

"Blaine's your policeman?"

I nodded.

"I'm sure he did. I'm sure he told you plenty." Sam steepled his fingers, squinted at the road. "I've made god-awful mistakes, honey. I can't deny that. But sometimes our mistakes are like rabbits. They mate; they make lots and lots of other mistakes without our help. I trusted the wrong people. And Kat? That is the gaffe that keeps on giving. That can destroy your entire life, especially if you're the last man standing when the smoke clears. It's the survivor's privilege to take the blame, just as it's the betrayer's prerogative how they want to frame the fairy tale, as long as they betray completely—and your mother did."

He said "your mother" like he was spitting acid.

"I made terrible mistakes, but I have paid for them. I paid for mine, hers, everybody's. I have earned the right to move on." Sam struck a particularly casual pose, like that teacher who insists you call him by his first name. "I can't undo what's already done. What I can do, and what I've risked my neck to do, is to offer you the chance to get to know me. That's why I came to Minneapolis. No other reason. And I want this crystal clear: you are not here against your will." Sam let that sink in.

"Okay," I said, after a pause. "What's—like, what's the plan?"

"We're lighting out for the West." He opened his arms, embracing all of eastern Montana. "We'll do some treasure hunting in Cali, then retire to Mexico. Haciendas, siestas, margaritas. And you, my dear, are free to come with us however far you care to. Tonight, we're bunking at a cabin in the mountains. A good friend of mine owns it. He called the caretaker—it's all set up for us, plenty of rooms. There's even a guesthouse. I figured I'd let you have that, give you your space. If you'd like."

Sam tipped the chicken bucket and poked around. I was listening closely for what lay beneath this at-homeness, his laid-back detailing of a life of crime followed by an invitation to the daughter he'd never met to join him on a renegade road trip. Other than his tone when talking about Mom, he'd sounded so at peace and balanced and reasonable.

Sam brought out a wing. I watched three of his demure little nibbles before blurting, "Can I go for a walk?"

He frowned at me, like: Of course.

"Of course," he said.

I had some trouble finding my balance. I couldn't shake the feeling he'd shoot me in the back, but I went, moving on a kind of cloud, toward the rest stop and then around it, to the ladies' room side. Here were the high windows. I heard a high giggle.

I was high. I'd reached the level of tired where tired had drugged me. But I had to assess some options.

Go with him to Mexico?

Mexico, Sam? You've got the FBI *and* US Marshals *and* Highway Patrol on your tail, but we keep hopping cars and sticking to back roads and you think that's enough to get us several *thousand* miles? Are you fucking cracked? It's a sweet invitation, but I'm afraid I have to decline.

Trust that he really had changed? The file Blaine had on Sam was a chronicle of incidents from almost two decades ago. Ancient history. Rehabilitation worked sometimes. Criminals went straight. Sure, Sam had robbed Harvey, except it was more like Sam had "robbed" Harvey, and that seemed less a red flag than—I don't know—a pale-peach flag.

So, fine—Sam was still inclined to petty theft.

But so was I.

Scary looks aside, he was kind of a doof. I'd been anxious in the convenience store, but that was with Blaine in my ear again, insinuating that Sam was a psychopathic mastermind who was going to eat my liver with fava beans and nice Chianti. When in fact, Sam's master plan pretty much sucked.

Which led me to another fact: the police would catch us.

We had the scanner. Johnny Blue respected speed limits. Outside of those factors, the continuance of our road trip hinged on luck. And when our luck ran out, I could play shell-shocked victim. If our luck held, I could exit stage left when I'd had enough bad puns and junk food.

Remembering the photo in my pocket, I took it out and unfolded it. God, Sam looked different—it didn't seem possible a person could transform so drastically. What must the rest of them look like now? The fat guy got skinny. The dude in the dress wore a suit to the office, and the girls pressing kisses to his cheeks had mom haircuts.

I put the photo away and went around to the building's other side. Harmony would never tell me where she grew up. Whether she had brothers, sisters, a dog, a bike. She'd brush it off with, "Let's focus on today," and she'd distract me with a snack or an outing, park me in front of the TV. Now I wanted answers.

Coming around the corner, though, I saw that the girl with curly hair was sitting in my spot, telling Sam: "A lot of vegetarians have a tendency to preach to people, and I'm not like that. I just have to live by my values. And I believe animals have souls." She scooped about a backhoe's worth of coleslaw from the tub. She was straddling the bench, her back to the leggy girl, who was chomping into a thigh with the commitment of a jaguar.

"I admire that," Sam said. "I tried to give up meat. Couldn't make it stick."

Curly noticed me. Sam turned around. "There she is. How was the walk?"

I took a seat opposite the girls as Sam introduced us. Their names ricocheted off my ears and went zinging into the ether. Legs didn't stop chewing to gag a hello, but Curly'd adopted a nasty smirk that hid in her voice when she said, "Hope we didn't scare you. In the bathroom. You know, when you found us asleep?"

I grabbed the last biscuit. "No, you didn't scare me at all."

"They're hitchhiking," Sam said. "I've given them my lecture already, but since you're just joining us: The last time it was safe to hitchhike in this country was before it had a space program. The last time hitchhiking was safe, automobiles had not been invented yet. It was not safe when a man on horseback offered you a ride on horseback." He pointed between himself and me. "Is this getting through?"

"What about rickshaws?" I said.

"No rickshaws. No gondolas, no bicycle package carriers."

"No ice-cream trucks?"

"No snowmobiles," he said.

"No dogsleds?" I broke first and laughed. "No unicycles?"

Sam rolled his eyes. "Now you're being ridiculous." Still trying to play straight man, he offered up one more: "And no skateboards without a helmet." Which wasn't that good, but somehow that made it better. I applauded. He took a bow.

"You guys are great," Curly said. The pitch she used cut across my laughter perfectly. "Really great."

"She's great. I just work here," Sam said. "These ladies would like to tag along with us for a while. The cabin we're going to has plenty of rooms. Plus, I've got some travel board games in the car, and those are always better with more players." He glanced at the highway and cupped his hands around his mouth. "Heeeeere's Johnny!"

The station wagon sailed up the ramp. Curly'd turned to watch it, and she was clapping, hooting, wolf-whistling, for reasons that were beyond me. I got up and collected our garbage, registering how mad I was by how anal I was being, fitting the small bowls into bigger bowls into boxes, wanting to get the shapes right, arrive at the smallest possible package.

"One thing." Sam nudged Curly's backpack with his toe. "I can't have you doing drugs around my daughter."

Curly turned to Legs, who put down her third piece of chicken and hiccupped.

"I didn't fall off the turnip truck yesterday," Sam said. "I'm in no position to judge, but I do have to set an example. I'm going to need you to give me your stash. I'll hold it for you and return it when we part ways."

Curly looked at me like this was my fault, and I couldn't resist: I gave my nose a quick scratch with a carefully chosen finger. Legs was unzipping her backpack, extracting a baggie with a few tablespoons of white powder at the bottom, as well as a razor blade and a mirror. Curly snatched it from her and gave it to Sam.

"Thank you," he said, folding it into his jeans. "You two go ahead. Kat and I will clean up."

The wagon parked. I admired our new Montana plates as the girls hefted their bags, pouting. I kept my voice low out of some weirdly misplaced desire not to hurt their feelings. Mostly Legs, since she appeared to have feelings. "Are you sure this is a good idea?"

"What, bringing them with us?" Sam put our bundle in the garbage bag and tied the handles tight-tight. "You want to leave them here?"

"They threatened me. In the bathroom."

"You weren't upset."

"They don't scare me."

"Then what's the problem?" He put the bag on the tips of his fingers, shot it like a basketball—and got nothing but net. "You'll be in the guesthouse. Johnny will make sure you have everything you need. They won't bother you, I promise."

"Yeah, but what about you?"

"I'm a big boy. I'll be okay."

I yawned. The yawn spawned another, and another. I heard Sam say, muffled, "You poor thing."

I staggered toward the car in an apathetic daze. He was advising I should take the back, and I was only too happy to comply. I crawled in, tossed the FOR SALE sign to the floor, and took off Blaine's coat, rolling it into a pillow. The wagon's heater was on. It blew soothing, warm wind. As I lay down, Sam was digging in his paper bags. He brought out a board game. "You ladies up for it?"

He murmured, hushing them anytime they said above a whisper, "Sorry!"

Rolling the dice and whispering, "Sorry!"

Knocking each other back on the board and whispering, "Sorry!" "Sorry!"

I dropped through the bottom of consciousness like a lead anchor, and hit dreams.

ELEVEN

There was a knife. That's most of what I remembered as I started the waking-up process. The low-angled sun was getting hacked up by some tree branches, flashing into the car, each flash as sharp as a dagger.

Dreams were the brain's compost pile. Mine were so vivid when I was a kid that I'd wake up thinking they were real, and I'd run down to Mom's room to tell her. She'd get mad. Interrupting her sleep messed with the sleeping pills, but she'd give another reason: nobody wants to hear about dreams. As it happened, I agreed with her. Still, I dreaded the violence mine always contained, the solitude.

The radio was playing that Superman song. Not 3 Doors Down. The sad one. Usually I hated it, but tonight it tugged at me, crooning at very low volume. The girls must have picked the station. Mountains had us surrounded. A WATCH FOR AVALANCHE sign blipped past. I imagined looking out the window and saying, There's one.

"Wild," I said.

Sam undid his seat belt and lifted the armrest so he could sit sideways, his legs filling a gap between the seats. "We'll be at the cabin in a half hour." He spoke quietly, lifted the shopping basket from the floor. "Do you need anything?"

I leaned forward, wondering how the girls could lie down and sleep in that small an area. "The cigarettes," I said.

Sam handed them back. He remembered the lighter. "Stop me if you've heard this one, but cigarettes are bad for you."

"I've heard this one." I tore cellophane, smiling cutely. I had nothing to ash into, but that was never true. I dug into a hip pocket and hit the remains of Blaine's money. In the other hip pocket, I found an old quiz paper. I folded a firm cone with a double-enforced bottom. Instant ashtray.

Sam laughed. "I would applaud, but then I'd wake them for sure." The radio was fading; he shut it off. "Not much reception up here."

Go ahead, I thought. Go ahead, ask me whatever.

Sam said nothing. He gazed at me with frank adoration. It got old quickly.

"When did you meet my mom?" I said.

"'75."

About ten seconds went by.

"Where did you meet her?"

"San Francisco."

"What was she doing?"

"Waitressing," he said. "She ran away."

"Where'd she run away from?"

"Oakland."

"Why?"

Sam's cheek twitched, and he looked down. He stirred the basket. Held up the powdered doughnuts. "Mind?"

"Go for it. Why'd she run away?"

"She had it rough at home. So did I." He dropped his snack. "I prefer not to discuss the past."

"Why?"

He peered sideways, where the road dipped into a valley. "You'll understand when you have children of your own."

"I'm not having kids."

"You'll change your mind about that." Sam said it casually, a truth so unimpeachable it didn't require an inch of room on any side.

This boat of a car was suddenly small—much too small and much too stationary. He watched the road ahead, oblivious that my fuse, lit, was sparking toward an ammo cache I'd been storing since my earliest lesson in what it means to be ignored, your convictions deemed unworthy.

"I'll change my mind, huh? Why will I change my mind? Because having children is noble? It's an automatically selfless act? I disagree. People have kids because their limbic systems tell them to pass on genes. Cop to it; say that. Say that and I'll respect it. I'll respect it more if you're dead honest and admit that you had a kid to give yourself a sense of purpose. To give *yourself*. A sense of *purpose*."

My voice rose on the emphasis. I heard Curly grunting awake, sensed the wagon angling downward—but those things were dull input, because Sam and I had one of those eye locks going that builds a metaphysical tunnel between two starers. There was the itch of my chromosomes knowing him, wanting to see an expression other than this friendly giant, whose smile was fading as sure as Top 40 radio in a deep mountain valley.

His grin narrowed; mine widened. I couldn't keep my mouth shut. "Wanting a kid's got nothing to do with the kid. With who they are, the person they are—the kid doesn't exist yet. It's maybe got something to do with the person you're making the kid with. You want a sense of mutual purpose. You want a camaraderie that isn't present in the relationship, so you figure the kid'll be the glue. Look around—it happens all the time. Babies are great glue. You're too fucking tired to fight with each other."

Curly was stirring, waking.

"Or, in Harmony's case, you're too tired to fight with yourself. When I was a baby, she was the greatest. Her insanity had to take a backseat, because here's this simple simian thing with a brain the size of a peanut who shits its diaper and cries about it, gets hungry and cries about it, wakes up and cries about it. She changed it and fed it and rocked it, and she felt like a hero because it worked. It was simple. It was one-to-one."

A giggle bubbled from the middle seat.

"Problem is," I said, "kids grow. They get more complicated. It happens wicked fast. And those parents who wanted purpose discover wicked fast: Purpose. Is. Hard. They wonder how this project of theirs went so awry, like the human being they brought into the world is a fucking basement remodel that's going overbudget. It's too much work. It shouldn't be so much work. 'Hey, you piece of shit, you shouldn't be this much work!'"

Sam twitched. A new face was being born from the placid mask. His chin, his forehead—jumping, contracting. I was excited; I wanted to see it. I felt powerful, midwifing this shift, making him push with my provocations.

"So they disengage. They pink-slip it. They know they're wrong to be doing that, and sometimes they'll play a sexy trick and get all up in that kid's grille, bitching at them about grades and why don't you get a boyfriend and why don't you have a job, giving such a conspicuous damn that nobody can accuse them of quitting. But they're done. And kids aren't stupid—we know when you're out. Most of us still get our three meals a day, the roof over our heads. But so do prisoners. Right, Sam?"

The valley grew around us, more pines and shadows. Sam's attention veered to those in lieu of me. He was almost here. His eyes were slits. His mouth was convulsing—he'd open it, and then I'd meet my father for real. He'd tell me what he really thought about who I really was, and I could not wait. “See?” I said. “Do you see now? I’m ruined. Harmony ruined your kid while you were weight training.”

“Nice,” Curly said, disentangling from Legs, who was glaring at me, too. They got on their knees and crawled to him. “It’s okay,” they said, stroking the veins in his muscles, “That’s okay.” Legs used the cuff of her hoodie to wipe his tears.

Even Sam’s *tears* were huge. “What was I supposed to do?”

The van went dark. We’d driven into the tree canopy.

“Nothing,” I said.

Sam was taking gulps too large for his throat. It was an ugly sitting-down dance, and he was shaking his head, like he knew how sick it was to witness. The girls patted him, whispered to him, while I apologized and apologized—in my head.

I’d never needed to have somebody understand as badly as I needed Sam to understand in that moment. But how to make it make sense? If you’re lucky, your childhood makes sense. If you’re not, you do your best to impose sense on it, heat it like a red-hot piece of iron and slam it with a hammer until it’s a shape that at the very least jibes with the future you want. How to convey to him how much work it was? I had this idea he’d be proud of me if I could only say it right: Another person’s crazy is viral. If you’re in it enough, it affects you. If it’s your mother, it infects you. You can’t help it. She decides you don't exist, and you find a way to make her viciousness the jet engine that powers you forward, even if you have no real clue where you're headed, which means you take wrong turns and run over people all the time.

The road snuck right. The car was slowing, coming to a halt.

I had to try. "Sam—"

"Guesthouse is down the path," he said. "Let Johnny Blue know if you need anything."

The van stopped. We were at a lake. There were a few stairs leading up from a tiny dock. A red fence was next to us. When Legs opened the door for me, it clipped the red paint, and snide comments about her clumsiness splashed across my brain. But I kept quiet, realizing that right now cruelty was the only eloquence I was capable of. I groped for the bulk of Blaine's coat and hugged it, getting out.

"I'll see you in the morning," Sam said.

The door slammed. The car drove away. In a couple of seconds, I heard the soft whir of a garage door opening, closing. I put the coat on and sat by the fence, my feet on the top stair. My father had known me for one day, and he already needed a break.

Like I could blame him. Like I wouldn't love a break from me, like I enjoyed being the thing I'd become.

"Stop," I said. "You can stop."

The lake's still surface was black, with blacker lines of branches reflected in the water. Hardy winter birds were screaming at each other; I searched for them, but they were invisible. That got me anxious, got me looking around. At the cabin, tall and narrow. It had huge, posh windows, and stairs that terraced to landings with squares of garden—just space and soil now. Past the driveway was a break in the trees. Johnny stood there, smoking. He was spooky-thin; I'd already divined that much. His shirt billowed at the sides, and light showed through it. I still had no idea what he looked like, which was illogical and understandable at the same time. I'd been so focused on Sam.

A half-or-less moon cleared the trees, whitewashing the gravel road. The mountains were crowned with gold from the setting sun. My bare arms prickled. The driver scared me.

He scares you, he scares you: I told myself this.

So, what? What do you want?

I got up, started walking toward him. His name's Johnny Blue; his occupation is driver; his hobbies include stalking girls in rearview mirrors.

He'd found the gap between the sun's gaudy exit and the moon's graceful entrance, a pocket of shadow. He moved deeper into it. He threw his cig by his feet and blew a long V of smoke. I was five yards away, getting closer, and all I could see was the part of his dark, messy hair.

"Hi," I said. "I'm gonna go ahead and be blunt here. I realize you probably know my dad from prison, and he's got you, like, guarding me for the night. So if you're gonna rape me, could we get that out of the way now?"

His head snapped up. His face was pretty like a girl's. And horrified. I felt regret, but not for offending him: I was bummed that the most beautiful male I'd ever seen outside of an Abercrombie ad had to be wearing pure disgust. Johnny Blue just needed a pair of wings on his back, then he could fly up and report to his boss what an icky person Rainy Cain was.

"Kidding," I said. "I was kidding."

He turned abruptly and walked down a terra-cotta path that curled to the right. He followed it into the woods. I jogged to catch up. The path seemed longer than it was, farther than it was, since forest hemmed us in. The main house wasn't visible. I was squinting hard to look for it, and I bumped into Johnny's back. "Sorry."

He took a key from his hip pocket. "Guesthouse" was too generous. This was a shack. The terra-cotta led right up to the threshold. The exterior was very vinyl, very pastel, very ugh. At either side of the faded front door sat a giant tire heaped with marigold carcasses.

Johnny pushed the door open, stepped aside. He drew a circle in the dirt with his toes.

"Johnny, right?"

He nodded at the ground.

"Could—" Go ahead. Embrace the idiocy. "Can we talk or something?"

Johnny shook his head at the ground.

"We can't talk?"

He reached for his back pocket and brought out a pack of Newports. Bit one, lit one.

"Well, this hasn't been weird at all. You'll be right here, I'm assuming."

Nod.

"All night?"

Nod, nod.

"All righty roo." I went in and batted the door shut. It had an inlaid window; the blinds shook. The guesthouse looked perfect for the Seven Dwarfs. My knees would poke into my armpits if I sat on the sofa. A twin-size bed was behind it, down three pointless stairs. To my left was a dinette set with two chairs, a mustard-colored kitchen, a fridge straight out of *Leave It to Beaver*. A framed needlepoint on the sofa's end table read HOME SWEET HOME.

A bunch of brown and amber bottles glowed on top of the fridge. I took one, not caring which. I unscrewed the cap and knocked it back, forcing as much down as I could before the taste hit. I coughed and found I was conveniently bent over the sink. Also, I was elbowing the stove.

"Only two dwarfs," I said. I snorted, picturing how they'd still bump into one another while cooking breakfast. Bidding each other good morning. Asking, How'd you sleep?

I stepped on the backs of my sneaks and unbuttoned my pants, shuddering, panting, doing a one-woman bum's rush for the bedroom, hoping the bathroom was next to the stairs. It was, and I walked into a shower the size of a casket, shucked my shirt and jeans and underwear, cranked the spray. Uproariously funny, the two-dwarfs thing. So funny I had to sit down and laugh about it. I was laughing; that's all I was doing. I was alone, so no one could say I was doing otherwise. I was alone, and it wasn't fair.

It's not fair, so okay, cry about it. Cry, you fucking crybaby. Cry here in the dark, that's all you know how to do.

The water never got warm. When it got butt-cold, I had an actual shower. A shelf held a mini shampoo and conditioner, plus a mini soap still in its wrapper. I took a towel off a rack. The medicine cabinet offered a buffet of travel-size hygiene, labels facing out. I used the Visine and the Neutrogena and the Jergens and the Oral-B and the Crest, and then I stopped and sat on the toilet, too drained to move.

The alcohol had kicked in. It didn't make me happy or mellow, as it had the handful of times before when I'd imbibed: sleepovers with fizzy Boone's Farm. The thick syrup upstairs was liquid maudlin. Maybe I'd done it wrong; maybe I needed more. The bottle, in the kitchen, out this room, up those stairs.

I may as well have been fighting a g-force keeping me on that crapper. Which of course was absurd.

That flash of self-awareness didn't help at all. None. I missed her. I wanted to watch TV with her while she ate ice cream and pretended I wasn't there. I didn't want to be dragging past the front door, where its window showed me Johnny was gone. Just me in this cottage in a dark, dark forest, scrambling past this dinette table, past this counter, toward the bottle that I saw now was Wild Turkey. These objects existing in a world where she was dead.

The fridge hummed. There'd be food inside. This place had a caretaker, and that's what a caretaker does—puts towels in the bathroom, puts food in the fridge, and leaves the fridge unlocked. I opened it: Take-and-bake spaghetti, lasagna. Macaroni salad, chicken salad, tuna salad in plastic convenience containers. The door was lined with beverage choices. I rested my head on the freezer door.

My hand was hanging at the end of my arm. I had to concentrate to make it rise, settle on a Nantucket Nectars orange-juice bottle.

Orange juice to cut the bourbon—that'll work.

I picked it up. Numbness spread through my fingers. I heard glass shatter, far away. Sticky wet splashed my ankles. I put my hands over my ears, not knowing I'd pinched my eyes shut until I opened them wide, startled.

Johnny walked out of a shadow by the dinette set. I was about to jump, but he moved too fast. He caught me, threw me over his shoulder in a fireman's carry. I screamed and pounded on his back, wriggling like a caught fish. When he set me down after about four steps, I toppled over, onto the table.

Johnny stalked for the kitchen. He disappeared behind the tiny counter. Glass crashed together. He stood, holding a white rag that I realized was his T-shirt. He carried it to the trash can, pushed the pedal, raised the lid, and slid a load of glass shards into the garbage with a sound like chimes. He went back and did it again. And again, the pieces getting smaller. He went back, and the sound became that of mopping. He got up, stormed to the sink, and wrung out his shirt, peeking down at his visible ribs, his unbelievable pallor. He put the T on awkwardly, pulling the wetness from his chest, making a face at the sensation. He turned and looked longingly at the guesthouse's door.

But I was in the way. Braced against the table with my towel, which was, by whatever miracle, still hiding everything important. I gaped at him with extreme stupefaction, remembering what Blaine had said about shagging strangers to cure loneliness: it helps for a little while.

The terry cloth felt itchy against my skin. I moved exactly right, and it fell.

Johnny made a sound like something trapped. I walked the two steps to him. He was too tall. I reached to pull him down; he wouldn't let me. I took fists of his sticky shirt. "Please."

He peeled my hands away. Under his belt, the teeth of his zipper glittered, pushing forward. I grasped at his wrists. Weird mews came from far back in my throat.

"Shh," he said. "Shh."

I stepped back. He let me go. The moon by now was daylight-bright. He glowed.

I boosted myself onto the table, propped a foot onto either chair and lay back. Trees outside were silver, hung upside down. I reached with my right hand and covered my mouth with my left. He could just watch if he wanted. I unfolded me and goaded me, and it was wretched, my sounds muffled by my palm.

Johnny pulled the hand from my mouth and pressed it to the table. “I have HIV,” he said, “but I brought condoms.”

I was shocked, but not. “Okay.” I sat up. He stepped between my knees. I worked at his belt buckle while he pulled a string of six condoms from his pocket, flapped them onto the table. He helped with his zipper. We shoved his pants and boxers down.

I’d never seen one so close. Johnny’s looked huge, but what did I know? He was wincing a condom on, got it to the base. I grabbed the bowl of his pelvis. He said, “Wait,” and put a second condom over the first.

He had me lie back again. “Don’t cover your mouth. I wanna hear when it breaks.”

His fingers were uncertain and cautious and a complete waste of time. I moved his hand to my hip. He leaned far forward, focused.

Oddest feeling. You know, logically, that there’s a space, and that it can be filled. Except knowledge is no match for the sanctity of your own body: the mine-ness, the you-can’t-come-in-ness.

He checked on me. He was being careful, and it was excruciating for him. I tilted, put my heels on his back and arched up. Proud of myself when he gave a high yip of alarm and fell in. Proud of the pain, which was instant and blinding. It sprang to either end of my body like a cut piano wire. It hurt too much to scream.

Johnny held the border of the table. His wet shirt suckered our fronts together. After a few seconds, I understood that it was over. "It's okay," I said, and licked the shell of his ear, suddenly so fond of him. "Everything's okay."

His grip on the table relaxed. He pushed off, standing. I hissed, catching at emptiness. Johnny waddled in the shackles of his pants to the trash can. He stepped on the pedal, unrolled the condoms, tied a knot, and tugged paper towels off a roll by the sink before wrapping the condoms and placing them—not dropping them—into the garbage. He returned to the sink and scrubbed himself thoroughly. He shut off the water, tore more paper towels, dried the basin and the floor. He shuffled to the trash can and threw a final fistful of paper.

Then he stood there. Looking longingly at the guesthouse's door.

But I was still in the way. He looked from the door to me. He crossed his arms, his pants heaped at his feet, his shoes still on. His penis dangled.

I had assumed we'd snuggle. Movies made this seem so easy. Though nobody seems to have HIV in the movies. "Have you had sex before?"

"Yeah." He sounded amused.

Outside, a bird called.

Johnny bent down and picked up his pants. He was doing the button when I got to him and jerked at his jeans, letting them drop. I wasn't sure what I wanted. I didn't want to put my clothes back on. And I didn't want to be naked while he had clothes on, so he needed to be naked with me. I liked him. Or I wanted to like him. Or something.

Nothing—absolutely nothing—made sense right now.

His arms hung stiffly at his sides. I shifted up. I wasn't tall enough to get his shirt off. I hopped once and laughed. Johnny pulled the shirt over his head and looked at me inquiringly.

"How tall are you?" I said.

"Six three." He gave me the shirt, like I might want it for a reason. I tossed it by my towel, took his hand. He stepped out of his pants, and I remembered his shoes. I bent down.

He seized my shoulders. "You can't. We can't do that. I read up on it. You can get it from one drop, the book said."

"I'm . . . I was gonna take off your shoes."

Johnny let go. "Oh." He put an unsteady hand on the kitchen counter.

I got on my knees and undid his laces. He'd double-knotted. I lifted the back of his heel. His feet smelled like he tried to keep his feet from smelling: pine. I skinned off his sock, did the other. I took his hand again, leading him past our christened dinette, toward the stairs and the bed at the bottom of them. His hand escaped. He went back and hunkered down to his pants. I guessed what he was getting, even before I saw the cigs. I nabbed the condoms off the table.

The bed's comforter featured fish with hooks in their mouths, smiling. I folded that to the foot of the bed, then the sheets, and got in. Johnny stood with his Newports and Bic until I patted the mattress. He got in like beds were foreign to him.

"Can I have a cigarette?" I said, thinking he needed to calm down.

He lit mine first. An ugly silver box in the shape of two linked hearts sat on the nightstand. He set it between us for an ashtray.

"You went to prison for stealing cars?"

"Yeah."

"How old were you?" I said.

"Eighteen."

"How old are you now?"

"Twenty-four."

Johnny was ashing after every puff, using it as an excuse to glance at my boobs. He stubbed a butt and lit another one, absently adjusting an erection that tented the sheet in his lap. The athlete in me admired his recovery time.

I put my finger to my nipple. "Do you wanna touch them?"

Johnny nodded. He picked the Newport from between my fingers and doused it, hitching toward me.

I reached for him. He stopped my hand and set it on my thigh.

"We have four more." I picked up the condoms.

"That's twice. I'm using two every time. It's safer." He took the condoms and placed them at the foot of the bed like they were precious. He reached for my breasts the same way. "Can we do it once at sunrise? Right before you go?"

"Go?" I climbed onto his lap. "Why sunrise?"

"I've never done it then. I slept on a cot. My girlfriend didn't like cots, so every time she left right after." He tipped me backward. "At night, it's a secret. But in the morning, it means you stayed all night. You can't go now anyway. A lot of animals hunt at night. I read up on it."

I had no idea what he was talking about, but I had zero inclination to ask. He used his hand, the way he'd seen me do it. When I bucked and cried out, he was hovering above me, watching as though I were the series finale to a show he'd been a fan of for years.

"How do you know me?" I said.

He said nothing, just stared.

"For real," I said. "You're looking at me like you know me."

Johnny gathered a section of sheet and pulled it off the bed, tucked it under the mattress. He picked up his Newports and shook them. There was a rattle at the bottom. He tweezed the cigs to the side, held the pack over his hand. A pill fell out, and he dry-swallowed it.

"What's that?" I said.

"Ephedrine."

"What for?"

"Keep me awake." He put the pack back and touched my knee, but then quickly moved like he'd made some wildly inappropriate advance. "Sorry."

I rolled up, leaning toward him. When I tried to kiss him, he recoiled. I tried again, more slowly. He recoiled more slowly. I asked, and couldn't believe I had to ask, "Can you kiss me?"

"I forgot how. He never wants to kiss."

"He?"

Johnny bit down.

"Who's he?" I said.

"Nobody."

My brain was endorphin soup. I laid my head on his shoulder. "Where am I going? In the morning."

"Town. There's a trail. I'll show you at sunrise. It's eight miles, but you'll make it."

"Won't Sam be mad at you?"

"I'll blame it on the girls."

"Don't blame them. What if he leaves them stranded?"

"He won't."

I bent Johnny's chin to me and kissed the cleft. "I'm not going anywhere in the morning. I wanna do this same thing tomorrow night. And the next night and the next. Wherever we stop, we'll—"

"You have to run at sunrise. You have to, Kat."

"Rainy."

"What?"

"My name's Rainy. Call me that, okay?"

Johnny got up and moved in jitters, his every nerve needing to fire. "I'll try. I've been hearing him call you Kat for four years, so it might take me a while. Rainy. Rainy, Rainy. That's nice. That's nicer than Kat."

It was novel watching a naked man pace—loose, swingy pieces chicks just didn't have. I put my feet to the floor, sitting almost primly.

"Your part's easy," he said. "If you tell me where the money is, I can take Sam to it. Once he has it, he'll leave you alone."

"What money?"

Johnny's foot froze. His weight came forward with pure inertia. "The money. The robbery money, the four million your mom hid. Sam says you know where it's buried."

I threw a pillow at him. "Right."

"Tell me you know where it is."

Any of my remaining happy-head chemicals got set alight by Johnny's obvious panic. He resumed wearing out the floor. He smacked his fists together. I thought he was overselling. He needed to learn proportion—low six figures; that I might have believed. But I was touched that he was creating a scenario to make the sex more exciting.

"Don't worry," Johnny said, kneeling in front of me. "It doesn't matter. It doesn't change your part. I'll show you the path in the morning. You run, get to town. Call your cop."

I pulled him to sit on the bed and set his arm over my shoulders, moving him like a prop.

"Blaine?" I said.

"He's been on the scanner all day. He's got everybody but the National Guard after us. That's why we're sticking to off roads." Johnny's heel tapped the floor. "He made great time. That '55 he's driving isn't an easy car. He must've customized it with rack and pinion—that's the only way I'd push a hundred on the highway. Even then, one bump and it's over. He's got the top up, but still, it'd—" A pat to my shoulder. "Never mind. Five more hours and the sun comes up. I'll show you the path. I talked to the same guy Sam talked to, in the House. Guy who owns this place, he's in for tax evasion. They couldn't get him on his real stuff, so they got him for tax evasion." Johnny's knee began to bounce. "Guys in the House blab about escaping all the time. Where they go wrong is, they make it too complicated—Sam just bribed a guard. My plan's even easier. You just run."

"And call Blaine."

"He'll have to double back. Or maybe he's doing that anyway—it's what I would do. If he ran the math on an '89 Outback versus a 'Vette, he'd have expected to pass us. Blaine, you said?"

"Right."

"Did he do the work himself? The steering?"

"No clue."

"Not an easy car." He squeezed and released me. "I gotta get up, Kat."

"Rainy."

"Told you it'll take me a while."

I was thirsty. I went to the bathroom, turned on the light. Now that I'd finally tried it, I wanted to fuck again. In the mirror, Johnny was giving his cock a dirty look. He shoved it down; it sprang back up.

I shut off the bathroom light, walked over, and got in his way. "I can remind you."

"Mmm?"

"How to kiss."

"You don't have to do that." He hummed as my fingers crawled up his neck. "Kat—"

"Rainy."

I didn't tug, just bumped him toward me in gentle intervals. He undid some distance every time, but not all of it. "What's wrong?" I pecked him.

"I don't wanna give it to you."

"It's kissing," I said. "I won't get it from kissing. Trust me."

His hands moved, stopping low on my spine. He set his forehead to mine and said, fast, "You don't have to do this. I'll help you anyway. I'll help you get away anyway."

I let go of him and went to the bed, got on my hands and knees, looked with what I thought was primal sexuality over my shoulder.

"Not like that." He said the same thing four or five more times as he rearranged me. Sat me as if for fine dining. He backed up and examined the result. I slouched. This was way too tedious. "Ka—" He caught himself. "Rainy?"

That's when I quit. I fell back on the mattress. "Chill, okay? Sorry I pushed. Whatever your problem is, please just relax."

After a minute, he came and settled beside me. "It's a face." Johnny pointed at water damage on the ceiling. "There's the nose. There's the chin. That's the hair."

"Or a vase. If you look at the light part." I outlined the contours. "Or a naked lady—the curves, see? Or a candlestick. Or a mountain road like we drove down today."

"You were always really good at this." His mouth closed audibly.

"When was I good at this?"

The tendon by his ear hopped, holding things in.

"Hey, what's that mean? When was I good—"

He kissed me, a peck but a firm one, a "shut up" one. He rolled me under him, and I laughed down his throat: Gotcha. I snarled my hands in his shaggy hair, taught him tongue. His reeducation on kissing took about five seconds. After that, we lost our minds. I got on top of him; he didn't like that.

"Please," I said, since it worked last time. Except this time, it came out tender.

He hid his face in the crook of my neck. "Always," he said. "You were always good."

I was so wet that the extra must have flooded my eyes. It was the only explanation. It wasn't how he shook reaching for the condoms on the nightstand. It wasn't his glad agony putting one on, and another, and bracing his forearms to plank above me. His noticing my tears and changing, diametrically. "We don't have to," Johnny said. He took the sheet and dabbed. "You'll go in the morning. You'll be okay."

We'd been building up too long; we were so primed it was scary. Nobody tells you about this part. How would they? We stared at each other, moving, tandem-breathing. Beyond sheer pleasure, to something other, where the self has no meaning so the guards leave their posts, forfeit borders.

"God! Oh my God!"

TWELVE

The bathroom light flicked on. The ceiling had supernovas. My hips reached for where he'd been, aftershocks, and my skin seemed bubbly, blistered in a superpositive way. I started laughing. I looked toward the light so he could laugh with me.

Johnny was at the sink, scrubbing his penis with a washcloth. Lather slopped off the tip. He was standing with his legs far apart. Harsh white light reached to the crack of his ass.

I didn't understand. Between his buttocks was a one-sided game of tic-tac-toe. Some of the scars were old, and some were new. Two still had fresh stitches. The lips of the wounds were red, angry. Of course they were. Of course, of course.

Beautiful boy in prison. He never wants to kiss.

Oh my God.

The faucet shut off. "Rainy?"

I didn't think about it, racing upstairs, leaping into my jeans. I just did it.

His shadow was long and thin across the bed. "Rainy, are you—"

I tripped outside, thinking I'd black out or barf and that either would be fine. I found a surface with some give, the tires, their grave of dead flowers. I was expanding—getting pulled from all sides, becoming larger to accommodate this new reality. I had to let it in. I didn't want to; I fought the stretch, curling inward. Trying to integrate what I'd seen with all I'd been through before it, the too much I'd been through before it, but my efforts kept being crossed out with red lines. Jagged red lines teethed in black thread.

"My God, my God, my God—" My refrain, vamping. My brain improvising: *Na-na-na,* I'm just secondhand news, my heart will go on and— "Shut up. Shut up, shut up."

The door opened. "Did I hurt you?" He sounded five years old. "Do you want me to leave?"

I did. I wanted nothing more. Leave, go away, I'm not ready. Whatever the hell any of this is, I am not ready.

I reached out, snared Johnny's hand. "Sit by me."

The tire sagged. I went sideways, laying my head in his lap.

"What happened?" he said.

"I saw your scars."

"I won't do that to you. Not ever. Don't worry."

"Who did it to you?"

"Doesn't matter."

"Yes, it does!"

"Shh. We're not that far from the main house."

"Who did that to you? Who did that to you?"

"It isn't bad. It doesn't hurt anymore. I go somewhere else." He set a tentative hand to my hair. "What can I do?"

"Talk. I like it when you talk."

"About . . . about what, though?"

"What'd you mean? 'You were always good'—what's that mean?"

Johnny's hand got bolder. He combed. That's all he did for a while. I was about to ask again when he said, "It's gonna sound crazy."

I had no rejoinder for that. Honestly, what was sane?

"I weigh one-sixty now," he said. "I was one-fifty when I went in. For a guy, I've got, like . . . I guess I've got a prettiness or whatever. My second day inside, a guy in the shower, he goes for me. And Sam swoops in and he saves me. Like he's Batman or something. I didn't really have a dad. And my mom wasn't . . . y'know?"

I sat up, nodding.

"Sam got me transferred to his block. He paid off some guards so I could have my own shower time, got me a job in the auto shop. He protected me. He didn't let anybody mess around with me. And he didn't mess around with me, either. He was my friend."

I experienced such a lift at this I was surprised I didn't levitate. I wanted Johnny to stop right there.

"Sam didn't have a cellmate, and I was terrified of mine. After two months—in the House, that's forever—Sam got it fixed so we could be cellies. I was so happy, I mean just so happy, had my blanket and my stuff. He steps aside to let me in. And I cross the bars, and he shoves me on the bunk and he does it."

That wouldn't compute. Does what?

"And I'm suffocating in the pillow, so I look up. All I can see is his mirror. But that wasn't what I was looking at. He thinks I like to watch us, but that's—he's not what I'm looking at. When he does it."

Johnny paused. He'd related the horror with the disinterest of a bad tour guide while my lungs turned solid and the ground dropped to a depthless pit where Sam haunted the very air.

"Around the mirror, there's . . . He used Scotch tape." Johnny's words were thick with humiliation: up to here had been the easy part. "The first one, you're a baby. A woman's holding you. She's got a swimsuit on. There's another mom and baby at the edge, so I think it was a swimming class. You're laughing, and you've got your hands pressed together like you're clapping for whoever's holding the camera. The next one, you're three. Exactly three. You're wearing a purple party hat, and you've got a cake with Scooby Doo on it and three candles. Your lips are orange but only in the middle. So you must've drank some orange punch or juice. Or soda. Could've been soda."

Johnny's beatific smile was fixed on the trees. "This one's my favorite. I don't know how old you are. You're wearing purple overalls with a pink shirt, sitting on red Keds, and you're holding this book that's as big as you are. One of your teeth is missing. That's why it's my favorite. It was a door I could go through, and Sam couldn't get me there. He could hurt me, but he couldn't really hurt me."

Johnny lit a cigarette and pulled deep. He held out the pack. There was one left. I took; he lit. "They're school pictures after that." He tipped the empty pack above his mouth, swallowing the capsule that fell out. "I don't sleep much. I don't like to—I dream funny. Sam doesn't know about the ephedrine. He thinks I have insomnia. He gets me all kinds of downers for it. I save 'em for when I need a break. Then I can tranq him."

Johnny stood and started pacing like a windup toy. "So when Sam's asleep, I can look all I want. It's boring in there. That's what really drives guys nuts, not the other stuff. I made up—it's kind of a game. I look at one of the pictures. The baby one, I usually start there. And I go from that one to the next one. But I've gotta go through every single day between them. I've gotta think of what you ate for breakfast and what clothes you put on every morning. Who you talked to. Did you play with a Lite-Brite? Or a Slinky, or did you practice a yo-yo? What'd you have for lunch? Did you watch TV? *Sesame Street*, *Reading Rainbow*? Or maybe game shows? *Where in the World Is Carmen San Diego?*—that was good. And when I finished that game, I made up another one. In that one, I'd go into the pictures. I could talk to you. Sometimes I was a baby along with you, and we'd swim together. And sometimes I was grown up, like I am now, and I'd push you on a swing set. Or this one time, when you were eight, we went fishing and you caught a water snake. And you just completely panicked. It tried to bite you, but I threw it back."

I rose, shaking my head. Johnny started talking faster. "Sometimes we were both grown-ups and we'd go places. I'd get books out of the library, and we could go anywhere. We went everywhere, all over, and, I'll be honest, last year, the . . . that red sweater. But before that, we were just friends. We were best friends, so if I look at you like I know you, or I talk and talk like I haven't seen you in a long time, then that's why. And it's"—he fired a finger gun into his head, mimed brains spraying out the back—"it's crazy. But you gotta believe me, there are crazier guys. There are way crazier guys."

"So . . ."

"So when Sam said he was coming to get you, to make you take him to the money— He trusts me. He thinks I'm his bitch. And I owed you. I owe you big-time. Y'know, for helping me get away."

Johnny picked up a pinecone, threw it past the guest-house's far corner. "Path's back there. In a couple hours, you run it all the way to town. Call your cop, game over."

“And Sam goes back to prison?” I said.

“He’ll still try for the money. If you knew where it was, I’d tell him and we’d go get it. But I can just make a place up.”

“And what happens to you? When the money’s not there?”

Johnny shrugged.

“We can go get the car,” I said. “We can go right now.”

“Sam keeps the keys.”

“I watched you hot-wire a bus in, like, three seconds.”

“You’ll be all right. The path isn’t hilly or anything. I asked.” He frowned at my frown. “Is it the dark? You’re going at sunrise, remember? I wouldn’t let you go in the dark.”

We stared at one another. It was like we were speaking two different languages.

I followed the side of the guesthouse to its back corner. There was a stump for chopping logs but no ax, and behind that, a mat of darker dirt. The woods didn’t split for the path. It got lost about five feet in.

I went closer, wanting to trace the route. Each of my steps was twinned by one of Johnny’s in the dry leaves behind me. “Careful,” he said.

“Of what?”

“Bears and mountain lions live up here. Snakes.”

It was December, but I didn’t argue. In spite of my significant defiance, I was watching the past change. In it, somebody gave a shit. Like, really, really gave a shit. Conceptualizing Johnny’s version of our shared, merry years, I tried to go all in. I imagined stumbling, skinning my knee, and he picked me up and carried me inside and used the stingy stuff and put on a Band-Aid and said, "Go play for another hour but not any longer, because supper's almost ready." I imagined we went to the zoo and I liked the panthers and I wanted to get closer, and he said, "No, no," and picked me up to protect me. At the water park, we did the slides all day. All day, every day, the entire summer.

Yet I couldn't ignore the false memories' sloppy construction, the gauze I'd put over the lens. There's a reason that's done, thinking back over a perfect day. It lends the scene a haze, blots out any grimace of annoyance at this unbelievably high-maintenance child and how bad you want to throttle her. Nor could I get around my own formulaic choices. His fishing trip with the water snake was better.

"I'm a real letdown, aren't I?" I'd never meant an apology more, though I told it to the forest. The affection in Johnny's gaze was so powerful I knew I'd make fun of him if I didn't avert my eyes. "I'm aware I'm pretty much a giant bitch. And I'm not saying that so you'll contradict me, like women do when they say they're fat so the guy will go, 'Oh, no, honey, you're beautiful, you're not fat at all.'" I backed up, fit my side to the house, picked at the paint. "I know I'm a nightmare. Sorry for that."

"I thought you would be. A nightmare. You're Sam's daughter, y'know? I thought you'd be spoiled as hell and a psycho on top of it. But then you saved the cop."

I spun around like a figure skater. "I what now?"

Johnny was literally scratching his head. “In front of his house. When we hit you. Sam stomped my foot on the gas, we hit the cruiser– You remember, right?”

“Yeah. But–”

“You had a chance to get away. I heard the cop tell you to go, and you didn’t.” He was getting really worried. “You remember, don’t you?”

“Anybody would’ve done that.”

Johnny went from regarding me like I was a pipe that’d sprung a leak to regarding me like a pipe that was stupid. “No, they wouldn’t.”

I felt my temper rising. “I’m an asshole. Okay? You maybe haven’t been around enough to fully appreciate it yet, but it’s a fact. We’ll fuck at sunrise and I’ll run right after, but you should come with me. Come with me as in driving, not . . . But that, too.” Holy no way–I was blushing. “Or you can go separate or whatever you think will work. Because I’m not worth it. What you’re talking about doing, I’m not worth it. I’m not.”

Johnny was beaming at me. “Yes, you are.”

I went to him and grabbed his hands. He had to absorb this. “Listen. I want to live by the ocean. I want to take walks on the beach. I want to learn guitar so I can sit on my fire escape and play ‘Moon River’ and maybe someone on the street hears and thinks, ‘Hey, that’s not awful.’ That’s my whole résumé, that’s–oh, for fuck’s sake, what?”

“‘Moon River’?” Johnny said. “There’s a guy on the top tier who’s got a record player. He plays that song every night before lights-out. It's my favorite." The heat he radiated was cloying and uncomfortable.

I lifted a foot to get some distance between us, but instead I went nearer, the burn increasing. "Remember that time we went to the mountains?"

"We had a snowball fight," Johnny said, his head bobbing yes, yes, yes. "I let you win. One night, the heater busted and I fixed it. Easy fix, just the converter."

"Paris?"

Johnny laughed—all air, still a nice sound. "I wasn't crazy about that. I'd never flown before. You held my hand the whole time. You really wanted to go to that big museum. You liked the guy who did the pond with the bridge and the flowers. I told you I liked these bendy clocks hanging on a tree branch. You said that meant I was sad, but I wasn't sad. I was happy."

"That week in Hawaii—remember?"

"Yeah, you liked it there. That waterfall—it looked a thousand feet high. You wanted to jump off of it. I wouldn't let you, not in a million years. You got mad at me, but then I climbed a tree and picked you this piece of fruit. You said it was the best thing you'd ever tasted."

"We hiked back to shore," I said, touching his ribs through his shirt, "and there was a boat tied to the dock. You rowed us out. I was thirsty, so when it rained, you cupped the rain for me to drink. I got hungry, so you caught a fish."

"You sang to me when it got dark," he said, putting my palm on his heart. It was pounding, "because I don't like the dark. You sang 'Moon River.' We saw this ship, right when you finished. There were people on the outside, by that railing part. The girls had sparkly clothes, and the guys were wearing tuxes. We could hear them talking. They were complaining, most of them. About how cold the night was or how warm the champagne was or how bored they were. And you looked at me, and I looked at you. And we laid back and went to sleep."

I had to sit. I hobbled back to the tires. "It's cheesy—that song. I don't know why I like it."

"It's sad we can't like cheesy things," he said. "Somebody's probably happy like that somewhere. Like the song says."

"Where?"

"Here. Me, now. I'm happy like that."

"Knock it off. None of that actually happened."

Johnny sat beside me. The cloud of his happiness evaporated. Our hands were two hopeless prayers between our knees.

"See?" I said. "I'm not good. It's too late for me to be any good."

"No, you're right. That stuff's not true. It's good, you reminding me." He watched his toe draw a figure eight in the soil. "You're better than how I imagined. You're infinity better."

I laughed. One more time: "How do I convince you I'm shit, man? Tell me what I have to do, and I'll do it. Whatever it is, I'll do it."

Johnny glared at the moon's angle, its effect on the trees. "If you have questions about Sam," he said, "about your mom, about anything, I'll tell you what I know. And once the sun's up, you're leaving. You're getting out of this. I pinkie-swore. I told you, 'Whatever it takes.' So whatever you need from me, it's yours." He bumped me with his shoulder. "But you can't make me not love you, Rainy. You gotta let me have that."

"Why?"

He raised a finger, tapped the side of his head. "It's all that's left."

THIRTEEN

Johnny kept his word. I asked, and he answered.

"But remember, half of what you hear in the House is rumor and another quarter is bull." We'd raided the fridge and spread a picnic on the bed. Complete meals with demonstrable nutrition didn't appeal to either of us—we chose a smorgasbord of preservative-heavy junk. I gummed gummy snacks too small and too sweet to be real strawberries. He squeezed Easy Cheese on Ritz crackers, and the uppers he was on made his aim hit-or-miss. "So, y'know. Grain of salt."

Sam had gone to San Francisco in 1975, searching for free love. He found hopheads using switchblades to dig hallucinated bugs out of their arms, two-pound babies born addicted to heroin, and their mothers wandering the Haight, days after labor, offering five-dollar hand jobs.

"At least, that's how Sam talks about it. I wasn't alive yet."

He went to a 7-Eleven, bought hot dogs and buns, ingredients for s'mores. He built a little fire on the beach, and anybody who came by could have some supper for nothing. Sam talked to all of them: "We got the bum end of the deal. It doesn't have to be like this." His audience wanted to know the other way it could be, so he told them certain crimes were acts of patriotism, certain violations were expressions of love. He portrayed himself as the authority on what counted as what when. It was those in dire need of authority who stuck around, but they were many. And they listened.

The Cain Gang robbed their way up and down the California coast from 1976 until 1982. They were small-time—convenience stores, liquor stores, mom-and-pop markets. They'd make camp on the beach between jobs, somewhere nobody ever went, and fritter their profits away on pills and pot and acid. When they ran low, they got on the road to another county, and another robbery. Their constant travel was important. Police jurisdictions sucked at information sharing, and ViCAP didn't exist yet. Even if it had, Sam's crew wouldn't have made the cut. They weren't violent. When a cashier was too frightened to put the money in the bag, Sam talked her through it. He'd ask whether she had kids, what their names were, what sports they played.

He'd say she was doing a terrific job. More than once, the woman thanked him before he left.

Johnny guessed there were probably cops who put together the fact that the robberies were serial, but they must've dismissed it as a bunch of dumb hippies. Faces in the gang came and went. Lots of turnover. The only constants were Sam and Harmony. She drove for him, wouldn't carry a gun. Sam carried a gun but never used it, and he liked to wear Looney Tunes masks for the jobs. In a time when beret-clad black men were pointing out that slavery wasn't over, and a radical faction from Puerto Rico was explosively demanding independence, and upper-class white kids were detonating houses in Greenwich Village, a guy doing stick-ups disguised as Bugs Bunny didn't really rate.

It was six years before California got hot for Sam, and it happened because he discovered two things: cocaine and banks, in that order.

They were utter failures at bank robberies. They'd go in with guns waving, then guns blazing. Inevitably a silent alarm got tripped. It was upsetting for Sam. He was a people person, but coke short-circuited him. It took his flexible temperament, his ability to adapt, and converted it to pure volatility. Back then, Sam did coke all day.

Johnny shuddered. "He's mostly pills now. He knows more about pills than I know about cars, and that's a lot. He taught me the basics—what's an up and what's a down, what you can mix and what you can't."

The gang did fourteen banks over four months and raked in $8,000 total. Sam killed three tellers and wounded five more. His trigger finger got jumpy on the powder, plus he didn't like taking lip. Tellers had a way of giving him lip even when their lips were pressed tight together.

Now the FBI got interested. It was 1983. Radical politics were tired, and greed was getting good, but only if you worked on Wall Street and wore a suit to the office. The seventies were over, and the sixties were very, very over, and somebody was going to teach these kids a lesson. The Cain Gang hopped in a van and headed east.

"They did more little stuff on the way, but by the time they got to Jersey, they were broke. Sam decided their next score should be big." Johnny and I were scooping our emptied snack containers into a trash bag. I felt stuffed, sated, and wide-awake. "He started casing, but banks had cameras now, security guards. Then one morning, Sam's getting coffee, and across the street at this mall, an armored truck pulls up to do a money pickup. Just two guards, and the back of the truck chock-full of cash. Sam thought it'd be easy. I see why—he drew me a friggin' map, took me through the plan. It looked good. Sam made it sound damn good."

Johnny's face lit up. He began unpacking our garbage, building a kind of diorama.

"Here's their car." Easy Cheese.

"Here's the mall." Ritz crackers, Triscuits, Chips Ahoy.

"Armored truck." Ben & Jerry's container.

Johnny steered the Easy Cheese to the Triscuits and parked. Ben and Jerry arrived not long after, stopping parallel to the curb. Johnny dented in the empty pint of ice cream—it took a lot of bullets—and he pushed the Cheese car, fast, toward a gridlock of single-serve trail mix and fruit-snack packets.

"They didn't think of the traffic," he said. "They forgot there'd be other cars. Sam figured three o'clock on a Tuesday, everybody's at work. But he didn't count on—"

"School," I said. "Kids were getting out of school."

"Here's the elementary, and here's the junior high." Johnny put a granola bar box and a drained Hawaiian Punch jug behind the mall. "Cops and state troopers were there in ten minutes. The gang got half a mile, to the bypass. Two troopers and three bystanders killed. They were a hundred feet across the New York State line, which is why he went to Sing Sing. Which is why I wound up meeting him."

Johnny wrinkled his nose at the mess and started junking it again. "Your mom must've noticed the schools when they were planning the whole thing. Sam thinks she had kids on the brain just then, since she was pregnant with you." He froze, holding the juice jug. "Sorry, I skipped ahead."

"That's okay."

"I'm not used to— My brain doesn't really work like that anymore. *A, B, C,* one, two, three."

"You're doing great." I kissed him. "Where'd you skip ahead from?"

His sudden joy made the state sound sacred. "California," he said.

Around '82, when their exploits started showing up in the Crime section of the *LA Times*, Harmony decided she wanted out. Easier decided than done: Sam ran a tight ship, with the girls especially. But Harmony had been married to him for two years, and with him for seven, and she knew his blind spots. He developed tunnel vision when preparing for a theft. The bigger the prospective take, the truer this was. After they got to Jersey and Sam saw so much money under so little guard, he became possessed, ignored her completely. She was even able to get to a doctor after a week of nonstop vomiting to find out her uterus had a tenant.

A week later, Sam assembled everybody to outline the plan. He also assigned each member their roles: Harmony would drive, as always; he and five others would subdue the guards; and the gang's most athletic member—a girl who was a nationally ranked sprinter before she met Sam and dropped out of college—was given a vital task: raiding the truck and running with the money bag.

Harmony saw her chance. Soon after the plans were laid, she went to the money runner and told her a top secret new plan. Something Sam didn't want the others to know about.

After a couple of weeks' practice, it was time. They drove to the mall and arrived at five minutes to three, Harmony behind the wheel of their van. She kissed Sam good luck. He got out with the gang behind him, all armed. The runner followed, ready with a duffel bag.

"Now, here's the awesome part."

Harmony had parked by a corner of the mall. She claimed, to Sam, that it would afford them more choices for a getaway route. Once her best friends and the father of her unborn child were thoroughly engaged with the armored truck, she got out and walked a few blocks. To where she'd parked another vehicle. It must have been a real chore to acquire that car without Sam knowing, but Harmony had done it—and it was a car that no one would ever APB.

"The guards in that truck put up a good fight. They died, but they took three of the gang with them. Sam was the only one who didn't at least get wounded. Then he—"

Johnny set a fist on his lips. His laughter got out anyway. "He turns around, and there's the girl, right? With the money bag? She's running right past their van. Sam thinks of chasing her, but this is why he picked her, 'cause she's so fast. Even carrying four million cash, she's just gone. He gets in the van, and he sees your mom's not there. Sam says he knew right away what Harmony was doing. A couple of his guys aren't dead, they get in after him, and Sam guns it for where the money went. Except there's the school traffic. A couple hundred cars, easy, and he doesn't know what he's looking for. He takes the turnpike; he doesn't have a choice. The cops catch up, and"—Johnny cleared his throat, shook his head—"the shoot-out on the highway isn't funny. I mean, none of it's funny. But it is, sort of. Your mom had serious balls."

Sam never implicated Harmony. His codefendants rolled on him like cheap sleeping bags in exchange for reduced sentences. During the appeals process, Sam made friends with his lawyer and persuaded him to research abandoned vehicles with Jersey plates recovered nationwide in the weeks after his capture. There was a black '73 Datsun catalogued in San Luis Obispo with a passenger seat soaked so maroon it looked like the factory had fucked up and put red interior in that one spot. Next, his lawyer looked into bodies. The girl was found on a Pennsylvania roadside two days after the robbery. Her autopsy revealed that her femoral artery had been nicked. Most likely it happened while she was running from the armored truck, toward my mother, with the cash.

"So your mom rode west with four million bucks while Sam got life."

Johnny scooped up the garbage and cinched the trash-bag ties with finality. Outside, dark was going gray with pre-sunrise. I recalled agreeing to some dawn sex. He tossed the bag on the floor, looked at the window, and stopped talking. It had to be the least aggressive seduction move ever made.

That suited me; I could pretend not to notice. I was occupied trying to square my housedress-and-heels mother with an outlaw getaway driver. Her rules about shoes on the carpet, her repeated felonies.

How often she checked behind her while walking down the street. Moving a slat of the blinds so she could see out. I'd always assumed she was scared of imaginary monsters. But five years on the run, a little LSD, a lot of marijuana, ripping off your husband for several million—he's in the clink and you know he's a chatty guy. What do you do? You put on a costume. You play the part. If the authorities show up at your door, you say Sam's mistaken. They'll leave long enough for you to grab the essentials, throw your daughter in the passenger seat, and tell her this is not a drill.

It was wonderful, in a way, to have Harmony make some sense. It was atrocious, too.

"I don't know how much cash can be left," I said. "She never had a job, and her wardrobe was pretty considerable."

"Sam's lawyer checked into that. She skimmed a quarter mil, but that's all. She did something with ladders or CDs or—bonds, I guess? I don't know. Sam said she was smart with it. Only nice thing I ever heard him say about her." Johnny scooted closer. His voice dropped low. "Sam said some really, really mean stuff about her. Stuff he'd do if he got a hold of her. I can't repeat it. Or, y'know, I won't."

I touched his arm, grateful.

"Sam thinks she kept the rest of the money hidden as a bargaining chip. So he couldn't kill her if he got out. He knew she was getting weird, but he didn't think she'd—" Johnny took my hand and held it in both of his. "I'm sorry your mom killed herself. I am."

"I wasn't surprised," I said, observing his thumb rolling over my knuckles. "But I was. It was strange. It's still strange."

"The bad stuff is like that. The horrible stuff. It's all strange. Sometimes I think it's because horrible stuff's not supposed to happen. It doesn't fit. Things are supposed to be good." He grinned, sheepish. "It's nice to think that, even if it's not true."

I crawled onto him. He hugged me shamelessly. Light was seeping into a dark corner behind the bed, where a mousetrap was set with a plastic wedge of cheese.

"This can't be all we get," I said.

"It's not that bad. It's better than a cot."

"I meant tonight. We can't just get tonight."

"I'm gonna draw a shape on your back. Try and guess what it is."

I laughed, kissed him neck to nose to chin, and at his lips, I married the moment to uncountable others, the many others we'd had and would get.

"Are you listening now?" I said.

"Mmm."

"Come with me. Run with me."

"I can't."

"Then meet me after. When it's all over."

"Don't cry."

"Say we'll meet after, and I'll stop."

He lay sideways, bringing me with him. A crumple under my head turned out to be our two remaining condoms. I unwrapped one.

Johnny stole them, flung them aside.

"You'll come find me," I babbled, resisting his efforts to hold me, calm me down. I didn't want to be calm. "After it's all over, you'll come find me and we'll go get an apartment. I'll wait tables. Mechanics can work off the grid. You'll get home, and I'll be there on the fire escape, with my guitar, and you can come sit with me, and we'll decide if we want to cook dinner or go out. Or see a movie, or take a walk. We'll get a dog, so we'll have to walk him."

I left off there for Johnny to contribute. He had sex hair, lovingly disarrayed. I touched it as a dopey smile spread over him. "Home," he said.

Pop! *Pop pop*! From upstairs, the kitchen.

No, outside.

I puckered to form the word "what," but Johnny was off the bed. He bolted up the stairs, out the door.

I went after him. Blaine's coat. I thought of going back but didn't. We'd handle this, we'd go back, Johnny and I would make sweet daybreak whoopee, and I'd get Blaine's coat and return it the next time I saw him; it's interesting—part of me really did believe all that. I was running through the woods, getting nipped by branches and needles. Curly and Legs: I'd forgotten they existed. Ahead, I heard a giggle, followed by a shush, same as in the rest stop bathroom. I cleared the trees. There were the girls, pushing the station wagon toward the road. The gravel made a sound like popcorn under the tires. They had it in neutral, were each at a door, straining, ass muscles rounding. Johnny was lying in the dirt, holding his crotch. I got to him as the van arrived at the turn.

"Stop them," he said.

Curly saw me and shouted, "Now!" Legs stepped into the passenger side, holding the window frame. She pulled; the door clicked. Curly hopped in the driver's seat. She yanked the door, but my shoulder was there just in time. The armrest conked off my hip, and the door wagged open again. I got a foot inside. Curly's fist smashed my left tit, and I shouted an incoherent cry of offense. I started slapping at her, a totally inept fighting technique, but she was about as much a pugilist as I was. We threw open palms, doing no damage. Legs reached for the ignition. I reached, too, and Curly tried to scratch at my hands. She missed, because I wasn't going for the ignition.

I pulled back and up, bouncing off the door as the transmission jammed into park. The car rattled to a stop; I crashed to the ground.

"Hurry up! Hurry up!" Curly yelled, catching her door and slamming it shut. Something fell out of her pocket. "Come the fuck on!" she was saying, but I was looking at the ground.

She'd dropped her phone. I checked on Johnny. He was cradling his groin, trying to stand. No sign of Sam, and Curly was cranking at the transmission lever, while Legs was yelling at her to hurry, hurry, hurry. A red wash of sunrise hit the treetops.

I snatched the cell, flipped it open, and dialed, doddering around the wagon to get a plate number. Blaine answered before it rang once. "Rainy?"

"Brown Subaru Outback with wood trim. Don't know what year." Gravel ate my knees. "Hang on. I'm almost to the front."

"Are you hurt?" Blaine's voice was like a balm. "Are you—"

Out of nowhere, my wrist bent wrong. I screamed, looked up. Curly was shutting the phone, putting it in her back pocket. “Fix this,” she said, kicking the fender. “Right now.”

She stood over me, trying for scary, but it didn’t work.

“Where’s my dad?” I said.

Curly smirked. “He’s a little tied up.”

“Ellie, it’s fine,” Legs squeaked from the car. “We can walk.”

“Shut up! Kat here broke it. She’ll fix it.”

I got to my feet a little unsteadily. I wasn’t 100 percent sure where I was going, but I wanted to get there, so when Curly got in my way: “Move.”

“I don’t think so,” she said, cricking her neck upward, trying to compensate for the eight inches I had on her. “You owe me a car.”

“How about you suck my dick?”

“No, thanks.” She patted her belly. “Ellie’s all full.”

I went around her. She came with me. “Fucking move,” I said.

She reached behind her back. I should have been afraid, but I was too angry. I did what she’d just done to me—grabbed her arm, tweaked hard. The gun fell from her hand. I jumped, thinking it might go off. Curly took the opportunity to wind up and throw a haymaker. I flinched, and her fist connected with the top of my shoulder. Heat came up my neck, to my hot head. I threw my weight at her, and we rolled against the hood. She got a knot of my hair and pulled. I dug my nails in her arms and drew blood.

For my first fight, I thought I was doing fairly well, until pain seared into my right eye. It didn't come from Curly, but from a pebble that got kicked up as Legs sprinted past us. We both watched, unmoving, as one of those fleeing knees blew out in a cherry spray. I saw the impact before I heard the shot rend the dawn, a big-throated boom!

Legs had made it almost fifty yards. She folded to the road and rolled to face us, fumbling for her knee. She found it. She attempted, for a futile few moments, to gather it together before she realized how many chips of bone there were in the hole, and how many there were in the road. Comprehension pried her mouth open, and she screamed, "Help me! Somebody help me!"

"Get off of her," Sam said.

I thought he meant me, that he was ordering me to get off of someone, maybe Legs. Maybe I was making her scream like that. Over and over and over and over, the "me" getting longer and louder. "Help maaaay! Help maaaay!"

Curly kept pushing me back down. "Sam, hey. We were just messing around. We wanted to go grab doughnuts for everybody. We didn't want to wake Kat, so we were being quiet."

Sam smiled; he didn't look mad. If anything, he looked sleepy. A friendly bear coming out of his cave after hibernation. A couple hundred pounds of affability, a hug waiting to happen: that's the story his smile told.

But it's still ringing through the valley, astoundingly loud: "Help maaaay! Somebody please help maaaay!"

And the gun hung at the end of his hand. And his wrists were cuffed in rashy red. "Smart of you," he said. "Wearing me out first." His brow knit at me. "Are you all right, honey?"

"Dad," I said. Legs was on her back now, screaming at the sky. "She needs help."

"The two of you need to get out of the road." Sam grabbed Curly by the front of her shirt. She was off the ground, kicking, her feet hitting mine in short, desperate timpani taps. Sam held the gun a few inches from her nose. "This is not what I do," he said.

Her face disappeared in a blob of jelly. Sam threw her. She bounced off the car door and crumpled. The tire obscured her. A dark-red pool poured outward, around the tire, dyeing the dull rocks. I was scuttling away, so it wouldn't dye me. I made to grab the grille, climb the car, but I didn't want to touch it, because she was touching it.

Sam took a breath of the cool morning and embarked on a stroll. He grinned fondly while Legs got up on the knee that would hold her and tried to limp away. He arrived by her side and walked along, nodding as if with encouragement. Curly's blood had sprayed him, wetting the neckline of his T-shirt. Legs hopped and staggered and cried, shrieking strange sounds.

I stood, took maybe two steps.

Arms wrapped around me from behind, skinny but so, so strong. "Don't," Johnny said in my ear.

"Don't!" I hollered at the absolute top of my lungs. "Sam, don't, she didn't do anything!"

Her knee caught a bad angle. She went down, and where she landed, she simply curled over, like the dirt was her childhood bed. She looked right at me. Quiet hiccups made her shoulders jump.

"Pretend to faint," Johnny whispered.

But I stayed locked with her. Her stare was saying: "I don't need to be afraid, do I? I'm daydreaming, right?"

I made mine say: "Yep, you're watching a bad episode of *CSI*, and you turned to see what's happening out the window. It's fine, you just checked out."

The shot startled her. Her eyes widened—surprise more than pain. I felt it, too. A distinct shredding, into the arm, through the chest, out the other side, opening a compartment for life to flow out of.

"Faint," Johnny said, hissing it.

Sam was walking toward us. He had hulk shoulders, high and furious. "What did I say?"

I slumped. I committed completely. I went fainting one better—I was dead.

"Put her down."

I was dead, so I didn't hear how Sam's feet pounded to a stop inches from where Johnny was setting my corpse to the ground. I didn't hear the blow connect, just Johnny's grunt, his fall.

"I forgot," Johnny said.

"What did you forget?"

"I don't look at her. I don't talk to her. I don't touch her."

"Did you touch her?" A click. "I've got three left, did you touch her?"

"No, she slept. I stayed outside."

"Then why is she here?"

"The gravel under the tires, it was loud. I came running when I heard it. The short one kicked me in the balls. She was making a phone call; there's a cell in her back pocket. We should hurry."

"Are you telling me what to do?"

"No."

"Say, 'No, Sam.'"

"No, Sam."

"What's wrong with the car?"

"Transmission's stuck. I can fix it."

"How long? Say, 'Five minutes.'"

"Five minutes."

"Get started," Sam said. "I'll take care of these."

I imagined Sam getting a solid grip on Curly's ankles and pulling. Don't picture it, I told myself. That sound could be anything. It doesn't have to be Curly's ruined head picking up grit like a wet mop.

It faded, giving way to clicks and maneuvers with metal—Johnny messing with the car's transmission. I couldn't breathe.

"Kat—sorry, I have to call you that or I'll get confused. Kat, you can't cry." Johnny knelt beside me and began untying his right shoe. His eyebrow had split down the middle, but he was focused, disciplined. He jerked his sneaker off, peeled the insole out, held up two black capsules. "These'll hit you hard."

I gulped the pills, hyperventilating.

"Good," Johnny said, throwing a glance in the direction of the house. "They'll take a while to kick in. Until then, no matter what, you're asleep. I mean it, you're sleeping. Okay?"

"He-his guh-hunna ki-hill uh-hus."

Johnny put a hand over my eyes. "We're . . . we're in the mountains. Nobody around, just us. I lit a fire in the fireplace. You made hot chocolate."

I lost it. I actually went to the mountains. Me and Johnny, on a couch, in a room with a spectacular view. I had a mug of Swiss Miss. The fireplace blazed.

So Sam's heavy feet hitting gravel, passing me—they were the wood, crackling as it burned. A minute later, Legs being dragged.

"Good," Johnny said. "That's good, Kat."

It was good. The Sierras wearing their white winter beanies. Our seclusion so complete, so perfect. We needed to put another log on. The fire was going out.

FOURTEEN

It ain't me. Creedence Clearwater Revival, ha! It was going to be a good day. Even if my body seemed to be a boneless pile, strapped into a car's front seat.

"Turn that up," Sam said, from the back.

A dirty hand on a dial complied. Numbers on a sun-bright clock read 4:42. Johnny, in the driver's seat, glanced at me sideways. He raised one finger off the steering wheel and looked in the rearview mirror. The cut on his eyebrow had sealed into a hard line. It connected now to before with cruel efficiency. I felt my heart pop to the memory of gun-shots. They were so vivid it felt like they were happening in the car. I would have thrashed or screamed or freaked out somehow, except now I knew who the man in the backseat really was, what lived behind his endearingly tone-deaf and slurred sing-along with the radio.

Johnny reached to the dash, grabbed the bag of sunflower seeds. He put them in his lap and swirled them. Two objects hilled out from the gray shells. They were thirty-five-millimeter film canisters. He picked one, popped the top, tipped it. A glob of black capsules fell out. He shook them all back in, save two. He tossed a single seed in his mouth then reached over, fed me the pills. My throat was bone-dry, but I got them down.

Our tires bounced on the shoulder. Johnny guided the car back onto the road, bulleting through terrain the color of rust. Slabs of rock in stand-alone walls, cracked soil like broken leather. My seat was leather. This wasn't the same car. I ruminated on what state our plates were from now, on what song would play after "Fortunate Son." On the mental image of Sam crooning to the roof of the car, his eyes shut, savoring the sound of his awful singing voice and therefore not seeing when Johnny slipped me the downers. On whether the dead girls were back in their hometowns yet, or if they were spending a few hours' quality time in a sterile room, prone on cold metal beds, their youthful perkiness covered in clean sheets.

I was sure I'd be joining them soon. I saw no possibility of escape, and my drug hangover had annihilated all my capacities to search. Having just swallowed another dose, it seemed too soon for the meds to be taking effect. And yet they spoke to me. “Come with us,” they said. “We’re your escape.” I let my head sag, shutting my eyes.

“Is she awake?” A mean fug of liquor filled my nostrils. “Did she move? It looks like she moved.”

“Yeah,” Johnny said. “A little.”

“She’ll wake up, right? Say ‘She’ll wake up, Sam.’”

“She’ll wake up, Sam.”

Clumsy fingers tugged the skin of my face, as though trying to mold it. “I didn’t mean to scare her.” His voice cracked. He sounded drunk, but it was more than that: plaintive preteen boy not liking what was for dinner. “I didn’t mean to.”

Johnny waited for his line. None came. “She’ll be okay.”

“Right. You’re right.” The seat belt tightened across my front, over my thighs. “I didn’t have a choice, did I?”

“No, Sam.”

“No. No, I didn’t. They slutted up to me all night so they could tie me to the bed and steal our car. That isn’t appropriate. Kat would never do that, would she?”

“No, Sam.”

“Say ‘Never, Sam.’”

“Never, Sam.”

“She’s a good girl. She’s her daddy’s sweet baby girl. She just needs time. Then she’ll take us to my money and decide she wants to stay. It’s understandable she’d have misgivings, but I did nothing wrong. They were whores.” He seemed to draw strength from the word. “Whores, Johnny. We don’t need more whores. We’ve got enough whores, right?”

"Right, Sam."

"Good boy. Tell me if she moves again."

"I will," Johnny said.

Creedence faded. I went with it.

It wasn't full blackout. I'd surface to wind that skimmed cool across my forehead, a powerful whiff of Stove Top stuffing, musical snippets getting cut together into discordant classic-rock medleys. The sedatives had turned me into a calculator where only the CLEAR button worked. I'd slip into recent, terrible events, then reset to zero. I'd experiment with questions: Where am I? Are my arms and legs attached? What do I do now? Back to zero.

How much time is passing? I didn't want to wake, but it was happening.

Sam had moved to the driver's seat. He grinned at me like: Good morning, sunshine. He took a can of Dr Pepper from the cup holder, sipped. We were parked at the curb of a side street that fed into a one-way, its four lanes scattered with taxis and a few nontaxis. Palm trees reached third and fourth floors of enormous buildings.

My body shook like it was trying to expel something stuck in a gear. I was yapping random syllables, pulling and pulling at my door handle. The childproof locks were engaged. My vision got fuzzy.

"Kat? What's the matter?"

My fingers hurt. Sam's mitts appeared, and he tore my nails from where they were digging into the armrests. I searched for Johnny. He was sitting back on his heels, picking at the carpet. Showing me the part of his hair in a clear signal: "Look at him. Don't look at me; look at him."

"All right," Sam said, unbuckling my seat belt. The car creaked. He folded and slid to the passenger side, putting me on his leg. It should have been much more of an operation than it was. I should have struggled, but I was flaccid, and his solid iron shape gave me a shape. He breathed the sour reek of yogurt gone bad. "Is that better?"

Twenty feet away, a yellow cab cut off a Hummer. They took turns honking. Others got in on the game. I found it familiar. Relaxing. I observed the chaos, pretending Sam was background noise. "Yes," I said.

"Tell me what's going on in that beautiful head of yours. Gimme the skinny, Minnie."

"Nothing," I said.

"The feds are at the cabin." Sam poked the police scanner with his toe. "Your cop tipped them, and it's intriguing to me. Why would that naughty little girl call your cop?"

"Blaine had cards in his coat pocket. I could've dropped one."

Sam rubbed a firm, slow circle on my back. "Why wouldn't she dial 9-1-1?"

"I don't know, Daddy."

"Ooh, I like that. Say it again."

"I don't know, Daddy."

"Just 'Daddy.'"

"Daddy," I said.

He pressed a line of three kisses up my neck. They pricked like thorns. "I believe you. I believe *in* you. Do you believe in me? Say 'Yes, Daddy.'"

"Yes, Daddy."

"I love you. Daddy loves you. What do you say?"

"I love you, too, Daddy."

"Now tell me what had you so upset a minute ago, and Daddy will fix it. Is it Johnny? Did Johnny—"

"No." I turned. I had to sell this.

Sam had a sunburn. He'd started to flake and peel, revealing baby-sensitive pink underneath. It dawned on me that that's what he'd resembled all along: a baby, a record-breaker-big baby. And a happy one right now. All his teeth were on display, and all but a few had been drilled, filled, colloided. His breath was fetid and horrible, and he didn't care. Perhaps it was possible to be too at-home in the world. To see it as a show that's just for you. Then there's no ethics, no core. There's only what you want.

Sam wanted a sweet, innocent child.

"I'm really tired, Daddy," I said. "It's like I'm running the miles instead of watching them go by. Y'know?"

He shook his head. Shaking it like: Wow—wow, this love I feel.

"Do Daddy a favor. Reach down and get that bag on the right." The grocery sacks were in the legroom of our seat. "That's it. Johnny, come join us." He dug in the bag and brought out a trio of masks. They were cheap plastic, a thin white band to hold them on. Sam became Bugs Bunny, with trademarked chubby cheeks, threatless buck teeth, ears that stuck up.

I was coming apart. I'd never thought that an apt expression before, but now it was perfect. I was splitting at some molecular level. I turned back to the street. I heard Sam say, "Kat gets the cat," and my peripheral vision got lost as he slid a mask on me.

Johnny was negotiating with the driver's seat, getting his legs to fit. Sam handed him Tweety Bird. "How you doing, buddy?"

Johnny gave a thumbs-up, setting the canary on the dash.

"Nyehh," Sam said. "Time to wake you up, doc!" He rattled the grocery bag. I didn't theorize about what he was getting, how it'd wake me. I grinned at a guy playing air drums on his steering wheel. I wondered what he was listening to.

Sam dangled the baggie he'd taken from the girls for safekeeping. He oscillated it two feet from my eyes, as if trying to hypnotize me. His other arm came around, and I watched his expertise at the process. He extracted the mirror, held it flat. He poured such a measly quantity of dust on its surface that there seemed no way it would have any effect. The razor slashed its own likeness, creating three short dashes. Sam tented his fingers under the mirror, holding it like a waiter, and shook a dollar bill from the baggie, already rolled into a tube. "Go ahead."

"I'm okay," I said. "Thank you, though."

"Katherine."

"I'm fine."

"You're not fine. You've slept for more than twenty-four hours, and that is enough."

I made no move to take it.

"Have you ever done this?" he said. "Is that why you're nervous?"

I nodded wretchedly. I was nervous because I knew that coke's not dose-dependent. No matter how small the amount, it can kill you.

"Watch Johnny."

I was grateful to watch Johnny, for any reason, for any length of time. Even if he was taking the mirror and the tube and snorting, not missing a crumb. His head inclined subtly, as if telling me to just do it, as he gave Sam the stuff back.

"I'm fine, really," I said.

Sam's voice honed to an edge. "Take it."

In the mirror was Sylvester the Cat, my eyes showing between two lines of white powder. I pinched the tube and lodged it in a nostril, bent to the mirror and sniffed, moving with the straw. Sandpaper on my sinuses.

That's the last seminormal thought I had before the cocaine blew through every synapse/organ/system, popping to a morning gone white-bright! I went to move my neck, and it jolted, my body as or more alive than my mind, going three thousand miles a minute, sea to shining sea and back again. At our right was the entrance to a bank—corporate behemoth, large lobby. I breathed fast as Sam took the last hit. He sealed the accessories with the cocaine and had me return the bag to the floor.

"I'm proud of you," said Bugs, the sight of him a nauseating jitter and jive. "I couldn't be prouder, you stopping those girls. Johnny told me you did, that you both did. Daddy's so proud of you."

Sam reached in his pocket and gave Johnny a teeny-weeny gun. Johnny accepted it as one would a pack of cigs. Sam fitted his paw to Johnny's delicate jawline, and Johnny turned his head, kissed Sam's palm. The gesture looked sincere. Sam opened our door, sneaking out from under me. I landed on the seat. The car door slammed, and I watched as Sam's wide body squeezed through the bank's narrow entrance.

Johnny's hand closed over mine. "Why did we stop them?" I asked. "Why'd we stop the girls, why didn't we just let them go?"

"He'd have been mad." Johnny hit a button on his door. The childproof locks disengaged with a synchronized click. He kissed my knuckles, tenderly. He pointed. "See that street on the left?"

"Yeah."

"Get to that street. Follow it. Run in one of the big hotels. Put the gun down first."

"I don't have a—"

"Run inside and start screaming, okay?"

I touched Johnny, same as Sam had, though my arm shook so badly I sort of slapped him. "Come with me."

He manipulated my fingers 'til my index stuck out, used it to tap his temple. "I can't."

He put my hand between both of his, pulling my arm to a downward angle. I was about to ask what he was doing when my whole shoulder kicked. The sound was too huge; I didn't hear it. His jeans shredded on his calf. Blood appeared there by bad magic.

Johnny didn't scream, but his expression did. "Run," he said.

A hot wash of adrenaline joined the cocaine. I clawed the door open and tripped into the street. Tires squealed. A nudge at my knees made me fall on a hood. The car's driver got out—suit, tie, spray tan, angry. "What the hell's your—"

I raised the gun. He paled and ran up the lane line. He looked back. "Take it!" he cried, hands above his head. "Take the car!"

I went to the driver's side. The car window showed me Sylvester the Cat. I took him off and threw him so he was smiling at me from the passenger seat.

I jerked the transmission to drive, heard the peal of my tires before I knew I'd pressed the pedal. I seized a hole in the traffic left by somebody moving too slow. I heard a horn bleat, and a woman called me names. I goosed the gas and went left, sparing a sec to check the rearview, where the bank shone beacon-like and a car was still waiting in the no-parking zone. I gunned for a lucky green arrow. I looped around a median doing forty, skewering between surprisingly few compacts and minivans and airport shuttles, mild impacts rollicking me around in the driver's seat, until the many, many lanes opened wide and let me through. There were fountains shooting stories high, more neon signs than I'd ever seen. I paid them little attention, because ahead another sign said highway; I took it. A sign for an exit to another highway, and I took it. I kept taking exits until I was on a forgotten road with no one on it and nothing around it. I rolled down all the windows and turned on the radio. "I Want to Know What Love Is" by Foreigner. I belted along, ad-libbing with the gospel choir singing backup. More songs should have gospel choirs singing backup. I laughed, checked under Sylvester. The gun was there. Beside it was a cell phone, flipped shut and shining silver. I put the mask back over it.

The land was parched, homogenous. I saw it in unclear shutter-clicks that told me only: sand. I pressed the gas into the floor with my full weight. Home wasn't far now. It wasn't this; it was this's antithesis. I cranked the music. "We Belong" and "I Wanna Dance with Somebody" and "Never Gonna Give You Up" and "Don't Stop Believin'." Journey sang it how many years ago, and here it was, still playing. A miracle.

There was a girl on the highway, skipping rope. She was wearing a black-and-white polka-dotted dress with pale-pink tights. I had years to ponder her. To think about how that was my Easter outfit when I was six or seven. I swerved, but I could fix it. The road was so long.

Tires free, spinning. Me free, spinning. The windshield showed a sweet bath of blue sky, then a thicket of brush and spines coming closer. Had I called him, Blaine's first question would have been "Where are you?"

The answer filled me up and made me float above the desert, balloon-light with relief: I'm here.

I'm right here.

III

ROAM

FIFTEEN

Somebody'd hung the room wrong. My hair dangled over a floor—ceiling?—covered in glass. Big hunks and tiny diamonds of glass. They threw light, and inside was dark—freaky dark. I heard breathing. It was speeding up, a downbeat to panic, because I was upside-down, suspended by a seat belt. How long had I been out? I remembered fragments about how I got here, all of them surreal.

I wanted to teleport. I'd take the whole car with me if necessary. A ditch in Minneapolis. December— fine, I'd take the snow, too. As long as there was an ambulance, fire truck, cops: "Miss, can you hear me? Sit tight, we're here to help." Maybe it would be Blaine.

"Blaine?" I said. I tested my neck. It turned okay.

I waited for the Sylvester the Cat mask to say he told me so, but he wasn't in the passenger side. The ceiling there had caved in. My window was walled in sand, as was the window behind it. So were both windshields. Like I'd been buried alive.

But the glass is shining. Where's the light coming from?

"Backseat, passenger side." And its beautiful wide-open frame. The stitch in my ribs complained. I concurred, aloud: "This is gonna suck."

I put my right fist on the ceiling. Floor. There was absolutely no good way to do this. I used my hands like brooms, sweeping as much glass away as I could. I planted my fist again and pressed the seat-belt button. Stunning flood of silver across my vision.

Pain is a lot of things in theory, and a lot of things in retrospect. Pain is only itself when you're in it. Pain is pure, and it makes people pure, and no matter how bad they are, it makes their motives pure: stop the pain. That's why torture works. It's also why torture doesn't work. I performed actions that were countereffective to making the pain stop, such as oscillating on my glass-covered square of ceiling/floor. I tried to put my right hand to my side and found I couldn't. When I brought my wrist up for inspection, it was swollen and achy, and there was a fat bulge where that little bump's supposed to sit parallel to the pinkie. I'd also broken my pinkie.

Crawling hurt. Surprise of the century. I squished around the headrests and knocked random crap out of the way. I peeked my head into sunlight and greeted a world that was amazingly beige, dug with my elbows and pulled into merciless heat, army-crawled until I needed a breather, turned my head, put my cheek to the ground, and checked out the car. The front end was crumpled into a thatch of bristled spruce that grew about five feet from a cement irrigation ditch. The driver's side dug into a hill of sand deeply enough that a backhoe might've done it. Kinked like this, I noticed my back was iridescent—a few dozen puckers of skin winked widgets of glass. The blood painted rings on my tank top. It reminded me of the sign for Target. Or, I suppose, a target. I spared a few minutes to pick out the bigger pieces, straddling bleak emotional collapse and fierce euphoric ascension because, yes, I was hurting and I was stranded and I was hotter than an egg frying on a dry skillet. But Sam was not here.

I decided to take five, celebrate. I put my other cheek to the desert floor. There, a few feet away, was the cell phone. A short length of snakeskin was trapped under it, inflating wind-sock-style on a breeze I didn't feel.

I got on my stomach, got a mouthful of sand. I coughed once and shrieked, curled up, and that made it worse. I arrived at the cell and picked the snakeskin free, flipped the phone open. The screen showed a bulldog with a Christmas star on his head. He was not pleased.

I dialed, awkward with my left hand.

"Listen," Blaine said. "Tell me where you are. Right now, first thing."

"I don't know." I did my best, but my best was, "The desert."

"Are you— Never mind, look around. Tell me what's around you."

"There's a road."

"Look at the road. Is there a sign?"

The sun was baking me stupid. My view profoundly dull, dry, and repetitive, an overlay of the same three frames behind that indestructible bird who never said anything but *meep-meep.* I tried a maneuver to get on my knees.

"What happened?" Blaine said. "How bad are you?"

"Bad." I stumbled to the car, leaned on the flipped front tire. It was slack and wanted to turn. Everything went gray. I dropped the phone and sprawled across the wheel and held it still, and it held me still. I searched for a route I could walk.

That hill. You'll see more.

But that's a mile, easy.

The phone was yelling. I bent to pick it up. My entire body rang with pain. "I broke"—where to begin?—"a few things."

"Check the charge. How much charge has your phone got?"

The screen reminded me of video games. Numbers made of squares. I spied nothing that would indicate its life span. "Don't know," I said. "I have to move, Blaine." I limped. Some exotic instability was going on in my leg. Fortunately, it paled in comparison. "Remember when you told me there's no pain like breaking your hand?"

I could hear his engine revving to obscene speeds. "Yeah?"

"Try ribs. Pretty awesome. Every time I inhale, it's like I'm rolling in broken glass. Which I did, too, so I can vouch for the metaphor."

Blaine swore, a nifty cuss combining "shit," two "fucks," and a split "goddamn." "I need you to do something."

"'Kay."

"I'm gonna hang up."

"No, don't." The earth underneath me was scorched. I was eyeing those scaly squares, to focus on his voice. His voice was sanity. "Please don't."

"Feds can trace your phone," Blaine said. "I have to call them, and the cell they're tracing needs to be on. Trace doesn't work with no battery, understand?"

"No." And I meant that on a few levels. Didn't know they could do that. Didn't understand how. But mostly, "Don't. Don't hang up."

"I'm sorry. Don't call me back."

"Blaine!" I blared it into dead air. My ribs grated, and I was grateful: it brought me back to the fact I was in serious trouble here. I surveyed how far I'd come, the car a greasy blot on a flat of cracked tan, long skid marks the roof had left, like somebody tried to erase a mistake and only made it worse. The road I'd been driving on was endless, stretching nowhere in both directions. Slight undulations of arid windsweep lacked even those cactuses that look, to a desperate person, like people. Their prickly arms raised in a kind of welcome.

I went for the hill, more an embankment, more a slight rise of gathered dirt. I was getting hotter. I recognized backtracking to the car as the best strategy, crabbing into that swelter of shaded ninety rather than this sunny hundred plus. But coherence had exited, giving way to dumb animal drive, and I tipped forward like a spilled glass of water—water, how great was water—kicked another foot into another step, and so on, like that. Once I was on top of the repulsive void, I shook my head. Buildings appeared in a little bowl of valley not a half mile away.

I had to be hallucinating. Though if I were, I doubted the buildings would be falling over. I counted structures and got to nine, but most of them weren't buildings anymore. They were lean-tos. Whole slabs of edifice had sheared off, leaving crumbled lumber and scabbed drywall. The pieces still standing were a petrified gray color, bulging out in splintered angles, and those were the handful not yet overwhelmed by sand, slithering in the available gaps and massing into dunes as if saying, Nice try.

That big one's got four walls. It even has a door. Fancy.

I blinked aggressively, trying to get a better read on what that squat rectangle was and why it'd been better built than anything around it, before asking myself why the hell it mattered. I got going. Between me and it sat the irrigation ditch, the two-lane, and a long pass of land spotted in spiked bushes and canker-like rocks. I didn't guess at the distance. I rationed my glimpses. If I checked my direction too often, the buildings seemed to get smaller. I could feel my scalp burning, my hair on fire. I'm telling myself: A ghost town—neat, never been in one of those.

Shambling onto Main Street. More like Only Street. Standing in the middle of the real deal, you can't help but think: "Ghost town" is right.

"Hello?"

I heard rattles and scuttles. Whatever owned this territory was gossiping, calling me a varmint, a goddamn interloper. A crooked window stared at me, mean idiot eye. That unfeelable breeze caught a ravaged piece of cloth in the shattered pane, making it flutter. I could tell that one was a house, but the others defied the usual labels: general store or school or saloon. They were broken boxes. I had to marvel at anyone attempting to settle here.

The building with its ostentatious door—it was actually double doors, hanging open—I went in. Blunted, groggy. The temperature plummeted twenty degrees. The darkness was total. I sat. I didn't mean to sit, but it happened. I crawled: the farther I got, the cooler I'd be. I went until I couldn't go anymore. The edges of my broken ribs rubbed together. It was like my most appalling menstrual cramps took a wrong turn north. I curled on my side and remembered that Legs did that, in the road, before Sam shot her. I tried to roll on my back and couldn't. My life began its death-prep slide show. It got stuck on Sam, Sam saying, "Daddy loves you." I wished he hadn't meant it. But he had; his love was real. It just didn't have anything to do with me.

An incredible heaviness descended. I weighed a quadrillion pounds. I fought sleep, that marketing genius. Sleep! No money down, no interest, no payments 'til brain swelling!

I looked around, to keep conscious. I realized it wasn't as dark in here as I'd thought—that'd been the contrast with outside. The roof boasted holes big and small. Sun beamed through. The walls protruded with miniwalls that divided the room into compartments. Each had a latch for a square window. I was in a horse stable. How this knowledge helped me, I did not know, yet a flower of cockiness bloomed in my chest anyway. I catalogued evidence, piled in corners, of a long-ago party: tall boys, cigarette butts, a blanket, and a pair of women's underpants, its lace yellow or yellowed.

I visualized the central switchboard of my body, where alarms went off and warning lights flashed. The cell phone was still clutched in my hand. It didn't seem melodramatic, wanting to tell him goodbye. I pressed buttons, but the screen stayed blank. The battery was dead. I searched for and found the nobility in giving up.

Hey, God? Your rules are dumb, I quit. Take your best shot.

A predatory growl came from outside, a distant rumble. I told God, Pshh, eaten alive by a wild beast? You're not even trying.

Then I gathered it wasn't an animal. It was getting closer. I heard gears shifting, an abrupt stop. A car door slammed shut.

"Rainaaaay!"

"Uh?" I said. And thought: Yeah, that'll cut it.

"Rainaaaay!"

The secret to good singing is breath. Engage the diaphragm, expand the lungs, which expands the ribs: "Heeeaaaaaaare!" Which terminates in a spate of clogged-toilet noises.

I shallowed my air intake to quarter teaspoons and watched the last moisture I had stick my eyelashes together. I listened to a powerful engine race for me, but I had no inner hurray about it. I was mostly wondering whether Blaine would shoot me if I asked him politely enough.

Fast feet moved across the ground outside. The bright-to-dark rendered him sightless, too, and he would have tripped over me if I hadn't moaned.

"Jesus Christ," Blaine said, his outline crouching, his hands searching my sprained wrist for a pulse until it noodled and I gasped and he said, "Sorry, sorry," putting it down.

His gun was strapped to his hip. He had on jeans and a T-shirt. The combo was incongruous, as was his being here, side by side with me in our ecosystem's toaster. We belonged on cold doorsteps. In dens and living rooms strewn with secrets, in police cruisers bound nowhere. I was suddenly, stupidly happy. Maybe the happiest I'd ever been—and this was also incongruous. But I went with it. What better time to make a fool of yourself?

"Hi," I said. "How's it going?"

Blaine's jaw jumped. He didn't like my heart rate. He began to palpate, glancing at and returning my goofy smile with his phoniest one. He showed me his bloody hand, fresh from a visit to my back. "What's this from?"

"Glass. You look tired."

His eyes traveled over my injuries. I'd forgotten his magnificent powers of blanding, on display now at their most potent. Blaine could've been handling auto parts for how engaged his face was in the process. Unless you were me, the auto parts he was handling, and you felt how terrified he was of making a mistake. His palm glided to my ribs. I mewled. He winced but nixed it fast, went back to strong and stoic and blank. "Okay, that's done. I won't do that again, I promise. I'll be right back."

I grabbed his shoelace. "Don't leave."

"I need to go get a few things."

"Don't leave."

"I'm not leaving. I've got a first-aid kit in the trunk." Blaine stooped and pried at my hold, stopping at the pinkie. "Rainy, this is broken. You shouldn't bend it. Let go."

I did, but: "Don't leave me here."

"Twenty seconds. You can count 'em. Ready?" Blaine didn't wait. He ran out the door.

The pain throbbed, and the throbs became strangely restful. "Whoa, whoa," he said. "Whoa, whoa, whoa." Moving me. I grabbed on to him. We got to the nearest stall, and he set my good side against it. I had bunches of his shirt. I squeezed, heard a popping sound.

"Look at me, Rainy. Look right here." Blaine was slipping. Fiery panic peeked through his cool. He had a butterfly bandage at the end of his eyebrow. His breath smelled of cinnamon. “Let your hand open. Let go.” His grip fought mine, and I watched, rooting for him. My pinkie knuckle was breaking the skin, bone hatching from the flesh like a chick’s beak. He won of course, but only on that hand. My other held around his shoulder, shaking with exertion.

He got to work with something on the floor. “This’ll sting,” he said.

Cold bit into my back and went hot. “How’d you find me?”

“Called the feds, had them triangulate the signal. Like I told you I would, remember?” Blaine used a dozen cotton pads, making a pile of the bloody ones. “They’re on the way from Vegas. Sam shot a guard in the bank. Guy was DOA at the hospital. I told the feds there’s not a snowball’s chance in hell Sam’s hiding in the city if you made it out.” He was relating all this like I knew what he was talking about. “That road’ll be D-day in a half hour.”

“Vegas?”

“I beat the others there. Heard a teenage girl with white hair stole a car and hightailed it for the desert.” Blaine opened a few bandages and used them on the deepest cuts. “You’ve been holding out on me. That must’ve been some driving.”

“Did I hurt anybody?”

“Just insurance companies,” he said. “I’ve been trying to cover every shitty back road in the Mojave, hoping I’d get lucky or you’d call.” He checked me for more problems he could treat. He wiped under my nose. “This keeps bleeding.”

"Sam made me snort cocaine."

Blaine's forehead crimped. I wouldn't have noticed, except it made a runnel for his sweat. A drop snuck down the side of his nose, almost like a tear. He wiped it off, rolled a cotton pad and dabbed at my nostril.

I thought I'd lighten the mood. "Coke's like weaponized coffee, huh?"

"Dunno," he said. "Never tried it."

"Square."

He didn't laugh. He uncapped a bottle of water. "Sip this. You'll want to chug it, but sip. Otherwise you'll throw it all up."

It tasted phenomenal. I whined when the bottle went away.

"There's more," Blaine said. "Don't move, I'm opening another one."

I breathed in to thank him and inhaled a water drop. I coughed. It was like a nail gun firing into my side. I screamed, which killed, then I still had to cough, so I did, and it made me need to scream again, creating a fun round-robin rib-jab competition, where everyone was a winner but me. My legs flailed, and that didn't feel great, either.

Blaine pulled me to him, trying to brace me, letting me hack and pant in his face. "Slow down. Slow down and breathe." He observed that this advice took absolutely no effect, my arms starting to beat at him as I strangled, my skin going tingly.

"Rainy? You don't need that much air. Watch me. Breathe with me." He aped a gradual inhale I couldn't have duplicated if my life had depended on it. Which it was starting to. "Good. Do that again," he said. "I'm with you, same thing again."

I heaved and managed to ask on the exhale, "Shoot me, okay?"

"In a minute. Do it again."

I tucked my head under his chin. That made it easier. We tilted. Rough, musty warmth encased me—the blanket with the balled-up underwear. "You don't know where that's been," I croaked.

"Think I do. Wish I didn't. What else hurts?"

"Leg."

"But you walked here?"

"Kinda."

"You might've cracked a bone. We'll have to put off the marathon. How's your head?"

"Fantastic."

"Then you need to stay awake. I'd put you in the 'Vette and floor it, but I don't want to move you any more."

There was an athletic bag on the ground, overflowing with medical supplies. Leaning against the hydrogen peroxide was a pack of Parliaments.

"Bum a cigarette?" I said.

"You're kidding."

I reached for them. My wrist was as fat as a tire.

Blaine returned the hand to my lap. "We'll quit together—how 'bout that? I made it eight weeks on the gum once."

"Why are you here?"

I don't know what I expected, exactly—"I was due for a vacation," "I've always wanted to see Death Valley," "I found an extra sock in the laundry and thought I'd come ask if it was yours." I looked up at him, nothing but curious.

He wiped blood from under my nose, his own nose flared, irritated. "In my driveway, when they hit us, I told you to run. You didn't. You went and got in their fucking van."

"No big deal," I said, figuring he'd get all mushy.

"It is a big deal," he said. He wasn't yelling, since I was about five inches away from him, but he bit into his consonants like jugular veins. "It was the dumbest thing you could've done. It might've been the dumbest fucking thing I've ever seen anybody do. And I'm a cop, Rainy." His chin dipped as if the implications of this should be totally clear to me. "As in, I once arrested a guy trying to break into his ex-wife's house by sliding down the chimney. As in, last year, I'm taking a statement on a burglary, and one of the things stolen is a tub of potato salad from the fridge—perp's a messy eater; he leaves a trail of it all the way back to his place. As in, a few months ago, I got called on a report of a couple kids having sex in a tree. They said, 'Why not? Why not in a tree?'"

"Was there a tree house in the tree?"

"What? No."

"Wow," I said.

"Look here." Blaine put two fingers under his eyes, bloodshot from endless highways and no sleep. "Look and listen, because this is important. You getting in their van? That took the cake. That's my new blue-ribbon winner. And you're coming back to Minneapolis, and so long as the bureau doesn't slap me with an obstruction charge, you're staying at my house until you learn some common fucking sense. As in, you don't get into a van when a police officer is specifically telling you not to."

I was still mulling the logistics of sex in a tree. I didn't see this as much of a debate. "Sam would've shot you if I hadn't."

Blaine shrugged violently. It moved me, and I hissed, and he said, "Sorry, sorry," his mad-itude shifting, exposing what was veiled behind it. "I'm no big loss, Rainy. I wake up, I go to work, I come home, I go to bed. Who cares if I'm not there to do that? Some nights, I go out and I don't go to bed alone, but I leave before first light. What's that make me? I'm a piece of shit. I'm a lost cause. I'm nothing. Putting yourself in harm's way for me, it's the stupidest thing you could do if you wracked your brain a hundred years. You can't do it again, not ever. I'm not worth it."

Oh. So that's how that sounds.

"Don't cry," he said, wiping the tears with his thumbs. "You're dehydrated, try not to cry." As if I were enjoying this particular cry. As if I wouldn't prefer informing him, in a well constructed set of bullet points that left no room for doubt, that he *was* worth it. But Blaine would never believe me. I understood, because I was sitting here clinging to him after he'd driven how many days breaking how many laws, and I'd asked him *why.* And now that he'd answered, I wanted to ask again, and ask and ask again, until he admitted he didn't do it for me at all, that he only wanted Sam's buried millions.

We were such messes. Such pathetic messes.

"Did Sam . . ." Blaine shaped the question in his mind. His obvious revulsion was too eloquent for words.

I shook my head. "Why's he like this?"

Blaine freed an arm from around me, placing items in the first-aid bag. "Same reason most of them are like this. Upbringing."

"Did you see the girls at the cabin?" I cut off any condolences that weren't mine to receive. "You're going to tell me it wasn't my fault if I tell you it was my fault, but it was my fault. Johnny said stop them, I stopped them. Sam shot them, I kept them there to be shot. He wasn't bad yet. 'Til then, he was nice."

"He's fooled a lot of people. More than you know."

"That's not it," I said. "Sam didn't fool me, it wasn't fake." Blaine packed bottles and containers, wrappings and rolls of bandage, arranging them carefully. I grabbed the crew neck of his T-shirt with my bad hand. Threads popped, and so did my finger. He abandoned the bag, went at my grip, but this time I held fast. "What were their names? What were the girls' names?"

"Ellie, I think."

"Other one."

"Rebecca," he said, gently pressing my knuckle joint, holding the bones in. "Becca for short."

"Ellie and Becca, Ellie and Becca, Ellie and Becca."

"Calm down. Try and calm down." Blaine's collar tore. A flap of it in my fist. "Hey, I'm gonna splint this. Means you've gotta open your hand."

I cried up at him, miserably, "Why are you here?"

"I told you—"

"You were lying," I said. "I know when you're lying. Why are you here? Tell the truth."

He opened his mouth. I filled with horror at what might come out of it.

"And if you say you love me, I'm gonna punch you in your fucking dick, I swear to God."

Blaine's laugh came high and thin. He glanced around the stable, as if for assistance. Landing on the med bag, he reached in.

"I like you," he said, and held up his cigs. "You're my brand."

My hand fell open. All of me, basically, fell open. I wasn't sure if he'd convinced me or I'd worn myself out, but I no longer cared. Blaine took two tongue-depressor sticks and sandwiched my finger between them, had me hold while he tore tape. He scoffed and shook his head as he worked. I wanted to say he could quit it, that I didn't need him to bland down for me, that I'd take him complicated.

I more wanted to tell him . . . I don't know. Things you can only show someone.

"There they are," he said.

A hem and a haw. A motor, its noise careening free around the desert, nothing to interrupt or dilute it. Nothing to hide how it was alone, and not in the best condition.

"What the hell, guys," Blaine said. "If there was ever a time to use your sirens."

I built a great argument about how this was an individual policeman or FBI agent who drove extra-fast to get here, outpacing his peers. They were right behind him. I'd hear them any minute. If I'd outspeeded Sam to such a reckless degree, he'd have had to be checking every route from the point where he lost me, happening to be close-by when my whereabouts hit the airwaves. No luck could be that bad.

I convinced myself effectively enough that I was able to say, "Sam has a police scanner."

Blaine stiffened. Lines of argument formed in his head, too, and he followed them to conclusions that were at odds with a single car.

"No," I said.

He extricated himself using a set of movements slick enough to cause me no pain. He ran for the barn doors. I grabbed after him, causing myself a ton of pain, blathering that it couldn't be. Blaine turned around, and I read him.

"No," I said. "No, no, no."

He hurried, picked me up.

"No, no." The Corvette was faster, for sure, but on open road. If we met Sam at a ramp, he'd T-bone us again. Blaine put me in the corner stall closest to the entrance.

"No," I said, my new favorite word. "No."

"Rainy, listen." I thought he was going to give a speech, but then it dawned on me he meant the motor, listen to the motor. It was much louder. He fluttered the blanket, covering me. "Stay here. Stay still. I'm good for something, okay? This is a piece of cake."

I wanted to tell him to hand me over, but I was too big a coward. His steps rushed from the front of the stable to the back, and back to the front. I was trying to put together a fat helping of bravery. I fabricated a scenario for five minutes from now. Sam dead, Blaine standing over him. Blaine shaking Johnny Blue's hand, because Blaine knew without knowing how he knew that Johnny wasn't bad.

I had to tell him Johnny wasn't bad.

"Blaine?"

The motor got louder and louder. It finally quit. Heavy hinges screeched. A weight met the dirt in two impacts, *pum-pum*.

"Here, kitty kitty."

I spontaneously grew new hairs, just so they could stand up.

"Rainy's not around, Sam," Blaine said, as if addressing a telemarketer who'd called during supper. "Thanks for stopping by."

There was a hole in the blanket by my ear. I shifted so my eye found it. The stable's front wall had gaps between the boards. Sam was standing five feet away from me, outside.

"I think you're fibbing, Officer Friendly."

Blaine squatted behind a divider. The two in front of that one were more drastically bent. He'd pushed them over. I didn't like that, or that he was diagonal from my corner, at the most extreme opposite angle this space could manage, minimizing the likelihood I'd catch a ricochet. He unholstered his gun and unsafety'd it. "Get in your car and get out of here. My backup is ten minutes away."

"Try this," Sam said. "If you give me my daughter, I'll still kill you but I'll leave you your scrotum. If you don't, I'll cut it off while you're still alive and shove it down your throat."

"Wouldn't fit." Blaine checked his watch.

"Unless you hid her in one of these other–No, you wouldn't. You'd want her near you, pedophile that you are."

"Gotta call rubber and glue on that one, asshole."

Sam advanced, pivoted, and put arms and hands around the door. A blast filled the stable. A chip sheared off Blaine's cover. Blaine was safely behind it, having moved with Sam as if they were partners in a dance. Now Sam spun back outside and Blaine shifted to get his sights on the door again. I shouldn't have been surprised he excelled at this, but–I mean, how do you practice?

Sam picked up the conversation like nothing had happened. "Why's that? Have you heard whispers about me?"

"No, Sam. I read your file." Blaine said it with a strange, sad weightiness. "Your hospital records are in there, from when you were a kid. I know your dad was a mean drunk who beat you anytime he felt like it. I know he once held you face-down in the thresher because it was raining outside and he thought it might swamp the fields. He had your arm twisted behind your back; he broke it. You told the doc at the hospital your dad beat you for the weather, and you went home after and your dad broke the other arm because you snitched."

"Stop talking."

"There's family interviews. They met with your sisters—"

"I said stop talking, pig."

"And your sisters told about how he saved the worst for them. For late at night, when everybody was asleep. They told how your dad brought you along on your twelfth birthday, taught you the ropes."

Sam got two shots off. I barely saw it—he moved so fast. His aim was high and wide. New holes appeared in the stable's ceiling.

"I read your psych eval," Blaine said. "I know you think that four million's real. That Harmony hid it and she told Rainy where to find it and you'll go get it. But the bureau's about ninety percent sure Harmony burned it. Otherwise, it would've turned up by now. Secrets have a way of turning up, Sam."

Sam rocked back and forth. It made a light show out of the stripes of sun. Hypnotic refractions and the hunched, implacable shadow-thing that Blaine was poking like a bull in a chute.

Blaine got on one knee. “And I know you’ve got Rainy mixed up with some really fucked fantasy where the two of you go make nice in Mexico. But I’m not allowing it, and neither is she. Your favorite thing about her is she’s part you, but guess what? You can take what you’re made of and make it anything you want. Rainy’s gonna fight you all the way. And I’ve got her back.”

“Yes, you’ve got her back. You wish you were on her back.” Sam darting from foot to foot was vibrating our wall. “I’ve seen, too! I know, too!”

“Yeah, I’ve got that all planned.” Blaine’s expression crinkled from the center outward, such severe distaste he could’ve been eating excrement. “I’ll put a towel down. Knocking the dust off can get messy. Gotta save my sheets. Might even save the mattress, depending how hard she wants—”

An enormity filled the doors. Sam day-blind, charging in. He shot sloppy, anywhere, everywhere. His mouth was threaded with spit, an elongated caricature yelling ragged vowels. I didn’t know whether to giggle or go crazy. Here was Sam Pissed Off.

Blaine reared, target-range perfect. He squeezed rounds with such efficiency the reverbs overlapped. Sam danced a bullet-boogie. His shirt threw bits of cloth. Blaine stood to follow Sam down as he fell and kept firing into him until the trigger clicked.

Sam's right shoulder was lower. His elbow hit the dirt before the rest of him did, and his arm twitched up with the reflex. I genuinely thought Blaine's leap backward was a victory move. It was acrobatic, particularly the side spin in midair and the dramatic toss of his gun—but what ridiculous victory move ends with landing like he did? Prone, an arm trapped under his stomach, the other flung out.

The barn went quiet. Nothing stirred but ringlets of smoke. Soon, Blaine would sit up, say everything was okay.

He rolled, or he tried to. His arm was in the way. He coughed. Blood sprayed the dust beside him.

I flailed at the blanket and dropped to a crawl, forgetting my wrist. It crumbled, so my elbows took over. I pushed with my feet, wormed to him. He'd gotten supine. He had a hand pressed to his neck. Red dribbled between his fingers. He was gurgling partial syllables; I could tell they meant something. His eyes were wide but lucid.

I got up and went for the first-aid bag, my locomotion disturbingly imbalanced yet not importantly painful. The kit was heavy; I had to drag it back. "What do I use?" I asked him.

Blaine grasped the bag by the bottom and dumped it. He selected a packet, handed it to me. I got my teeth around a corner and tore, caught a wad of white netting. Blaine took it, laying another packet in my lap. A river of blood fell from the wound before he mashed the gauze onto it, using his fingertip to stuff some inside. He tapped the bandage I was holding, showed me a wheeling motion.

"Wind it around?"

He nodded, grabbing his own wrist and digging his nails in, loosening them.

"Tight but not too tight."

Blaine put a thumb up. He was weakening. He bounced his head to the ground limply while I got the bandage on. "Good?" I said. He nodded again. "You need to sit up. Come on, I'll help you." My groans of what a wonderful idea this wasn't coaxed him awake. He pushed us both off the ground. I set him against the stall. "Blaine, get your fucking eyes open." He obeyed. They about popped out of his sockets.

"You know how hard it is to get one of these?" Sam said.

I turned much too quickly. My rib cage revolted. I doubled over.

His shirt hung in shreds. The vest underneath was black, bulky, misshapen—pooching out on his stomach as he rose on steady legs. Towering over me, he knocked on his chest. "You have to deal with some real scumbags to get one of these."

My vision enlarged. All my senses did. My nose started bleeding again, so I licked the blood off my lip, tasting my own bright copper. Tasting what I was made of. I put my feet flat and pushed, stood up rickety.

But I was fine. I knew what to do. It was awesome, in a way, to know it was one of the last things I'd ever do. "What if he'd aimed for your head?" I asked.

Sam tore out of his shirt and undid Velcro. The vest slipped off sideways. "Pigs are trained to shoot center mass."

His sunburn was much worse, highlighted when he looked down, dark-pink chin on his colorless breastbone. "Pigs are trainable—did you know that? I trained one to herd when I was a kid." He touched fish-white flesh, wrinkling his nose at large patches going different shades of bruise. He glared at the superficial damage, then at Blaine. Sam corkscrewed to pick up his gun.

I stepped to my right and got between them, reaching for my back pocket. Awkward to unfold the photo one-handed, but I did it and held it up. "Your money's here."

Sam's feet were crossed. Untwisting to stand, he lost his balance, which gave me a moment of bleak pleasure. He approached me, pinched the photo from my hand. He approached me, searched the image.

"Mom told me exactly where," I said, as steadily as I could. "She buried it so you'd never find it without me. I'll take you right to it. But only if we leave now and you leave Blaine alive."

Sam's expression was an eerie melt of every human emotion sort of gooping together. I couldn't watch. "Interesting," he said, coming toward me. "An interesting proposition." He sounded so rational, so calm, like he was narrating a documentary on PBS. "The problem is, I'm quite persuasive. I think if I blew Officer Friendly's brains out, I'd be able to change your mind. I think I could make you beg for the privilege of giving me my money."

I had to look up, but not far. And I had to swallow some hesitation. But not much.

“Are you sure?” I said. The space between us seemed to waver. It was the heat. It was convection. It was a mirror we both looked into, and through. “Are you sure, Sam?”

Blaine kicked the divider. We ignored him.

Sam flapped the photo, fanning himself. “What if I don’t know where this was taken?”

“Mom said you would.”

“Did she?”

“Yes.”

Sam smiled winningly and leaned around me. “She has Harmony’s rebelliousness, pig. Don’t worry—I believe in discipline. But you know that, since you read my file. I invite you to imagine. Imagine what I’ll do.”

Blaine hmphed and grmphed in weak rage. I stared at the open door ahead, and I didn’t project my own imaginings onto that sun-white rectangle. I let it remain blank. When Sam tucked my wrecked wrist in his arm and pulled me toward the exit, a gentleman escorting a lady to dinner, Blaine’s mangled protests got fainter.

“He’ll bleed out in a few minutes anyway,” Sam said.

We walked outside, the sunlight a wave of scalding bleach. Sirens shrilled somewhere in the distance. From much closer came a car sound that was more familiar: Ding! Ding! Ding! My eyes adjusted. There was a truck that was a huge, unwashed, ancient automotive mistake. Its door hung open.

So I’m walking, indifferent to direction or speed, and my dad’s got my arm, my dad’s leading me. And I’m looking over at Sam, and he could be on his way to a semi-important appointment. Dentist, podiatrist—nothing pressing. And Blaine's Corvette is idling. Its topper is flipped in the dirt. Its plates now hail from California. Johnny, in the driver's seat, catches the full wrath of the sun. As his head lolls sideways on the headrest, the bloodless cast to his skin makes him match the dead truck, and the truck matches the dead town, and I'm sure I do, too, as I grumble and groan across Only Street. The 'Vette's red is shiny, despite its coat of dirt.

Sam knocked on the back of car, and the trunk popped open. "Get in."

I inspected the trunk, stretching every second as much as I could. Doing so, I caught sight of something that planted my lifetime's most annoying seed of hope. I bent my leg in a tentative, agonized attempt to climb inside, but Sam gave me a push. I landed in a sprawl and made whatever sounds felt like coming out as the trunk lid clapped me into perfect darkness.

Rainy's gonna fight you all the way, he'd said.

"Here we go," I sobbed quietly. "Here we go, Rainy, go get 'em."

The engine purred. A speed that couldn't be much slower than Mach 1 yanked us away from the approaching sirens. I listened for them to get closer. A slipstream blew over the trunk, obliterating them. I shivered, wept, beseeched permission to forfeit, not sure who I was asking or what form permission would take. I started a grotesque horizontal wiggle-rumba, turning around in a series of painful movements. This was a Minnesota car. He was a Minnesota cop. I was probably wrong. The bag I'd seen was probably just a castoff from some long-ago vacation.

The warm zipper glided easily. Exploring by touch yielded metallic cylinders, ribbed plastic wrapped in flimsy labels. I found a tube with a fat end and a switch on the side. I told myself that it wasn't a flashlight, and when it wasn't a flashlight, that was my sign.

I pushed the switch with a quavering thumb.

Blaine's winter survival kit was well stocked.

SIXTEEN

My favorite thing in the bag wasn't the water. I made a rule of a bottle every hour, but after five bottles, I had to pick an empty to pee in, a predictably moist procedure. My favorite wasn't the food, and not just because I couldn't work the can opener, meaning I was stuck with the pull tabs, meaning I forewent the precious Chef Boyardee ravioli for generic ham-and-navy-bean soup, which I ate condensed with a foldable spoon. It tasted like sodium squared. My favorite wasn't the cooking fuel—like I'd fire up some Sterno when I had a few square feet of space and I was swaddled in a polyester blanket. My favorite wasn't the blanket, though that was a close second.

My favorite thing was the watch. Still in its packaging, it had Day-Glo, a timer, an alarm, the whole nine. I read the instructions, took my best guess at the hour. Programmed it, played with its functions. It surprised me how much it helped. To know time was passing, that I existed inside it.

I put the watch facedown and rifled through the bag a bit more. Handled the road flare carefully, opened the buck knife. I entertained fantasies of giving Sam a surprise hello. Then I checked the time.

I popped more Advil, waited for it to take effect, checked the time.

I found a smaller, cuter first-aid kit and wrapped my wrist in an Ace bandage that did precisely nothing. Checked the time.

It was 7:27 p.m. when the roar of our momentum quieted. The car stopped. A door clicked open, and feet scuffed on pebbles. They became one foot, hopping, to where the top of my head kissed the side of the trunk. I heard Johnny open the flap for the gas compartment and unscrew the cap. He socked home the nozzle; fuel rushed in. Had he even bandaged his leg?

I could smell the desert outside. I didn't hear any voices, save the Stones on the car's radio, so I pictured where we were as another blank, tan haven for tumbleweeds, its vistas a tight contest for most boring. This was probably some miniscule fill station on a route rendered obsolete by progress. I imagined a geezer inside protecting the cigarettes. Maybe he didn't like the look of the big guy lazing in the passenger seat. Maybe he was concerned about the boy hopping on one leg. Maybe he was calling the cops this very second.

Johnny thudded a finger on the car's side in that classic "Are you there?" rhythm.

I tapped back, insanely grateful to communicate. I wished I knew Morse code. I had no idea what I'd tell him, but the fact I couldn't tell him got me desperate and weepy. I imagined the pain he must be in. I hoped his wheels were turning as fast as the ones underneath us, trying to find another way out.

We were back on the highway after four minutes and thirty-seven seconds. I timed it.

My mind wandered. I tried keeping it occupied by singing *Rumours*, the whole album front to back, but it wound up soundtracking these incredibly vivid visuals of the places we'd been. The stable, where the police were no doubt finishing up by now, Blaine in the back of a slow-moving ambulance, on the way to a morgue drawer. From there, I went to mountains, the cabin, where Ellie's and Becca's bodies were gone but the stains they made in the road had sunk into the soil. Was Harvey's two hundred still under the convenience store's freezer, or was he right now reaching to get it? Did that church in Nowhere, Minnesota, miss its bus yet, or were they right now noticing it was gone?

Right now, everything was happening right now.

For instance, the flashlight was dying. I began a frantic search for batteries. I glanced at the watch and saw it was midnight, which took my hysteria to new levels, because I couldn't account for the last five hours.

Winter survival kits have spare batteries; that's 101. I dug through the bag again, but there weren't any. Luminescence was dimming on my creepy little nest. The light went out. I banged on it, and it stayed out. I hit the watch's Day-Glo, its blue-green light soothing. My eyeballs rolled, tired wheels taking me somewhere.

The Future Is Now: Where's that from? It's true. It's laughing its ass off at your plans. Your cravings for getting good and lost—the future is saying, Here you go.

We stopped again, at 1:48 in the morning. I heard glass break. The tires echoed on a smooth grade. Inside somewhere. Sam and Johnny got out of the car. They conversed, and a short while later, a wrench tapped below.

I squeezed the Day-Glo button again. 1:57 a.m.

The trunk lid thunked, lifted. My space filled with blotchy moonlight. Footsteps scraped, and a big shadow covered me. I was curled toward the back of the trunk. I raised my head up. At first, I thought Sam was playing a joke, that he'd spray-painted himself for a prank. His bare chest and shoulders and belly were dark maroon. His face was scaly. The top of his head had sprouted bubbly white pustules.

Behind him were oil-stained floors, a smatter of old rags. A long door yawned open, letting in silver light. Beyond was a driveway cloaked in trees.

Sam sat on the rim of the trunk. “Johnny says there’s a bad sound coming from the engine. He wanted to check it before we went any further. In case you were wondering.”

I wasn’t.

“We’re close. I remember this place. They used to serve egg creams. Have you ever had an egg cream?”

I hadn’t, but they sure sounded gross.

“We were happy here, your mother and I. It was the only happiness I ever knew. What your friend the pig said about me isn’t the full story. It’s much more complicated. Not even I understood it until now. Now that I have a child of my own.”

It was incredible he could still confuse me. This should have had me laughing inside, but I listened, serious. I put down the watch and twisted to get on my back. The pain was amazing.

Sam stroked along the trunk lid. “It’s hard being a father. The disappointment. You can’t know how heartbreaking it is. You broke Daddy’s heart, Kat. But even if you hurt Daddy, even if you reject Daddy, he still loves you. Daddy loves you so much.”

I didn’t answer. There was no point.

Something was off about him. The way he fidgeted, picking at the rubbery stuff that insulated the trunk. He seemed oddly shy. I wanted to write his mood off to sun poisoning; his burn was definitely bad enough.

“Darling, I’m uneasy.” Sam reached with one finger and touched the top button of my jeans. His other hand joined, helped unbutton it, opened the flap to a row of four more. "Your pet policeman, the way he talked about you. If he was inappropriate, I think you'd be afraid to tell me." The tip of Sam's tongue peeked out, wetting his upper lip. "Daddy's going to check, all right?"

Any fear I'd ever felt had been practice for this moment. I couldn't wrap my head around what was happening. I was pulling my stomach in, to get it away from his fingers, which were weirdly decorous and well mannered. Like unbuttoning my button fly was part of a Victorian high tea. I wondered if I could I pull a my-mom and unplug from reality.

Could I get back if I did?

"Johnny?" I said. The wrench stopped tapping. A sliding sound along the floor.

"There's no need to speak to him." Sam said, one button to go. He'd only half turned when Johnny Blue appeared. He did a double take.

A bulky wrench was poised high in Johnny's hand. Sam flung himself backward—no time for anything else. The wrench winged him in the elbow. Sam cried out, going for his gun.

I battled to sit up, couldn't, push up, couldn't. Johnny brawled ahead with a crazed Geronimo yell. His pant leg was hiked, a soaked cloth tied around the hole in his calf. The wound tore as I watched, as he made it take his weight and ran at Sam, putting the wrench sideways while Sam's fumbling left arm found the gun, got it around. Johnny swung, and Sam fired. They sprang apart. Sam's gun fell to the floor.

I rolled and fell out of the trunk like a rag doll, crawled across the garage floor. I beat Sam by so little I pulled the trigger without aiming. The recoil jerked me into something soft. I nearly dropped the gun. I couldn't believe how heavy it was. In front of me danced a riot of blobs and surfaces, a blurry figure advancing. I pulled the trigger again. The kick-back made me squeal.

A stooped thing ran out of the garage, its footsteps chittering on pavement. My ears rang.

Slowly, the ringing became a whistling. The hole in Johnny's chest blew fizzy bubbles. His inhales were prolonged *hih*s, his exhales short *hoo*s. It didn't take a medical degree to grasp that his lungs were trying to pull air from wherever they could get it, including from this new portal, and that it wasn't enough or it was too much or not pressurized right. "Don't try to move," I said, getting around him. I put his head in my lap. "Don't move. You're going to be fine."

He held up a finger, pointed at the soot on the floor. He started writing in it.

He wrote: *RUN*.

"I will," I said. "In another minute, okay?"

Johnny was crying. And underlining and underlining *RUN*, hell-bent, gritting his teeth at that one word and how emphatic he could make it.

I took his hand and folded it. He fought me about putting his hand on his chest. "I know," I said. "I know. I remember." Because there was blood on his chest, lots of it. He didn't want me to touch it. He turned his face up, pleading. Muscles strained in his neck.

"Remember when we were in a boat?" I said. "I was hungry, so you caught a fish. I got thirsty, so you made it rain. And you were scared of the dark, so I sang to you. Remember?"

He nodded, a corner of his mouth lifting.

"Moon River. Wider than a mile." I sang him the whole thing, my voice a dry, broken wheeze. It was such a short song—where were the other verses? He stopped moving at "dream maker." His chest quit bubbling at "two drifters." I called him "my huckleberry friend," this dead boy in my lap. "Moon River. And me."

Far down in his eyes, our boat was bobbing away. "I won't leave," I said. "All I ever do is leave you." I gathered him, rocked him, told him I'd protect him. I noticed cigarettes sticking out of his hip pocket. I stole them.

"What do I do? I won't tell. I won't tell if you talk to me."

None of this was really happening. All of it had been a goof, a performance. Sam would come in through that door he just ran out of and take a bow. Blaine would follow, bow, pat Sam on the back for a job well-done. Johnny would spring up out of my lap and join them. I'd get up, unhurt, and give the whole ensemble a standing ovation. They deserved it.

This notion was so persuasive, so comforting. I used it to get myself under control. Budgeted a few minutes to actually believing that it was all a gag. Meaning: Your heart doesn't have to slam like this, you don't have to gasp for breath. You'll look down, and Johnny will be smiling at you like he does.

Once I believed it, I looked down. Johnny was the same.

I put his head on the floor and walked on my knees to the trunk. I pulled out the blanket and covered him, hiding all his wounds. I put his hands on his chest and set my hand on top of them. I had to say something. It had to not be bullshit.

"You were the best thing about the worst thing that ever happened to me."

That wasn't it. True but still wrong. I knelt there, pushing his eyelids closed and getting his hair in some kind of order, patiently awaiting inspiration. I found it in *RUN*, written in the dirt. A final wish that had nothing to do with him.

"Easy," I said, standing. "Easy, easy." I slapped my jaw, making myself wake to reality. I checked to see if the Corvette's keys were in the ignition, the visor, the glove compartment. They weren't. I set the gun on the hood for a few seconds so I could button my pants. I looked toward the door. I couldn't go out there. I couldn't; it was impossible. I should stay, stay with Johnny and wait.

My left thigh was wobbly. It didn't hurt, or maybe its hurt didn't translate through the noise of all my other hurt, but it definitely shortened each stride.

RUN. Johnny'd underlined it a dozen times.

This wasn't the desert. There were gas pumps. There had to be people not far from here.

I approached the unsheltered night, my walk peg-legged, my pulse thudding, my gun hand wanting to stiffen. I crossed outside, turning awkwardly in circles.

The garage had a store conjoined to it. A sign in the window read PEPSI 10¢. The gas pumps weren't digital; they had those numbers that whirled on dials. I kept rotating, expecting Sam to jump out at me. I climbed the driveway's steep grade to a ratty two-lane, thinking he'd be straddling the centerline.

Except there was no centerline. The pavement had cracked. Dandelions divided the lanes. I spun around, aiming the gun in all directions.

"Stop," I said. "You can stop." I was wrong, I couldn't. But I slowed enough to confirm where the moon was, and clock directions from that.

North and south, forest squeezed the road as if trying to smother it.

To the east, the trees canopied tightly, letting almost no light in.

West, after about two hundred yards of darkness, the road broke from the tree cover. Then the cracked blacktop shot straight and moonlit into a hazy distance. There was a sign not far away. I squinted, couldn't make it out. I thought the moon must be obscuring the print, but that wasn't the problem. The print had worn off. So had most of the paint.

It was orange once, now dulled to silver with stray streaks and dots.

Behind me, a spot of light shone through the garage's door. I could see Johnny's shoe.

Don't look back, they say. What you survive stays behind you, forget it, move on. But that never works. Pretending it does just keeps the damage sitting on your shoulder, until inevitably, you become your damage. It's the type of realization you want to pass on to somebody. It's the type of realization you get when all your somebodies are bodies.

I turned and limped west. Thinking: I was young once.

SEVENTEEN

Those woods were pure hell. My single attempt at running almost made me crash to the ground, so I sacrificed speed for vigilance, constantly verifying that the forest did indeed peter out. When I exited to open sky, I walked backward for a while, gun waving in my hand. I wanted to watch the muzzle flash, listen to Sam howling as he took a bullet right through the heart. I turned around only because the road was cracked in more places than it was whole. The thin moon lit the tripping hazards beautifully. It also gave an unnerving glow to the flats on either side of the asphalt. Thousands of stumps poked from the dirt, their wide bases covered with mushrooms.

Strange they'd build a logging road, harvest a football field to the left and right, and leave. I wasn't complaining—it would be tough for someone to sneak up on me—but there were no structures, no houses, no people, and no signs of people. I had to pep-talk myself pretty hard to avoid a despairing certainty that I was the only biped for quite a distance. Except for Sam, of course. And Bigfoot, if he was around.

The temperature was high forties, max, and my naked arms never tired of telling me this. My gawky walk had to be pulling fifteen-minute miles, if that. I didn't want to estimate this distance, so instead I watched the night sky and listened to the world around me. The forest came alive with birds, what sounded like infinite birds, arguing, taunting. The sky above them phased out of black, to gray, through all the purples. I'm not sure when I started smiling, but when the purple turned pink, I told it, "Thank you. Thank you." There was heat on my back and my shoulders, and I was grateful for that. Things had gotten easier, here at the end. The new goal was the oldest goal—don't stop.

A stench invaded the air, and I pressed my arm to my nose and hurried. A dead animal lay at the roadside. Its fur was matted. It writhed with maggots. Skunk was my best guess, but it was too big, inflated with death gas. As I passed it, the first blush of sun cleared the woods behind me, lighting a wet-and-wild glimmer of worms in soft meat. I retched and missed a step, but somehow didn't fall. I followed the crack between lanes, to where the sun spotlighted—

My finish line.

Everything stopped at this tree as if this were the whole point, the reason for being there. At this big oak, ugly but powerful. A wall of forest to either side of it was the deadest of dead ends.

I dropped to my knees. Birds cackled while I put down the gun and dug in my pockets, searching my jeans. All I found were Johnny's Newports, his lighter, and in my right hip pocket, about $2,000. I laughed, fanning it out, the bills flat and pristine. I thumbed the Bic alight, picked up the two grand, and put the pretty flame to its crisp edges. I lit a butt off their burn and inhaled 'til it hurt. "Best inhale's the last one," I said.

I picked up the gun. It looked mean, and smug in its meanness, and I didn't want to give it the satisfaction. Plus, shooting myself struck me as grossly immature.

I swiveled around, still sitting, to face where I'd come from. Johnny's pack had nine cigarettes left. I smoked them down to two, waiting. If this dumbass fiasco had taught me one thing, it was that the next disaster required me only to wait. If it had taught me two things, it was that Sam could be counted on to show up and tear up what miniscule scraps of peace I'd managed to collect, that he seemed to think it was his job. I strongly doubted he'd disappoint, now that I was cornered.

And he didn't.

At a mass flap and squawk, the birds rose in a cloud of what seemed like thousands. Their climb was the forest growing taller, moving inward. They changed direction, swirling north. Their cries were so loud they almost drowned out the sound of the engine.

The Corvette rammed from the forest, its bright red and shiny chrome a riot of color among earthy neutrals. I stood in awe; I'd never seen anything move that fast. Sam was going over a hundred.

The car grew. My feet yearned for a rearward march, but I planted them. Nothing behind me would help.

Make him go faster, I thought. He might swerve.

"Yeah, okay. With my handy-dandy telepathy?"

My head did a repetitive involuntary nod, a physical override of good sense. When a car's coming at you, you get out of the road. You don't stand there and bait it. You don't fool yourself you can jump out of the way when you can barely walk.

I lifted the gun. I brought my other hand up. The pinkie was busted and wrapped, but the middle one could still extend. I held it high. "Come on, come on," I said, "come on, come on, come on," as the engine got louder, as the car got close enough that I could see Sam. He was looking down, frenzied, bouncing in his seat. His seat-belt buckle twinkled beside his ear. As the Corvette's cherry hood roared toward me, I thought back to Johnny telling Sam we needed to stop. Getting under the car and ting-tinging with his wrench.

And I knew, without knowing how I knew: Johnny'd used his free hand to bleed the brakes.

Sam's head snapped up. He and I locked eyes in a momentary flash that spanned hours. His skin was red as a stoplight. An oddly gallant grin showed one side of his teeth, bewitching me. I couldn't move. I could practically hear him say, "Daddy forgives you."

A front tire hit the skunk, which exploded in a foul mash, its bloat acting as a springboard. The Corvette lifted off the ground. Tires on the passenger side corrected to the right, steered into the rotation, and the car launched into a spiral. A headlight came so close I could have spit on it. I turned, watched the car's underside sail past me. It landed upside down and did somersaults over the tree stumps, ejecting pieces of itself with each impact. It kept going far longer than I could have thought possible, finally finding inertia, and with one last roll, coming to rest.

The world went startlingly quiet. I looked back where the car had come from. The road was empty. I turned around again; the wreckage was much more interesting. The 'Vette's bent hood hung open. Bars of the frame were exposed. The interior was tussled, seats tilting drunkenly. Chunks of paneling were everywhere. I limped toward what was left, scanning, frantic.

I found him folded in half. Sam's toes were planted in the dirt, as was his chin. His spine had inverted and coiled to make this possible, and his forehead and temple were flayed, skin erased by gravel. His eyelid hung off the left side, flapping as he tried to blink. He stared straight ahead. His arm reached onto the tarmac. His fist opened and closed, fingernails scraping.

He paid me no attention as I went by him. I was desperate to never see him again, unable to look away—I shuffle-ran backward until I stumbled and fell. The gun went off, the shot cacophonous. Birds squawked, joining the concert of bullet reverb, my heavy breathing, and Sam's nails fighting to pull him forward. As the birds rose above him, his eyes rolled up to peek. His hand stopped moving. It continued not moving for some time.

I couldn't lower the gun. I decided this was okay—no rush. I said that out loud: "No rush. Take a sec. Time-out."

I took stock. I was not dead. Uncertain of that call, I checked my own pulse. It was tommy-gunning in my wrist.

I cried a little; I'd earned it. Actually, the skunk earned it. I put the gun down, saluted the greasy stain he'd been reduced to, and discovered I was sitting on tree roots. They carved up the blacktop to my right, then went snaking down a path. You had to be here under the big oak to see it, narrow as the trail was. Draped as it was with droopy, sallow leaves.

It led out of the woods, into a clearing. The leaves were from a willow, and there was a branch slung low.

Like a long bench. Perfect for taking a group photo.

I got up and limped, staring at my feet so I wouldn't stumble on the vines. Arriving at the dirt, I went on, to where the dirt ended and became sand. I lifted my head.

The Pacific embraced the sky, the two of them reflecting one another's blues. The beach must have been farther away back then, since the willow was healthy in the picture. Now it had warty salt-sores and leaves close to my natural hair color, a chromatic no-man's-land between yellow and brown. I went and stood where they'd put the camera that day. A bit behind, letting the chubby guy make his adjustments. He told Sam and Harmony to scoot in. She smiled and she meant it. He was gangly, mop-topped. The camera flash made me wince and turn.

There was Sam, sun-charred, skinned, and origami'd, lying at the roadside, his reaching arm in a perfect line to this spot. Did he die clawing to get here? Did he want to grab his younger self and shake him, tell that dumb kid what a terrible man he'd turn into?

I made an odd noise, a combination scream-giggle. I covered my mouth. I wanted to jump forward five, ten, fifteen years. I needed to hear it would be okay. I needed to hear I'd be alive and someone would give a damn I was alive, and I'd be different, better—or at least I wouldn't get worse. I wished my older self could be sitting on this tree. She was the only one I'd believe. The only one I'd believe who wasn't dead already.

I went to the willow and sat, regarding the water, the waves. The ocean put my mind at ease. At rest.

Suddenly, with a crash, I sank. My ribs found new places to stab me, and I howled. I slapped around, hitting desiccated lengths of bark that my bony ass had evidently caused to cave in. I whimpered at the placid blue sky and asked, "Really?" I was sitting on something mushy and dry—I figured it was another dead animal. My process for escaping was a graceless half cartwheel, which I caught with my bad wrist. I pillowed my head on the sand, groaning.

There was a duffel bag jammed inside the tree.

It was gray canvas. Wedged through that knot a few feet over and pushed in from the opening with a foot or a stick. Really cramming so intrepid trekkers on a PowerBar break wouldn't find it. My thoughts, always anxious to look at both sides of a contradiction, really outdid themselves here. I knew for a fact it was the money, and I knew with absolute certainty it wasn't. I got off the ground, maintaining my why-not approach. Why not tug it out of there? Why not see if it's abandoned camping equipment or an air mattress or Jimmy Hoffa or $3.75 million of your parents' decades-old robbery take? I mean, what else was I up to?

I grabbed hold, curled into a ball, and rocked backward. Wood snapped. The bag landed on my shins, larger than I'd thought—hockey-gear huge. I worked the stiff zipper across eighteen years of rust. She'd lined the sides in plastic. I tore it, and cream-and-green bricks tumbled over each other.

I picked up a stack. My thumb clicked through the petrified bills. They gave off a conspicuous smell of nothing, but I flashed to the everything they could buy. To a future where I had a bunch of nice stuff, where I had throw pillows. Where I owned a car with heated seats, shoes I referred to by men's names in plural: "These are my so-and-sos." I had guest soaps. College. Grad school, if necessary. A house is an investment; renting's a waste. Retirement: never too soon to start; no such thing as enough.

Awesome, genius. What's the plan? Drag it? How far, to where? I have a hunch Rodeo Drive is about six hundred miles south. Hide it and come back? You're never coming back here. If you get out of this, you're going to have the same attitude toward remote areas as that chick at the end of *The Texas Chainsaw Massacre*—and at least she could hitchhike.

"Yeah, yeah, I get it." I dug sulkily for a cigarette, cursing when I remembered I'd left the pack next to my flambéed two grand. But I did uncover a last treat from the bottommost of my pocket. Bending their bodies over the staple, I counted them. Four more matches.

I sneered at Sam. He was perfectly still, and still reaching.

"You want it?" I asked. "Hey, Daddy, want your money?"

Digging a pit around the duffel, I wished money could beg for its life. Part of me begged in its stead, giving the cash a heart and a mind that could know regret, and regretted being the excuse for all this fuss. It apologized; it was sorry for all the pointless dead. It was sorry for the madwoman who'd stuffed it into a living grave. But it was especially sorry for the daughter who'd freed it, who'd lost two totally fucked parents in its name, who'd never, never have the kind of uncomplicated life she craved. Moon River. All that.

I folded the matchbook. Popped, tossed. Fire scampered bundle to bundle, treating the hundreds like Duraflame. I collected the nearest pieces of willow wood to build some heft. The blaze grew good and dangerous. I tried not to get too comfortable, but it was hard. Too easy to decide I was safe now. That for sure, forest rangers or state park employees or someone would come soon.

The fire fooled me best. It told tales about the morning getting warmer. It said I could sleep, that I'd be okay, and the ocean concurred, hushing my worry about slowing breaths and heavy eyes. What it couldn't quell was my conviction, down-deep and deeply upsetting, that I was not alone out here.

"Whoever you are, come out," I tried to yell. "After the week I've had, you're about as scary as a baby kitten on ludes." I had my ears perked, attuned to a level that was almost superhuman. The wind picked up. The trees swished and clattered. Nobody stepped out of them, but the awareness wouldn't leave me. Someone was watching. "Come on and show yourself."

A grumpy sound came from the ocean. Far, far out, at a distance I couldn't begin to estimate, clouds in layered slabs were trampling the clear day. I nodded at the approaching storm like it and I had agreed on a matter of huge significance.

As I dumped sand on my fire, reason raised its hand. I must have called on it. "You should backtrack to the garage," it said. "You might make it if you hurry. You need to stay dry."

"Screw dry," I said, getting up, going to where land and sea shared their boundaries. The shore unwound in a wavy line as far as I could see and beyond. Behind it, the trees were thick. Behind those, sharp hills spiked in a wilderness of shale and dense pines.

Prevailing wisdom is, stay in one place if you're lost. I'd heard this. It was often excellent advice, but—

"We're not lost, are we?" Foam bubbled over my shoes. Weedy sea oaks slapped me, in a tizzy about the same fierce gusts of wind that were narrowing my path to a tightrope. I walked it, I'd fall off and get back on. I was dragging my bum leg, with a foot that had gone numb. This couldn't be the real ending.

I was being followed.

"There's more, right?" I chatted about other stuff over that last impossible mile—how there was a Wendy's around this next bend of bay, and I'd get a cup of chili and a baked potato so hot it burned my mouth, then the Frosty would feel so good—but I kept coming back to that. "This isn't it, right?"

The storm unleashed. My hair was strings in seconds, my clothes these wet sacks of waterlog the wind ripped at like sails. I bowed my head so exhales could stream off my chin; otherwise, I'd drown standing up. The sand disappeared in gushes of angry tide. I staggered to all fours, got up, got going again.

And I found I had enough left in me to shout. Whoever was there needed to hear this.

"Look, if all you're saying is, 'Well, who the fuck're you?' then you win. I'm nobody. But you're winning cheap. That's all anyone has to say is, 'Who are you?' And it's over?"

There was a roar of thunder, followed by lightning, weaving through the whole squall, bright, frightening. I ducked as if that would help. The air filled with the smell of ozone and a subtle high note. An adorable crumb of my psyche as yet devoted to rescue misidentified the high note. It was a release of ionized atmosphere. No reason to get excited, no excuse to turn around. It most definitely was not a siren.

I looked above me, at a boiling cauldron of gunmetal brew. Beside me, at the ocean all rippling and wild. At the trees I was grabbing for balance: they were mangy. They bent and snapped as I reeled by, my perception shot, imagining a stripe of coffee brown where the foliage gapped back there. I was imagining the gap itself—sure, I was—just as I was imagining that SUV coming around the turn way too fast, sludge spraying from its tires as they slid and corrected. This was followed by the shriek of brakes, the sound of a car door. They were figments of my imagination. Fragments of some coulda-been.

So when a man came running out of the trees, his momentum almost carrying him into the water, and he dug the sides of his shoes in and he saw me and froze, I'd decided to blow right by him. I couldn't see him very well, as though he were on the other side of a sodden windshield. The bandage on his throat was worrying. You're not supposed to get those wet. Delusion or not, I opened my mouth to inform him of this, and expelled whatever fumes of energy I'd been running on. The sand sped up to meet me. I was jostled, spun. I figured a wave, though I didn't seem to be entirely underwater.

"Rainy?" Blaine said. "Look up. Look at– Shit."

I couldn't move. My muscles had no volition.

"Okay, here we go. Up you go, we're outta here."

My neck sank over his arm. I wanted to ask how the hell he'd found me. I tried to force my eyes open.

"That's good, Rainy. Blink so I know you're awake. Keep doing that, okay?"

I tried. It wasn't easy; raindrops kept pounding into my eyes. I opened them wider.

That's when I saw the woman by the water's edge. She was just standing there, watching us. The deluge did a lot to hide her. The woods closing behind us did more. I couldn't make out any details, other than she was tall. Thin but not starvation-skinny, hair the colorless color of dun. She was tipping her face to the storm and smiling, like this was the most beautiful day she'd seen in a long time.

"What're you smiling about down there?" Blaine said, breathing hard. "Huh? Can you tell me?"

She headed south, her bearing not what I'd call regal or snobby or even confident. I'd call it itself. I'd call it content, if I weren't so afraid contentment is synonymous with complacency.

"What? What, Rainy, what are you trying to say?"

I was trying to say, "Put me down, Blaine, I have to go ask her one more thing."

But I doubted I could catch her. She'd covered a good distance already, bound for somewhere she considered important. She was a series of flashes through the trees—cutouts of rogue, unrelenting progress.

I watched her as long as I could. I hoped she didn't have much farther to go.

MY REFLECTION

County Road 42 was a strip of flypaper, clumped with suburbs. The weekend traffic was sporadic. A police cruiser appeared, driving eastbound. Its horn honked, and a hand waved out the open window.

"That's Dougherty. His handwriting's so bad the department made him take a class."

"In handwriting?" I said, talking with my mouth full.

"They gave him the same workbook his son used in first grade."

Blaine was trying to cheer me up. We'd done sandwich assembly, a thirty-minute drive. A climb up the water tower's ladder with him reminding me every other rung to be careful. He'd okayed it with the police in Savage first, and I'd have loved to hear his end of the conversation: "I'm gonna be up there with a friend this Sunday night around seven. Don't arrest us, okay?"

My class was graduating today. From where we sat on the tower's platform, Burnsville and Apple Valley and snippets of Farmington were visible. Dewey High wasn't. They held commencement outside. All those caps thrown in the air, birds rising in tandem flight—I couldn't take it. I never went back for spring semester.

My kidnapping was hot news for about three seconds. While I was recovering in Eugene, Oregon, Child Protection Services started yowling about how imperative it had suddenly become to find me the best foster situation ever—despite the fact that by the time I got released, I was three weeks from being eighteen.

But Blaine knew a lot of lawyers. And I didn't mind lying to a judge. The sale of Mom's house banked me more than enough to rent a frumpy studio apartment in Hastings. Emancipation was a formality after that. We put a futon in the living room/bedroom to make it look like someone lived there. Unnecessarily, since CPS rolled its collective eyes and went back to circle-jerking as soon as the courts decreed me an adult. I'd been ready for Blaine to fight me about school, but he hadn't. He'd met with my principal, who said I had enough credits to graduate. I was enrolled at the U for fall semester.

Blaine finished his sandwich, crumbled his wax paper. He held up a Wuollet bag.

"When did you stop?" I bounced, excited.

"Yesterday. Not as fresh as they could be."

I peeled the paper from my angel food with strawberry frosting and bit into it, making a noise that Blaine chuckled at. He wasn't into cupcakes. He always got a dainty little fruit tart. He picked off the kiwi and ate it in two bites.

The scar on his throat distended when he swallowed. It didn't get enormous, not even more noticeable than usual, but I remembered much too vividly the blood pouring out of there. No matter how many times he explained that it'd never really been more than a scratch, the fact he had emergency surgery and didn't come out of anesthesia for nine hours (at which point he ripped out his IV, left the hospital AMA, called the FBI, said his Corvette was LoJacked and gave them the VIN—cops love acronyms) it made me shudder when the line by his carotid grimaced in my direction.

I chewed more slowly than usual. We were here for grad day, but he also wanted to talk to me.

"So—"

"'M not done," I said.

He leaned to get at his pocket then offered the pack with a wry goody-goody pump of his eyebrows.

I took a stick of Nicorette and developed a deep fascination with the scenery. "It's not a big deal."

A peewee soccer game was getting started a block north. I observed the teams lining up in messy formation, young coaches with whistles around their necks nudging this kid forward or that one backward.

“I believed you the other morning,” Blaine said. The ref blew the whistle. Two kids scrimmaged, bumping into each other, trying not to fall down. “When you told me you couldn’t sleep. Next night, I started to wonder, finding you down in the den again, reading at five a.m. After that you got smart, sneaking upstairs before I woke up. But I could smell the coffee.” The smaller kid broke away, dribbling with all the coordination of a newborn colt. I could hear the cheers from here. “This doesn’t work if you lie to me.”

“You telling me to move out?” I said. “I can be out by tonight.”

“Is it the one where you’re in the trunk?”

I said nothing.

“Is it the one where we’re in the desert and I get shot?”

“New one.” I meant to sound testy but didn’t quite swing it.

“You need to tell me.” The goalie was hurling the ball back into play. He held on too long and basically punted. “What the shrink said, remember? These are poison. You need to let them out. It’s normal, I had the same thing.”

“You didn’t have this one. This one’s worse.”

“Why?” he said.

I bonked my skull on the water tank, gave him a face full of: Please. Please just this once let it go.

Blaine shook his head. He raised a calloused finger and pointed between my eyes. “I’m not leaving you alone in there.”

I hugged my knees, hiding my face in their convenient cave.

"Rainy, we've talked about this. You have to trust somebody. It's the hardest thing there is, but you've gotta try." He set a hand on my shoulder. It rooted me, so I wouldn't float away. "You can do it. I know you can do it."

I'M IN THE middle of a street. It's winter. There's snowdrifts all down a long row of buildings. I'm confused: Haven't the plows run? I look closer and notice there's no glass in any of the windows. The doors hang open even though it's the middle of the night. The facades are covered in graffiti, mostly boring tags, but there's this one, a kind of cartoon with a boy, in cutoffs and orange shorts, blowing bubbles. I peer over my shoulder and see the top of the Ferris wheel wedged over the roofs. Its peeling paint is bright canary yellow. I know where I am.

I go inside and upstairs, find a window with a view. The city rests in permanent stasis. Sleeping Beauty's kingdom, only doomed for a lot longer. I walk around an endless maze that was either a hospital or an orphanage—the rooms have dozens of dolls posed on naked bed frames. I sit in a desk at a school with indecipherable words scribbled all over the blackboard. I watch an old-fashioned theater stage with no players on it, unless you count the shadows the moon makes, and I discover a room full of gas masks. Tens of thousands of gas masks, the kind with an elephant trunk on the front, as if the designer had said, Let's make these as spooky as humanly possible.

It's getting light out. The snow is melting, and scary-thick icicles drip and break and drop. Once the sun rises, everything's different. It's spring. I go outside, walk to the river, and rest on a bench that's rusted but strong. I let the morning sun strobe my skin, listen to the wrens and swallows. For a long time, their heads were malformed and their throats were rock gardens of tumors. But over the decades, they adapted. Now they fly higher to bathe in the rain before it puddles with radioactivity. Now they pass on grit deep down in their DNA, nucleic resistance to their poison place. And they sing.

Human voices are singing, too. Hi-fi. Far off.

Nothing but *Rumours*.

It takes a while to get to the plant; the album's almost done. I follow "Gold Dust Woman" to the cooling pool. Sam's got a portable grill. He's turning burgers. He's scrawny, young, and his head's covered in hair. My twentysomething mom abandons her record player, hopping up to kiss me hello. Johnny waits 'til she's done and *really* kisses me hello. Ellie and Becca are shoving each other on a platform above the water, competing to catch the biggest catfish.

I say as I sit that this venue is creepy and sad, not to mention plutonium-rich. Johnny asks about plutonium, and I tell him that's the worst one. In fifteen more years, cesium's and strontium's half-lives will be over. But plutonium decays into americium, and that's over four hundred years. And that's a *half*-life.

"Oh, *pffft*," Sam says, handing me a plate. "You like yours medium, right?"

The cooler's packed with Mom's specialties: German potato salad, cheesy green beans, pie. We're bottomless pits for the food. We grunt compliments, and Mom smiles at them. I'd think it was strange she doesn't speak, but no one's talking all that much. I'd consider it the most boring meal of my life if it weren't for where I'm sitting, who I'm with, and how there's so much joy tingling in my body that I can barely eat.

The sun's beginning to set as we finish. Ellie says, out of nowhere, "We're gonna go check out the amusement park."

"You're ducking out of cleanup, is what you're doing," Sam says. He shoos them. Not mad. Just Dad.

"Do you think the carousel works?" Becca asks me.

I tell her, "Sure, probably."

She's so excited. They run off in that direction, skipping. Like adults imitating children much too well.

The rest of us wrap up what's left of our supper and gather trash. There's a trash can right over there but nobody to empty it. Sam says, "Throw it in the trunk." The Corvette sits parked a stone's throw away from us. I'm sure it wasn't there before, but that's why dreams are annoying.

I go to help Mom with the record player; it's heavy. Sam beats me to it, and to my surprise, Mom wraps me up in a hug. We sway together. I could die there, wearing the heat of her. She slips away, dances to the driver's side, and claims her seat.

Sam piles stuff in the trunk. I go to Johnny first, putting his arm around me like a flotation device. We approach Sam together. He's having trouble fitting everything in the trunk. Some asshole made a real mess in there. They even left a bottle full of piss.

"Dad," I say, "how could you?"

"How could I what?" He doesn't understand. He's not that guy yet. There's a heartbreaking innocence in his expression when it dawns on him: "Was your burger too rare?"

I wish, in the dream, that dreams were places for warnings. "A little raw," I say.

"I'm sorry, honey." He closes the trunk softly. "Nobody's perfect." He winks and goes to the passenger side, does a graceless leap over the door.

"It's okay," I say as the car coughs to life. They drive around the pool, toward the rear of the plant. When they disappear around a corner, I can't hear the engine anymore. I look in the amusement park's direction, hoping for lights, calliope music, giggles. Instead, it's static and silent.

Johnny takes my hand. The sun's mostly gone when we get to the forest. Stepping in, the red leaves crackle under our feet. Johnny lights a cigarette, and I tell him it isn't a good idea—this place is a tinderbox.

"Watch this," he says, and flicks his Newport.

The fire hits the leaves. They come alive. They're butterflies. They fly all around us, glowing—so many I can barely see him. I feel their little legs, hear their wings rush in my ears.

"I wish this was real," I say.

And Johnny looks at me and says, "It is."

"THEN I WAKE up." I'd related the dream in a flat and lifeless voice. I was about to give it a smart-ass grace note, a no-big-deal coda, but it came out a sob that bent me double with its force. Blaine reached out in what I figured was history's most enthusiastic hug before I understood it was actually a catch. He'd thought I was trying to pitch myself over the side. He let go when he realized that wasn't the case, and I ran out of tears after a few minutes.

"Help me out on something." Blaine handed me a napkin. "How's that dream so bad you're pulling all-nighters to get away from it? How's it worse than the others?"

"It's not," I said, and blew my nose most alluringly. "It's better. That's what makes it worse. I'm using them like puppets, making them say they're happy."

He frowned into space, letting my logic set in. I watched his cheeks get increasingly rage-rouge. He rolled his eyes. "Do you ever give yourself a goddamn break?"

I had a flannel on—it was May, but it was still Minnesota. From the breast pocket I took a kitchen match and two cigarettes. I smirked up at him.

Blaine laughed. He didn't want to. He wanted to keep fighting, say exactly the right thing, convince me, fix me, save me.

"Cheater," he said, accepting a Marlboro.

I scraped the match on the railing and lit us. "How many breaks did Sam give himself? Or my mom? How much slack do you have to cut yourself before you become a monster?"

"That's what I'm for. I'll tell you when you're cutting too much."

"I won't listen."

"You're listening now." He tipped his head back and exhaled. "God, that's good."

We settled into the final whistle of the soccer game, the onset of sunset. I saw why he liked it up here. Why he remembered it when most people thinking of their prom night would flash to the color of their date's dress, or the last song they danced to on a floor covered in balloons. I saw why he picked tonight, when by all rights I should have been sitting in a rigid folding chair listening to a boring speech about my future's golden possibilities.

Instead, I was on steel mesh, foot cocked against a chipped railing, watching today's golden possibilities founder and sink. I felt guilty bringing us back to the dream, but I hadn't told Blaine my real problem with it yet. "Why would I make Johnny say that? That it's real?"

He shrugged. "What if it is?"

"Then I'm a monster."

"Because?"

"Because they're stuck." I tapped my temple. "I trapped them. I'm free, but they're not."

"What if you didn't?" he said. "What if all you did was give the best parts of them a better place to be?"

"In a toxic wasteland?"

Blaine tic'd his neck at the night, smiling. "What if you gave the place a better place to be, too?"

A rebuttal was right there on the tip of my tongue: Then I'm still a monster, because how much of my gift is a lie?

But we were smoking our last cigarettes, and the soccer kids were lining up for team high fives. And it occurred to me that accepting defeat isn't always a loss. The sun did it every day. The sun was doing it now, ceding the kingdom. Burning down the clouds so it could build something brand-new tomorrow—oh, mirror in the sky.

"Yeah," I said. "Yeah, maybe."